THE ANGELS OF L19

'*The Angels of L19* asks questions about loss and faith – how it is practised, negotiated, and experienced – and brings both the fantastic and quotidian vividly to life. It is at once a grand metaphysical fantasy, and a story about teenagers coping with grief. The book is deeply serious, at times horrifying, yet also funny, poignant, and moving.'

– Amy Sackville, author of *Jack Glass* and *The Thing Itself*

'*The Angels of L19* is an adroit depiction of hell, wrapped inside a portrait of heaven, written from within real life. It challenges us to consider how madness preys on the innocence of faith, or maybe how faith preys on the innocence of madness. Jonathan Walker is a writer of real substance and intellectual curiosity.'

– Rónán Hession, author of *Leonard and Hungry Paul*

Also by Jonathan Walker:

Pistols! Treason! Murder!: The Rise and Fall of a Master Spy
(illustrated by Dan Hallett)

Five Wounds: An Illuminated Novel
(illustrated by Dan Hallett)

The Angels of L19

JONATHAN WALKER

Jonathan Walker

2021

175 /200

WEATHERGLASS BOOKS

For my true friends the Jenkins family

Come, Lord, come to Hell anon / and take out thy folks everychone.
'The Harrowing of Hell', Chester Mystery Plays

1

ROBERT

When he was born again, the walls began to sing.

On Sundays, it's fish fingers for tea, with watery potatoes and grey butter beans. Robert eats at five o'clock, an hour before Uncle Edward and Auntie Rose, but his aunt often sits with him at the morning-room table.

There are always fourteen to twenty beans: seven to ten mouthfuls, two beans at a time. Mix each mouthful with one-third of a fish finger to disguise the taste and texture. Half a gulp of orange squash to wash it down.

Auntie Rose is sitting at the other end of the table. Apron on; arms crossed. Her eyes follow the fork up to his mouth.

The fluorescent tube above stutters, as if there's something trapped inside.

By five thirty, Robert's back in the television room, at the far end of the sofa, near the window. Auntie Rose is at its other end, by the door; Uncle Edward's in an armchair in the far corner of the room.

'Aren't you going to church?' Auntie Rose asks.

'Not today,' Robert says.

'But you didn't go this morning either.'

He shrugs. He normally goes twice on Sunday, but last week he arrived at the evening service late, and before he entered the church, he placed a brown paper bag over his head with the words 'Shame and Disgrace' written on it in black marker. He couldn't see where he was going, so he bumped into a few pews before he found an empty seat near the back.

The speaker was from Jireh in Bebington. Quite a good sermon, on the theme of repentance. But Bill Forester said Robert was 'disruptive', and he should stay away from church, just for today.

No need to mention any of that.

The *Radio Times* sits on the empty cushion between Auntie Rose and Robert, folded neatly to tonight's page for BBC1. She picks it up. 'Do you want to watch *Songs of Praise* then?'

He winces. 'It's not the same thing.'

'Alright, I only asked.'

A choral 'Amen' comes through the wall from the Foresters next door. It's a collective sound: Robert can't distinguish the individual voices of Bill, or his daughter, Tracey, Robert's best friend, because their whole family comes round for Sunday lunch – aunts, uncles, cousins, grandparents – and they stay for the afternoon. And when they meet together, they sing.

Robert knows the Foresters' habits because he lived next door for several weeks three years ago, shortly after he moved to Liverpool. Auntie Rose was in hospital with golden staphylococcus. Uncle Edward went to the bookies every afternoon, and passed out when he came back. Even though Robert was twelve, the Foresters made him show his teeth at night after brushing. He didn't mind. He was happy there.

If Robert pressed himself against the adjoining wall, he could hear the singing with his body. WHEREFORE MY BOWELS SHALL SOUND LIKE AN HARP FOR MOAB, AND MINE INWARD PARTS FOR KIRHARESH. With his aunt and uncle in the room, he can't follow the sound down into the dead cavity between the two houses. But he can turn an imaginary volume dial up, chasing the echo back to its source. The background hiss in his head gets louder as the sounds from next door die away.

2

Robert keeps his eyes fixed straight ahead, but he can feel his uncle's gaze drifting towards him like a drunk at a steering wheel. If Robert jerks his head left, to catch him out, his uncle stares straight ahead at the television, even though it's turned off at the wall to save electricity.

Above the carriage clock on the mantelpiece, there's a seam of glue where the edges on the rolls of flock wallpaper go out of alignment. Solid resistance for a picking fingernail. Nits on a scalp.

His ears pop, and the pressure in the room adjusts. Here is a new thing, but at the same time, a very old thing. A presence.

It first appeared to Robert last summer, when he came home from church camp in Wales. He wasn't surprised to find it waiting for him. He was expecting a message from God, after giving his heart to Jesus. The only surprise was that the presence didn't immediately deliver the message. It's returned several times since then, but Robert's still waiting for it to speak. It's only for him. No one else can see it.

It stands in the centre of the room, where it arranges the other occupants around itself like the figures on a clock face. Tick-tock on the mantelpiece. Or is it coming from the presence?

Its body is ivory; at other times, wax. Always hairless, smooth. No articulations or openings, apart from a bubbled vertical slit in the centre of its head, like the line of glue on the wallpaper.

An egg. Sealed, but waiting to split.

Even though the central heating's on, Auntie Rose pulls her cardigan tighter. Uncle Edward stands up and turns on a bar of the electric fire, which pings and creaks as it turns orange. The light behind the fake coals rotates and flickers. Like the ticking of the clock, the smell of burning dust comes from the presence, not the fire. It draws all sensations into itself.

Silence in heaven for half an hour. Silence in the television room too.

Robert sometimes feels like his aunt and uncle have already died, and he's living with their ghosts. Or their empty bodies.

When the Foresters have left for church, Robert goes through to the front room, which Auntie Rose calls the dining room, even though they only eat there on Christmas Day. The table has carved legs, and takes up too much space. Around the edges of the room are two winged armchairs with vinyl upholstery in alcoves, and a display cabinet with glass doors and shelves. Inside the cabinet, there's a black-and-white studio photograph of Auntie Rose and Uncle Edward, and two commemorative plates: one each from the Silver Jubilee and the royal wedding. Below that, there's a junior-school photo of Robert in a cardboard mount, and a loose snapshot of his dad as a teenager, when he first went to sea. The picture of his dad is usually propped up against the edge of the mount, but tonight it's slipped down onto the glass shelf. There's no photo of Robert's mum.

He opens the cabinet door and picks his dad up, then closes it again and salutes the photo. He scoots round the table to get to the armchair at the back of the room. He leaves the curtains open and the light off, but the streetlamp outside is bright enough to make out the outlines of things. By special permission, he's allowed to listen to a portable radio in here.

He doesn't care about the Top Forty countdown, but he likes Annie Nightingale's request show, which comes on afterwards. Listening to the fraught messages from teenagers all over the country, he feels like an alien monitoring earth transmissions.

Robert has a Walkman, but there's no record player in the house. He usually buys albums on vinyl and gets Tracey to tape

4

them. That way it doesn't matter if his Walkman chews up the tape, and he can keep the vinyl in mint condition. The Foresters have a hi-fi in their front room with a graphic equalizer and a double tape deck. So the first time Robert hears a new record is next door, during the taping. If Bill's out, Tracey turns the volume and the bass frequencies up.

After coming back from church camp, Robert tried to convert his record collection and only listen to Christian music. But albums from the Scripture Union shop sound like *Songs of Praise*. Their lyrics are too obvious. The meaning's on the surface: nothing behind. Whereas, when he listens to The Teardrop Explodes, or Simple Minds, or – especially – U2, God is hidden inside the song, even when the words seem to be about something else. It's like the lyrics are in code, and Robert's got the key.

Tracey always goes to youth group after the evening service, so she doesn't come home until ten. Like Robert's, her bedroom looks onto the back garden and has a rectangular bay window. At about ten twenty, Tracey knocks the base of her fist three times against her side of the common wall between their rooms. Robert knows she's hitting an X drawn there in pencil; he thuds back at the identical X on his side, directly above the disused fireplace. Then they both go to the side panels of their respective windows, and turn to face one another.

Tracey has her Walkman on, the same model as Robert's, but red instead of blue. She touches her hands to the earphones, then holds her index fingers up in the air, parallel to one another, as if measuring the space between them. She swipes them through the air like drumsticks and mouths the words, 'This song is not a rebel song!'

Robert mouths in reply, 'This song is "Sunday Bloody Sunday".' From the introduction to the live version on *Under a Blood Red Sky*. He leaves Tracey alone at the window for a minute, while he goes to find his own Walkman.

In the studio version of the song, the bass is the easiest instrument to follow, just to the right in the mix. *Dur-der-der, der-dun; dur-der-der, der-dun.* A five-note pattern, although it sounds like four unless Robert slows it down in his head and counts it out on his fingers. The guitar's flat: dead chop. Marching forward, no time to waste. The cymbals spill everywhere, washing out to the edges. The violin cuts the song open.

Back at the window, Robert looks at Tracey's hands. Her fingers are hitting the sill so fast they're almost invisible. Eyes closed, but she knows he's there. He waits for her to open her eyes again and flutters an imaginary white flag on a pole above his head.

Her nightie is stitched in diamond shapes – like a quilt – with lace at the collar and cuffs. Eczema flares at her wrists, and out in a halo around the tiny metal cross she wears around her neck. Sometimes she uses a steroid cream, and then she glistens. Dragon skin. Beautiful.

When the presence delivers its message, everyone will know that God has chosen Robert. Bill and Tracey will know.

2
TRACEY / ROBERT

Tracey's watching the annual revue at church, peeking out from behind the door of the impromptu dressing room. There are a few topical skits referring to church business from the previous year, although it's really just an excuse for everyone to do their party turns. As usual, there's a sketch with an elder in drag, speaking in falsetto, wearing an orange wig (the same wig every year, but not necessarily the same elder). Tonight, it's John Cooper. He can't work a washing machine or cook anything except beans on toast, but he can boil a kettle, so he's pretending to be a tea lady.

Tea. The solution to all life's problems.

'I don't seem to be able to pray, and God feels very far away,' says Kevin Cooper, John's son, in the role of Joe Bloggs believer.

'Oh dear. Have a cup of tea,' John replies. His only line, repeated several times.

There's no happy ending – just the same joke over and over as Kevin's stated predicament and dilemma get worse. Dark, so big tick for that, but otherwise off target. The tea's not important; no one thinks it is. Someone goes to the trouble of making it, puts it in your hand. Someone *touches* you. That's why.

John and Kevin leave the stage area to polite applause. John plods through to the dressing room, but he has to go past Tracey to get there. 'Shouldn't you be wearing a hat?' she says.

'Eh?'

'1 Corinthians 11,' Tracey says. Women should cover their heads in church – a tradition Tracey has never observed, and which her dad has never mentioned. But John brought it up in the morning meeting two weeks ago.

'Very funny,' John says, adjusting his cushion boobs.

Tracey's about to go on and play the drums in a sketch with Robert, who isn't very popular with John – or with the women who make the tea after the service. Last week, he poured himself a cup, and kept pouring as it overflowed into the saucer and onto the table. Tracey had to grab his hand to get his attention. It took ten minutes to mop it up.

Jenny Spinks, the compère, announces a short break for Tracey to set up her drums. She only needs the bass and snare tonight; even so, she's brought the whole kit. Robert doesn't really need a proper drummer, but that's what she is, so that's what he gets.

Tracey looks at the audience. Nobody's wearing a hat – not even the old ladies. Because it's not a church right now, it only becomes one on Sundays, when people come here to worship.

She never wears a hat because there are no special places where God is more present than others, and no magic rituals to summon or bind Him. The whole world is God's church, and this is just a building.

The congregation funded and built Garston Chapel ten years ago. Tracey remembers playing in the sand in a roped-off corner of the construction site while her dad discussed floor plans with the other elders. There are two halls, with a blocked-off courtyard between: one hall for the morning service; the other for the gospel meeting in the evening. The courtyard's surrounded by plate-glass windows, which provide natural light into the halls; and there are linking corridors at both ends of the building, with a kitchen in the far corner. Tonight, the revue's in the morning hall, and the back corridor's the dressing room. So people take their drink and biscuit next door in the evening hall instead of the kitchen.

Are they ready for Robert's poetry? Tracey feels sick, but excited too. In the empty morning hall, she presses her palm against one of the windows and squeaks the condensation aside. There's snow falling outside, dissolving as it hits the glass.

Kevin Cooper, who wore his own clothes and therefore has no costume to change out of, comes up and says, 'What did you think?'

'Was it meant to be that dark?'

Kevin's chuffed. 'That was me. Dad just had the tea-lady idea.'

Tracey's known Kevin since she was four, but she's never paid much attention to him. He has shoulder-length brown hair, a little fuzzy at the ends, so he almost looks like he has a halo. She can see the top of the Motörhead logo on his black T-shirt, hidden under a white school shirt. She says, 'Robert wanted me to ask you …'

'What?'

Too late, because Robert now appears from near the front entrance, where he's been hiding in the bathroom, waiting for everyone to go next door. He's wearing a cut-out Morrissey mask, with two gouged holes for the eyes and a letterbox slot for the mouth. Two weeks ago he had a bag over his head. Why does he keep covering his face?

'Have you told him yet?' Robert says. His voice sounds weird behind the mask, as if it's coming from somewhere else – like he's a ventriloquist's dummy.

'I was just about to,' Tracey says.

Morrissey's forehead has the word 'This' written on it in black marker. Under his nose, the word 'Charming' forms an uneven moustache, since the second syllable has been crossed out and replaced with '-less', drooping down the left cheek. The word 'Man' makes a goatee on his chin, but it's also crossed out, with 'Boy' written underneath instead. To reinforce the last point, Robert is not wearing a Smiths T-shirt but one that reproduces the cover of U2's first album, also called *Boy*. A picture of a bare-chested child, gazing out at the photographer.

'Ask me what?' Kevin says.

Robert hops from foot to foot as if he needs to go to the loo – although he's just come from the bathroom. Tracey thinks he's laughing, but it's difficult to tell with Morrissey in the way. 'To play piano,' Tracey says.

'But I can't,' Kevin says. 'Only guitar. And I don't have it with me.'

'I know you can't play piano,' Robert says. 'That's the point.'

'I don't get it. What do you want me to do?'

'Whatever you want,' Robert says. 'So long as you do it on the piano.'

Kevin wiggles one hand down by his waist and the other up in the air near his shoulder. 'I'm a guitarist,' he says again.

Morrissey doesn't react. 'Will you do it or not?'

'Pretend to play the piano?

'No,' Robert says. 'Actually play the piano – but really badly.'

'Why didn't you ask me about this yesterday,' Kevin says to Tracey, 'when we had the rehearsal?'

'Robert doesn't do rehearsals.'

'No script,' Robert says. 'Plus, one person with no idea at all what's happening.'

'One person onstage,' Tracey says. 'Because the audience has no idea either.'

'Don't you remember,' Robert asks, 'from camp last summer?'

'No,' Kevin says. He strokes his own moustache, which is not as impressive as Morrissey's. He ignores Robert and gives his final answer to Tracey. 'But I'll give it a go.'

Robert says, 'All you need to know is I'll be reading some poetry. And you're my accompaniment. If you can't think of anything to do, just follow Tracey's lead.'

'Is the poetry about The Smiths?'

'No. It's a tribute to the Romantics.'

Kevin smirks. 'Duran Duran?'

'The *real* Romantics.'

No rehearsals. Well, that's a fib, because Robert and Tracey have practised adding a backbeat to the poems several times. *Thum-thum-thum* on the kick drum, keep it going while Robert breaks his lines down into syllables, one stress per beat. Then a rimshot on the snare at the end of each line. Simple, but that's okay because Robert's not exactly Shakespeare. For a start, his lines don't go *de-dum, de-dum* all the way through. So, even though the basic rhythm's simple, it's still difficult to get the drum pattern right.

She works at it on her own, and doesn't tell Robert. She needs to know exactly what he's going to say next and how he's going to say it, which means she has to memorize the poems too, and say them to herself while counting out the beats.

So 'no rehearsals' only means she doesn't know exactly what he's going to do before and after the poems. For example, no warning about joining The Smiths tonight. Robert wasn't very impressed with their *Top of the Pops* appearance last year. He did talk about it the following day, but what he said was, 'Moan, moan. Look at me, look at me.' Which is rich, coming from him.

'I'm surprised,' Kevin says to Tracey, when Robert's busy rummaging in a plastic bag at his feet. 'Wouldn't think this was your thing.'

For the *Two Ronnies* sketch Tracey did with Jenny Spinks earlier this evening, she taped a repeat showing and copied out the entire script, line by line, adding marks on the page for emphasis. Pause; rewind; replay. She tried doing it with Robert last year, but even when he knew his lines, he mugged for the crowd instead of playing it deadpan. Maybe she should have given him a mask.

Below Morrissey's face, the rest of Robert's outfit isn't quite right. He buys his non-school clothes at Topman and

Burton, but he only goes in the sales, so he gets the weird stuff. The colours are too bright, or the size is wrong. Tonight's shirt, which he's wearing unbuttoned to display the T-shirt underneath, is yellow to go with the daffodils he's pulling out of the plastic bag. It also has orange paisley shapes, which look like embryos and clash with his red hair, which he's gelled up into something resembling a quiff. Or a breaking wave, which is about to collapse onto Morrissey's face.

The crowd is returning from next door. Robert hands Tracey a sheet of A4 paper from his plastic bag. 'To stick on the bass drum,' he says, brushing off a pollen stain. The sheet says 'The Jones'.

'Shouldn't that be The Joneses? Or is there only one of you?'

'Jones-es. Jones-es-es,' Robert says. 'Never mind.' He retreats to the dressing room at the back of the hall, since he doesn't want to spoil the surprise.

'Are you sure you're up for this?' Tracey asks Kevin.

'Why not?' He walks over to the piano and sits down as Tracey slides her drum kit out from the back of the stage area. She sits down to adjust the placing of the stool and the cymbals. Kevin lifts up the piano lid. He interlaces his fingers and cracks his knuckles back.

Jenny Spinks announces them: 'Ladies and gentlemen, please give a warm Garston Chapel welcome for The Jones … es. With their hit song, "William Wordsworth, It Was Really Nothing".'

Robert flings open the door of the dressing room. It bangs so loudly against the wall that Mrs Evans in the third row spills her tea. Tracey starts drumming. The pattern doesn't matter at the moment, so she just does a basic snare and hi-hat combination. Robert is pulling more daffodils out of his plastic bag. He's also stuck one in the back pocket of his jeans. It looks sad, drooping down towards the floor.

Kevin stabs notes on the piano. He's a distraction already,

but she tunes him out and concentrates on Robert, who yodels and then starts doing a sort of waltz with an invisible partner, arm outstretched, making his way slowly from the door at the back of the hall to the area where Tracey and Kevin are set up. He pauses every few steps to throw a daffodil up into the air over the heads of the audience. The first one goes towards Mrs Evans, who lets out an 'Oh!'. Robert blows a kiss to the third row. He puts the plastic bag down and turns towards the audience to begin his onstage preparations: stretching and leaning down to touch his toes; jogging on the spot, huffing and puffing as he lifts his knees high.

He starts dancing. To Tracey, he looks like Ian Curtis of Joy Division, but the only influence he'll admit to is Bruce Lee, which is why he calls his signature move 'The Nunchuks'. He keeps his upper arms rigid, and flops his lower arms, wrists and hands around in circles in front of his face and out to his sides. At the same time, he moves his neck from side to side and steps backwards, forwards and sideways, while keeping his head fixed forward. It looks like he's in a mating ritual with Mrs Evans.

Mrs Evans is seventy-two. Leave the poor woman alone! But Tracey can't get this message across, except by hitting the crash cymbal harder. When that doesn't work, she throws a spare stick at the back of Robert's head. It hits the target and bounces off towards Kevin, who ducks and hits keys randomly.

Robert stops, and rubs the spot on his head. Then he seemingly has a bright idea, and eviscerates his plastic bag for the last of his daffodils. He turns around and nods to Tracey, which is her cue to go into the *thum-thum-thum* kick-drum rhythm.

'O daff-o-dils,' Robert says, addressing the flowers in his hand. 'You give me thrills.'

Kevin tries to follow Tracey by blurting out a crashing non-chord whenever she hits the snare. Or rather, half a second after she hits the snare. Still distracting.

'You are so yell-ow,' Robert says. 'And ex-ceed-ingly mell-ow.'

Robert's now into the swing of things – but so is Kevin. That's not good, because he's bored of following Tracey.

'I crush your head, With my train-er tread.' Robert demonstrates this action by grinding two of the remaining flowers under the ball of his foot.

'And you lie there …' Robert normally whispers this line for added pathos, but tonight he has to raise his voice because of Kevin, who's hitting the piano with his fists and elbows. And yes – bashing his head up and down on the keys, which means Robert has to shout:

'Utt-erly splat-tered.' He gestures towards the yellow pulp at his feet like a magician showing off his assistant: only in this case, he's stomped her to death instead of sawing her in half. Kevin redoubles his attack on the piano, so Tracey has to drum louder too, or Robert will lose the rhythm.

'And when I got home, I got bat-tered.' Since Robert's now screaming, this comes out funny peculiar rather than funny ha-ha.

Tracey's dad's sitting in the front row. He's trying to catch her eye, and he's about to stand up. She shakes her head at him: I've got this under control.

Robert takes a moment to gather himself before bellowing the last line of his poem: 'For be-ing such a com-plete and utt-er fasc-ist.' Tracey isn't sure about the stress pattern there, but anyway.

Kevin is now pretending to have murdered the piano. He shoves over the stool behind him as he jumps to his feet in horror at what he's done. The piano makes a last sound of distress, and falls silent.

Robert throws the rest of his daffodils out into the audience, but most people are looking at Kevin. Some of them have their hands over their ears. Tracey winds down the rhythm with the ride cymbal: quieter, quieter.

A general shifting in seats. Jenny Spinks claps her hands once, but then stops and mumbles an apology to herself. Tracey's nine-year-old cousin Sally laughs. Tracey looks at Kevin, who grins.

Robert's wobbling on tiptoe, with one hand pointing straight up in the air. He's silent, staring out into the aisle between the rows of pews. At the top of his outstretched arm, his hand opens and closes.

Fifteen seconds pass. Kevin whispers, 'What now?'

God's everywhere. He's here now.

There's a weird smell. Sour milk? Mouldy fruit? Tracey says, 'Robert.'

Robert's forgotten Tracey's even there. He's looking at the presence. It's standing in the aisle in front of the stage area. Its ivory skin is translucent, but the white flesh has thickened underneath. Curds and whey. Fermenting.

Its head has an opening now. A dry circle. An inverted cone cut into this wet dissolution, positioned somewhere between where the nose and mouth would be – if it had a nose or a mouth. An all-purpose sense organ, for receiving and trans-mitting, detecting and analysing. Light particles, sound waves, molecules changing from one state to another.

The cone advances towards Robert, out of the head. It's bigger than the head, even though it's coming out of the head. And now Robert is inside the cone, which means he's also inside the head. It surrounds him, like a caul.

The cone is black, and as it narrows towards the apex there's a red disc. So the cone's truncated. It doesn't end in a point but in another, much smaller circle. The circle flashes: red, then black; red, black. No, that's not right. More like it's sliding in and out. Red, black. A diaphragm opening and closing.

He falls into the cone.

'Robert,' the red disc says. It sounds worried.

'What?'

'Robert,' Tracey says.

He's standing in the church hall with his arm in the air, his hand blinking on and off. How long has he been like this? He flattens his feet, does a half-step shuffle and sweeps his arm down, his upper body following it into a bow. 'Thank you,' he says. 'Thank you.'

Tracey splashes a cymbal. A nervous cough from the back row of the audience; shuffling feet. A cup rattling in a saucer. Jenny Spinks claps again. Some people pat their fingers against their palms, but it's a feeble echo of Jenny, who can't stand the pressure and gives up after a few seconds.

The presence is still there. The cone has retreated back inside its head, and now it begins to vibrate as the red disc clicks in and out. 'I know you will never forgive me leaving you with this terrible mess,' the cone and the disc say. 'I would like to say "I love you", but after this you won't believe it.'

It sounds like an old record, full of scratches and crackles. As if everything it can say to him is fixed in advance. It's all been said before; it'll all be said again.

3
TRACEY

Mark Thorn's house is a motherless place. Kids come here from all over Liverpool, not just Aigburth and Garston. They spill drinks, pull the curtains off the rails, rip the wallpaper, chase each other on and off the sofa. Mark doesn't seem to care.

Peter Pan and the Lost Boys.

Every Tuesday evening, Mark holds a Bible discussion group. Tracey got here early today, because she wants to talk to him alone. Now she's in the kitchen, making drinks. She sniffs the milk – always a good idea, here. The sour smell's familiar. It seems to be following her around at the moment, as if the entire world's about to turn.

The house belongs to Mark's parents. Tracey's never met them; they live in Kent. They used to rent it out to students, but when Mark was released from hospital after he came back from the Falklands, they moved in here with him for six months. When they went back home, Mark stayed in Liverpool, and the house became a sort of unofficial church youth club.

Several people in church say they have an 'open door' policy, which means anyone can come round without asking first – Mark is the only one who puts it into practice. Or maybe the only one who Tracey's friends want to visit.

Mark lives by faith. That means he trusts God to provide for him. Everyone's inspired by this. They imagine strangers handing over tenners on the street, compelled by angelic voices.

Mark is vague on how it works in practice, but Tracey can guess. He has a navy pension, he doesn't pay anything for the house, and – Tracey knows this because she sometimes sits at the back during elders' meetings, waiting for her dad – the church gives him a payment every month from the collection. That's not including the envelopes her dad sets aside from his own money. She saw him hand one over before the evening meeting last Sunday. He didn't look at Mark; Mark didn't look at him: like spies on a bridge. Her dad doesn't even like Mark.

Tracey keeps quiet about all this, because she doesn't want to spoil it for everyone else. Anyway, it's still impressive. People with no money stay here for free, and Mark doesn't have any gadgets: no VCRs or hi-fi. Not even a television. He used to have an old Triumph Spitfire, which he restored himself, but he sold it and gave the money away.

His bedroom's downstairs at the front. During the day, he sits in state and receives visitors.

Tea for her, but Mark drinks boiled water – he's a show-off that way. She comes through from the kitchen, and puts his mug down on the bedside table. Mark's leaning back against the headboard with his legs stretched out on the coverlet, crossed at the ankles. He's wearing an Adidas tracksuit and a plain white T-shirt underneath. The sheets are all tucked in, shipshape; the whole room stowed neat as a cabin. Besides the bed, the most noticeable piece of furniture is a bench with a set of weights, which he uses every day. There's one decoration: a poster Blu-Tacked to the wall above the headboard. It's a reproduction of a Victorian painting, which shows a man, kneeling by a pool. A group of topless women in the water, pulling him in.

The poster's a subject of controversy among the Tuesday night regulars. Someone's drawn a speech bubble coming out of the mouth of one of the women, which says, 'Stop looking at my boobs!' Mark was angry about the speech bubble, because you shouldn't deface a work of art, but no one confessed, and he hasn't taken the poster down.

Tracey doesn't know how to raise the subject of Robert. It's weird, being in a man's bedroom. She sits down on a straight-backed wooden chair and puts her mug on the large dresser opposite the bed. She doesn't say anything.

The bedroom door stays open.

Doors stay open in Tracey's house too. It's a matter of prin-ciple. Except on the morning of her mum's funeral, when she stood outside her parents' room, holding a mug of Earl Grey: dirty dishwater, but her dad likes it. Three sugars – two more than usual – because she thought it might help. She held her breath for twenty seconds, as if she had the hiccups, then she knocked. That bed was tucked in too. Her dad sitting on the edge, in a stiff shirt and a fat black tie. Puffy face, like he'd shaved in cold water. Still in his socks, freshly polished shoes to one side. She looked down at his feet. His left big toe poked through a hole in one sock. His eyes followed her gaze. He wiggled the toe around. She put the tea down. Her dad didn't speak. She didn't touch him.

She doesn't touch Mark either.

He's had several operations. The scar tissue on his arm and torso contracts, so they have to cut it open again and do skin grafts. It's most obvious on the left hand, where the fingers are still fused together, but he has problems with the wrist and elbow on the same side. You can see angry flashes at his neck and waist when he moves.

Tracey doesn't believe in saints, and even if she did, Mark wouldn't qualify, but she envies him. He's been purified. She imagines him turning away from the explosion in the Falklands, his face protected by the hand of God. His skin sizzling as it hits the black Atlantic water.

She runs her fingers over the inflamed skin on her own neck.

Resists the urge to pick and scratch. She doesn't feel purified. She feels grubby, dragged down into her body.

'Does it bother you?' Mark says, looking at her probing fingers.

'What?' Maybe she's coming out in sympathy, the eczema spreading like a blush. 'No, no.' But it feels like an insult, this denial. Because it's Mark, who deserves the truth. About this anyway. 'Yes, it bothers me,' she says. 'First I prayed that God would take it away. Now I just pray I'll know how to bear it.' She glances at his hand, then winces. 'It's not the same.'

'It is the same,' Mark says. 'Because you feel the same.'

'I don't. It's not that bad.'

'It's alright.' Mark swings both legs over the side of the bed, so he's facing her. He places his hands together, as if he's about to pray, except that the right hand is curled protectively around the damaged left one, but then he squeezes both between his thighs. He's folded in on himself, and his hands are trapped, not raised to God.

He straightens up; his spine clicks. He unzips his tracksuit top and shrugs it off. Then he takes off his T-shirt. Smooth, in one go – even though he has to hold his left arm at a funny angle. 'Look,' he says.

She looks. Ridges and whorls, mountains and valleys. A changing landscape. When the burns were new, he must have been skinless. Without form, and void. A wet hole of pain. Then God made a firmament, to divide raw, molten flesh from the crust on its surface; inside from outside; who he was before from who he is now.

But Mark lives in a fallen world, and his body doesn't know how to stop making scar tissue. Now the burn is something it keeps doing to itself, over and over again, the landscape folding, cracking, splitting.

His burns are part of him. Or he's part of them. Her eczema just feels like a parasite. Chewing her skin up, scratching it off.

Should she touch him; put her finger in his side.

Mark puts his T-shirt back on. 'What did you want to speak to me about?' he asks.

'Have you noticed anything strange about Robert lately?' she says. 'Stranger than usual.'

Mark tuts. 'That thing at the church show. And camp last year. A lot of bottle, I'll give him that. But he takes it too far. It's just to please himself – he doesn't care what anyone else thinks.'

'It's funny.' She enjoys the reaction Robert gets. She enjoys provoking it with him. But she's not responsible; she can wash her hands. It's like being a participant and a bystander at the same time.

'I can see the attraction for you,' Mark says. 'Everyone can see you're a good person. Look after your weird friend when he throws an eppie.'

Tracey blinks. It's part of Mark's power, this willingness to say the unsayable, as if he's passed beyond vanity to some place where everyone's capable of looking at their reflection in the mirror and seeing it for what it is.

'He's different,' she says, 'lately. He has these gaps. Seems to go somewhere else.'

'Hard to tell what's normal, with him. Have you asked?'

'I tried. He changed the subject.'

'Are you and he …?'

'No. He's just my weird friend.'

'You seem close.'

'I don't think of him that way.' She goes to scratch her neck, touches the cross there instead. 'I've known him a long time,' she says. 'He changed, when he became a Christian. For the better.'

'So I'd hope.'

'He seemed happier – for a while. Now I'm not so sure.'

The front doorbell rings. Already? She glances at her watch. Still an hour until the official start of the Bible study. She had to rush her dinner to get here before anyone else.

'I'll keep an eye on him,' Mark says. He zips up his tracksuit top. 'We can talk again.' He nods towards the hall. 'Will you get that?'

She goes to the front door, feeling proud, like she's sharing the hosting duties.

It's Robert. 'Hi,' he says. He frowns. 'What are you doing here so early?'

Rebecca Miller's gran has just died, so Tracey's stuck talking to her in the kitchen. Tracey isn't close with Rebecca, who goes to Bethesda, but everyone remembers Tracey's mum, so she often finds herself in awkward conversations about death and heaven. Robert doesn't seem to have the same problem – not everyone knows his story.

Tracey's making another cup of tea. Only the one though, because making a drink for Mark or Rebecca is fine, but she doesn't want to set a precedent and end up as the group Wendy, tonight or any other night.

Although the kitchen's full of people, she focuses on the sound of the kettle as it struggles towards the boil. Kevin jostles her as he squeezes past into the lounge.

Apart from Mark, everyone here's a teenager. Well, apart from Sandy and Liz, the nurses who live upstairs. They're older. They help with Mark's dressings, after the operations. She doesn't *think* he planned it that way. Anyway, people move in and out here all the time.

The Lost Boys are just as likely to be girls though. They find the burns romantic. When Mark turns his attention on you – is that a feeling from God? Tracey's not sure. Maybe it's a gift, but he doesn't always use it wisely. Robert, who really is a Lost

Boy, follows Mark around from room to room, while the girls squeal and shout.

Well, she knows herself. Robert can be too much.

Mark powers through the kitchen holding a pile of exercise sheets for the Bible study. He types them himself, and photocopies them at church. There's a paparazzi swarm around him. 'Alright, alright!' he says. 'Time to get started. Sit down and shut up!'

Everyone moves through to the lounge at the back: a large room which seems to have been created out of two smaller ones, since there's a crude plastered archway in the middle, where the connecting wall used to be. The furniture's donated or rescued. The sofa smells of chip grease and engine oil, so Tracey usually sits on one of the wooden chairs. Or the floor. But the carpet's even dirtier.

She takes the seat next to Rebecca, who holds on to Tracey's hand like it's a soggy hanky. Robert's on the opposite side of the room, near Kevin, who's squashed into the middle of the sofa, next to his friend Paul. They're whispering to each other. Paul's a mod, so he's wearing a Ben Sherman shirt and Adidas trainers – though surely mods aren't supposed to have a perm and highlights? Kevin has a Led Zeppelin T-shirt – proudly displayed, since he's not at church – and Dr Martens boots.

Kevin usually says nothing during the discussion; Robert won't shut up. Paul asks awkward questions. Like Robert, he's a recent convert.

Kevin winks at her. What's that supposed to mean?

'Pray first,' Mark says, and lowers his head. Everyone else does the same – apart from Robert, who keeps looking at Mark, and Tracey, who watches both of them.

Sandy and Liz whisper something to each other. 'Oi! Shh!' Mark says. 'Tracey, do you want to open for us?'

Not really – but if you insist. 'Lord,' she says, taking the opportunity to get her hand back from Rebecca, 'please help us to learn something new about you tonight. Not assume we know the answers already. Thank you.' As she says these words, she discovers that she means them.

'Good prayer,' Mark says. 'We're going to look at Genesis 22. Difficult story. I've been struggling with it all week. God asks Abraham to kill his only son, Isaac, whose birth was a miracle. Why, God?' No one answers on God's behalf, so Mark continues. 'Who wants to read the passage?'

The usual awkward silence, until Robert says, 'I will.'

Everyone groans. Paul throws a balled-up piece of paper at his head.

Robert uses the King James Version. Tracey can't remember when it fell out of fashion. Everyone had it when she was little, or the Revised Standard Version, which is similar, but with modernized spelling and vocabulary. Even that's heresy for some members of the congregation. As Mrs Evans likes to say, 'If the King James was good enough for the Apostle Paul, then it's good enough for me.' But now over half the church uses the New International Version. There's also the Good News, in simple English, and the Living Bible, which is even simpler.

When Tracey was little, she knew every Christian believer. Now there's a bigger world. People debating God's Word. New ideas, new gifts, or old ones rediscovered – like speaking in tongues, which her dad doesn't like. He says that miraculous proofs of God's presence were special gifts for the early Church. He uses the RSV.

'Do we have to have the ye olde version?' Paul says to Robert. 'Nobody knows what it means.'

'God won't fit into normal words,' Robert says. 'When I'm reading, I want to feel that. I don't want the words to disappear.' His knee has begun to jiggle.

Where do people speak in tongues? Not in church – not their church anyway. No one does it here at Bible study either. Or is there a secret inner group who meet on a different night? Who would that be? Not Robert: he would've said. She doesn't want to ask Mark how speaking in tongues works, because she's scared it's contagious and he might pass it on. How would she explain that to her dad?

Mark says, 'Jesus came down to earth, to speak with us face to face. And used everyday language.'

Robert isn't giving up that easily. 'But no one understood Him.'

'And the people who made the King James, they were trying to do what Jesus did: make it easier. Even Shakespeare wrote for ordinary people. English changes, even if the Bible doesn't.'

Robert pushes his palm down on his jiggling knee. A lid on a boiling pot. 'The disciples had to ask Jesus what he meant.'

'And He told them.'

'But they still didn't understand. And what about Revelation? God hides what He means. Sometimes.'

'I think it's dangerous, this idea of hidden meanings,' Mark says. 'You end up with the Bible in a special language, and you need priests to explain it for you.'

Everyone here tonight has an NIV or the Good News, apart from Mark. He uses the Living Bible when he's reading out a long passage, but when he wants to concentrate on a particular word or phrase, he goes back to an interlinear edition of the NIV, which puts the English translation next to the Greek text. Mark doesn't know any Greek: he looks up the words one by one in *Vine's Expository Dictionary.*

'I'm not talking about priests,' Robert says. 'God has secrets. He doesn't share them with everyone. He whispers in your ear.'

'Robert, we can talk about this another time if you want. We need to get on with Abraham and Isaac.'

'I don't have the King James tonight anyway,' Robert says. He claps one palm against the pale cover of a new NIV. 'I brought this one instead. I just got it, for the group.'

'Okay. Can you read Genesis 22 for us?'

Tracey tries to concentrate on the reading. The stories are all so familiar. The best way to pinch yourself awake is to ask questions in your head. Try to make the story real.

Robert begins, 'SOME TIME LATER GOD TESTED ABRAHAM. HE SAID TO HIM, "ABRAHAM!" "HERE I AM," HE REPLIED.'

Abraham's not even surprised. He doesn't say, 'Can I really hear a voice? Is that you, God?' Not even, 'Oh flip, it's God again. He's already made me cut the end of my penis off. What's He want this time?'

Robert continues. 'THEN GOD SAID, "TAKE YOUR SON, YOUR ONLY SON, WHOM YOU LOVE – ISAAC – AND GO TO THE REGION OF MORIAH. SACRIFICE HIM THERE AS A BURNT OFFERING ON A MOUN- TAIN THAT I WILL SHOW YOU." EARLY THE NEXT MORNING ABRAHAM GOT UP AND LOADED HIS DONKEY.'

God speaks; Abraham obeys. But there is a gap. A night be- tween. What happened then? Abraham alone with his decision. Jesus in Gethsemane, sweating blood. Please, don't make me do this.

'AS THE TWO OF THEM WENT ON TOGETHER, ISAAC SPOKE UP AND SAID TO HIS FATHER ABRAHAM, "FATHER?" "YES, MY SON?" ABRAHAM REPLIED. "THE FIRE AND WOOD ARE HERE," ISAAC SAID, "BUT WHERE IS THE LAMB FOR THE BURNT OFFERING?" ABRAHAM ANSWERED, "GOD HIMSELF WILL PROVIDE THE LAMB FOR THE BURNT OFFERING, MY SON."'

Isaac has to carry the wood. Like Jesus carrying the cross. At least Jesus knew what he was letting Himself in for.

Mark's a burnt offering too. She blinks that thought away – like tears.

Robert reaches the climax of the story. 'HE BOUND HIS SON

Isaac and laid him on the altar, on top of the wood. Then he reached out his hand and took the knife to slay his son.'

On the other side of the room, Kevin lifts a knife-like finger and moves it towards Paul's throat. Paul swats it aside and tries to concentrate on his Bible.

God doesn't speak to Isaac, because it's not Isaac's test. But at some point in the story, Isaac makes a decision. Abraham's an old man. He can't carry the wood, and he can't tie Isaac up against his will. So Abraham decides to obey God, but Isaac decides to obey Abraham. Which decision is harder? Isaac's trapped in Abraham's story. Lie down and die, so *someone else* can prove a point to God. Your life doesn't belong to you. That's the real test.

Robert continues. 'But the angel of the Lord called out to him from heaven, "Abraham! Abraham!" "Here i am," he replied. "Do not lay a hand on the boy," he said. "Do not do anything to him. now i know that you fear God, because you have not withheld from me your son, your only son."'

The angel opens its mouth, but God's voice comes out. Like a tape recording. Or a ventriloquist's dummy. Can God possess you like the Devil does? Is that what happens when you speak in tongues?

Does Isaac hear the angel too? Double relief. Not just, 'You're not going to die.' But also, 'God really did speak to your dad. He's not mad.' Or maybe Abraham's staring at nothing, talking to himself. So Isaac has to keep believing, keep sacrificing himself on the altar of his dad's faith whenever he remembers this moment.

No mention of Sarah. No one cares what Isaac's mum thinks.

Earlier in Genesis, three angels visit to announce Isaac's coming birth. In that story, Sarah's there, listening outside the tent flap. She doesn't get to sit with important visitors; she just makes the tea.

When the angels tell Abraham that Sarah will become pregnant, she says to herself: You must be joking. Because she knows her own body.

The angel says, 'WHY DID SARAH LAUGH?'

Sarah denies it. 'I didn't laugh.'

'Yes, you did.'

The message is for Sarah, but God delivers it to Abraham. Like in church, where John Cooper thinks women shouldn't speak in the morning meeting. If they have something to say, they should whisper it to a man sitting next to them, and he can say it for them.

Abraham believes; Abraham acts; we never see him thinking. If there was a night like Jesus in Gethsemane, then it's private, hidden. But Sarah thinks, and her thought is a doubt.

Where's Sarah when Abraham takes Isaac away to kill him? She doesn't know anything about it. Because if she knew, she'd stop it.

Robert's finished the reading, and the atmosphere in the room's serious. Kevin puts on a childish voice and sings a Sunday school song, 'Father Abraham had many sons, Many sons had Father Abraham.' He waves his arms in the air to the rhythm of the words. 'I am one of them – and so are you.'

Rebecca perks up and finishes the verse: 'So let's all praise the Lord!' Everyone laughs.

Tracey can't ask most of her questions aloud. But she can ask, 'What's the difference between a test and a temptation?'

Mark must have been thinking about this too, because he doesn't hesitate. 'God tests; the Devil tempts,' he says. 'When God tests, he wants us to pass. To grow stronger in our love for Him. When the Devil tempts, he wants us to fail. To separate us from God. And God will never ask us to commit a sin.'

'What, you mean like murder?' Paul says.

'If a voice told you to kill me,' Robert says, 'you'd think it was the Devil.'

'Not necessarily,' Kevin says.

Tracey admires Rebecca's angora jumper, and then lowers her head to pick at the fraying elastic holding up her knee socks. What if her dad said, 'God told me to kill you'? Or worse, 'God told me to kill your mum.' Is that why she died? To test her dad's faith? To test Tracey's?

No angel for us; no message from God. No explanation. Silence.

She says, 'The devil can pretend to be an angel of light. To trick us.'

'God had a special relationship with Abraham,' Mark says. 'They've spoken before, many times. So Abraham recognizes God's voice. No room for doubt.'

'Abraham knows,' Robert says. 'But he can't explain to anyone else. No one will understand.'

'Abraham had a personal covenant with God,' Mark says, 'but today God's covenant is with the Church. If we want to know His will, we need to look at what it says in the Bible, talk to other Christians, pray together.'

'If Abraham did that, you all would've talked him out of it.'

Mark ignores this. He continues, 'This story is a prophecy about the crucifixion of Jesus too. God can ask Abraham to do this, because He's willing to sacrifice His son as well. The question for us is: What are we willing to do? If we hold something back from God – if we say, "You can have everything else, but not this" – then we're going to lose it.'

The Lord your God is a jealous God. But jealousy comes from fear; and PERFECT LOVE DRIVES OUT FEAR. How can Tracey love a God who'd take her mum away, just because she loved her too much? Or not enough.

Robert flips to a Bible passage and reads, 'IF ANYONE COMES TO ME AND DOES NOT HATE FATHER AND MOTHER, WIFE AND CHIL-

DREN, BROTHERS AND SISTERS — YES, EVEN THEIR OWN LIFE — SUCH A PERSON CANNOT BE MY DISCIPLE.'

Rebecca blows her nose. Tracey pats her shoulder and thinks, WHOEVER CLAIMS TO LOVE GOD YET HATES A BROTHER OR SISTER IS A LIAR. She doesn't say that aloud either, even though it's a Bible verse. She doesn't like arguing.

'If we let go of the thing we love,' Mark says, 'then we might get it back. Abraham believed God would keep his promise about being the father of a great nation, even if he killed Isaac.'

'How?' Paul asks.

'God would bring Isaac back from the dead.'

Paul laughs.

'God brought Jesus back too,' Mark says.

'Ah.' Paul blushes, as if he's been caught out. 'But what if God hadn't stopped Abraham?'

'He did stop him.'

Paul's trying to learn how to behave in Bible studies, so all he says is, 'Hmm.' He looks around, trying to catch someone's eye: someone else who agrees that this is nuts. Tracey keeps her face blank.

'Abraham was willing for everyone to hate him,' Robert says.

Mark says, 'Abraham was saved by faith. And faith means: be ready to answer God's call, to carry out His will. Whatever it costs. He looks down briefly. 'On your study sheet, there's two questions.' A collective rustle of paper as everyone confirms this. 'What have I given up for God? What would I struggle to give up, if God asked me to? We'll take ten minutes now to write down some answers.'

Silence for a while — or what passes for silence here. People tapping pens, muttering, giggling. The pens all come from a box. Tracey's has no lid — and the end's been chewed off.

When a decent interval has passed, Mark asks, 'Kevin, what have you got?'

'Who, me?'

'Nobody has to say what's on their list, if they don't want to. Maybe it's private, between you and God. But it would be good if we had some examples.'

'Well,' Kevin says, 'no swearing, no drinking, no, um, sex before marriage. That kind of thing. Which made me think. Why is it always about giving things up? A list of things you can't do.'

'Prohibitions,' Mark says. 'But when Jesus came, He said, BLESSED ARE THE POOR. BLESSED ARE THE MEEK.' He looks at Rebecca. 'BLESSED ARE THOSE WHO MOURN. All positives.'

Yes, well, Tracey thinks: you're the one who told us to write down what we've given up.

Mark continues, 'And then, the most positive of all: LOVE YOUR NEIGHBOUR AS YOURSELF.'

'BLESSED ARE THE PERSECUTED,' Robert adds.

'On your list,' Mark says to Kevin, 'they're all general things. Nothing personal.'

'Hang on a minute.' Kevin tries to buy time by excavating himself from his position on the sofa, where five people are sitting even though there's only space for three. He's half-submerged in the middle, so he has to elbow his way out.

Mark says, 'Paul, what answers have you got?'

'Politics,' Paul says. 'For both questions.' He crosses his arms.

Mark waits a moment to see if he wants to say anything else, then asks, 'Anyone else? What would you struggle to give up?'

'Music,' Tracey says. She nods at Kevin and taps her finger against her blouse. He grins and touches the same place on his Led Zeppelin T-shirt.

'How much time do you spend on music?' Mark asks.

'Playing or listening?'

'Both.'

'More than praying or reading the Bible,' Tracey says. 'More than the telly. It's probably the most important thing in my life – other than God. And it feels … separate from Him. Not necessarily opposed, just separate.'

'God speaks to me through music,' Robert says.

'The question isn't always: what do I have to give up?' Mark says. 'Sometimes it's better to ask: how can I use this to serve God?'

'Like David in the Psalms,' Robert says.

Mark asks him, 'What did you write down, for the second question?'

'What's the one thing I *don't* want to do?' Robert says. 'The most difficult thing. The thing I'm most scared of.' He slaps the cover of his Bible. 'Tell everyone at school about my faith.' He pauses. 'Therefore, I'm going to do it.'

Mark puts his hands together and leans forward. 'How?'

'I can ask to speak at an assembly.'

'You … could do that.' Mark's taken aback. He normally has to push people; he's not used to them getting ahead of him. 'I think it's a good idea,' he says. He'd just prefer if it was someone other than Robert who'd had this idea. He adds, 'We can pray for you.'

Kevin gives up trying to escape from the sofa cushions and sinks back into oblivion; Paul has his hands over his face. They both go to the same school as Tracey and Robert.

Sandy and Liz are whispering to each other again. Tracey notices some writing on the wall where there's a ripped corner of wallpaper. It's quite small: it reads 'Melanie fancies Chicken Skin'. Who's Melanie?

Tracey looks at her sheet of paper. What have I given up for God? My mum. What would I struggle to give up? My dad. She can't say that though. There are other things she can't say too. Things like: Please God, don't hurt Mark's beautiful face. But some things have to be said, no matter how painful it is.

She holds her hand up like Mark does in church when he's singing praises. Everyone stops talking. 'If God told my dad, "Kill your daughter,"' Tracey says, 'he'd reply, "Take me instead. Kill me instead. I'll die before I kill her."'

She looks at Mark, but she's talking to Robert. She says, 'I'll stand there with you. I'll speak with you.'

4
TRACEY

Tracey steps inside Robert's porch and presses the bell. *Bing; bong.* Old-fashioned metal chimes.

He never has any visitors – apart from her, and she never steps inside for longer than a few minutes. She feels too self-conscious, as if the rooms are larger on his side of the garden fence; as if there's an echo when she speaks. But today she's not going in, just ringing the bell to let Auntie Rose know she's here.

She walks round to the far side of the house, where there's a tall set of wooden gates blocking the driveway, with a smaller pedestrian gate set within the larger frame. Behind the gates, farther down the driveway, she can hear locks being turned on the back door, which opens from the kitchen onto the driveway. Auntie Rose is singing, 'La cucaracha, la cucaracha, Play it on your old guitar-cha!' She always sings the same lines. She's tone-deaf.

There are gaps between the planks on the gates, so when the kitchen door's open Tracey can see Auntie Rose, who stands on the threshold for a second and rubs her hands together. 'Brrr!' she says. Then she walks down the driveway to open the side gate for Tracey. She's wearing her apron.

'Good morning, Auntie Rose,' Tracey says. She always feels like she should bow for this daily exchange.

'How are you today, Tracey?'

'Very well thank you. Did you watch the ice skating last night?'

'Oh wasn't it *beautiful*. I was so pleased they won.' But she doesn't look pleased. She keeps rubbing her hands together. She says, 'I'm concerned about something.'

'What?'

'You can't have your drums in the garage any more.'

Tracey swallows. 'Okay. Why not?'

Auntie Rose slides the two bolts at the top and bottom of the pedestrian gate back in place behind Tracey. 'The noise upsets Edward,' she says.

Tracey doesn't believe this. Uncle Edward doesn't have emotions. But maybe Tracey's daily practice wakes him up. 'I'm sorry about that,' she says.

'Yes,' Auntie Rose says. 'So you'll have to move them.'

Tracey tries not to scowl. 'When do you want me to do that?'

'Today.'

She waits a second, and says, 'Can I practise now? I'll move them after school.'

'Well … alright.' Auntie Rose removes a Yale key from her apron pocket. She holds it out in the air between them for a second before she hands it over.

It was a condition when her dad bought the drums: she can't use them inside her house. And their garage is full of her mum's stuff. Her dad doesn't even keep the car in there. So every day, when she gets up, Tracey does her *Daily Bread* reading and quiet time, has breakfast, and then comes through to Robert's garage. She practises for twenty minutes. Then she knocks on the kitchen door to give the key back. When Robert's finished his breakfast, he then repeats her journey the other way round.

Today it's foggy, and there's frost on the ground. It's difficult practising on winter mornings, because there's no bulb in Robert's garage, so it's gloomy as well as freezing. In one corner, there are garden things: gloves, secateurs, a metal watering can and a rusty manual lawnmower, which her dad heaves backwards and forwards across the tiny front and back gardens for Auntie Rose. Why doesn't Robert do that?

The drums are in the middle of the concrete floor, on a few yellow sheets of the *Echo*. She sits down on the stool and checks the kit. Bass, snare, tom; a ride and crash cymbal, a hi-hat with a floor pedal. She usually listens to something on her Walkman and tries to drum along. Today, it's 'Blue Monday', which is impossible – that's why she's chosen it.

Robert seems to think that Larry Mullen Jr of U2 is Tracey's favourite drummer. But if he'd ever thought to ask, he'd know it's Stephen Morris of Joy Division and New Order. Listening to their records, she likes trying to work out which bits are Morris copying machines and which bits are machines copying Morris.

From the *NME* and *Melody Maker*, she knows that Joy Division's producer, Martin Hannett, made Morris record each drum part separately, in isolation, but Morris couldn't stop himself hitting the missing rhythms out on his legs; he had bruises after every session. 'Blue Monday' is different: it's programmed on a drum machine. Tracey knows from *Top of the Pops* that when New Order play it live, Morris abandons his kit and fiddles about with synthesizers. So there's no way for her to reconstruct the drum pattern by watching him move. Instead, she has to play the original recording on her Walkman in snatches of a few seconds, rewinding the same section over and over again. Like the VCR with a comedy sketch.

'Blue Monday' opens with a kick drum. She wasn't sure at first, because the compression makes the pitch seem higher. But yes, it's a kick, from the lower body. Except there's no twitching foot on the record – only hers, here in the garage.

Dum, dum, da-da-da-da-da-da-da-dum, dum, dum, dum, dum, dum, da-da-da-da-da-da-da—

It doesn't even sound that fast, until you try and copy it.

Maybe if she had two pedals, but one foot can't keep up. Especially today, when she can see her breath and she's bloated with boots and a puffa jacket. Last winter, she tried drumming in fingerless gloves. It's better when the sticks touch skin. And the blood gets moving in her hands soon enough. She can see her fingers getting redder.

Dum, dum, dum, dum, dum, dum, da-da-da-da-da-da-da—

The same pattern when the synth comes in, but it changes when the bass starts. Or rather, it moves down in the mix, and a new rhythm comes in on top. Much simpler: kick, snare, hi-hat. Clear, separate movements, like Morris in the studio, playing for Hannett. About one minute in, all the instruments drop out except for a fill on the hi-hat, then when the song comes back, there's a new drum sequence, and the impossible rhythm disappears.

Tracey hits the stop button and rewinds the tape. She goes back to the impossible bit, which helps her to think about another impossible thing. In about an hour and a half, she and Robert are going to speak to the upper-school assembly.

Dum, dum, da-da-da-da-da-da-da—

The Brethren believe in witnessing. Many evening meetings involve testimonials, in which believers describe how they first came to experience God's love and forgiveness. Faith is a story. You tell it to yourself; then you tell it to other people. And when they hear your story, it confirms their own.

It starts in darkness. Separation from God, the depths of depravity. Persecuting Christians, trading slaves. Alcoholism, drug addiction, prostitution. Tracey doesn't know any drug addicts or prostitutes, but Mr Harris was an alcoholic. He wasn't allowed to take Communion, and everyone used to watch his mouth and hands when the cup came round.

Then there's Robert's dad. *Dum, dum, dum, dum, dum, dum, da-da-da-da-da-da-da—*

She hasn't had sex, but she can still plumb the depths of depravity, inside her own heart. FOR ALL HAVE SINNED AND FALL SHORT OF THE GLORY OF GOD. THERE IS NO ONE RIGHTEOUS, NOT EVEN ONE.

Yes, but the story's better if you met God on the road to Damascus. A flash of lightning, dividing before from after. Mark found God in the Falklands. An explosion and a shipwreck. He definitely has the best testimony in church. He can even show where the Devil tried to snatch hold of him.

Tracey can't find where her lost self used to be, no matter how often she rummages through her past. As far back as she can remember, she's been surrounded by God's love. Waiting together, in silence, in the morning meeting; sharing the bread and the wine. She's never felt alone, or separate – until recently. Because the older she gets, and the more history she accumulates, the farther away God seems and the more she has to fight to clear a quiet place inside for His still, small voice.

Silence; noise. And somewhere in-between: *dum, dum, dum, dum, dum, dum, da-da-da-da-da-da-da—*

Tracey was baptized a year ago: that was supposed to divide before from after too. Go down into the water; come up clean, washed in the blood of the Lamb. Die to your old self; be resurrected in the Spirit. She had to go to discussion classes for a couple of months, but there was nothing new to discover there. At home, her dad said, 'I'm not going to interrogate you. It's not an exam you have to pass. You know when you're ready. It's between you and God.'

'How does it feel?' Bernard Sumner asks in 'Blue Monday' – then says it again but changing 'it' to 'I' – because, like Uncle Edward, he's got no idea what an emotion is. A robot asking what it means to be human. He doesn't want a description; he wants instructions.

God is all around her – and He's hidden somewhere inside. She thought baptism might bring Him back to the surface.

At church, the baptistery's hidden under the floor in the evening hall. Beneath the wooden cover, there are steps leading down into it, with handrails. When there's a service scheduled, Tracey's dad stays on after the morning meeting to take the cover off, fill the pool, and turn the water heater on.

A year ago, she put on a special white robe, like a dressing gown. She stepped down into the pool, where John Cooper waited, immersed to his waist. Like entering a drooling mouth.

The robe ballooned, and she pressed the water out from underneath before waddling her way to John. A smell of chlorine. Probably no one had ever peed in the baptistery, but someone might have had a verruca.

She turned her back to John; he placed one hand on her stomach and the other on the back of her neck. 'Do you accept Jesus Christ as your personal Lord and Saviour?' he asked.

'Yes,' Tracey said, and then, to make double sure, 'I accept Jesus Christ as my personal Lord and Saviour.'

'IF YOU DECLARE WITH YOUR MOUTH, "JESUS IS LORD," AND BE-LIEVE IN YOUR HEART THAT GOD RAISED HIM FROM THE DEAD, YOU WILL BE SAVED.' John dipped her under the surface while the organ music swirled into her ear, filling it up.

She imagined Mark under the water with her, his hands on her stomach and her neck, fire and shrapnel raining down.

'I baptize you, in the name of the Father, the Son and the Holy Spirit,' John said from somewhere above, through the water. A distorted voice, like Bernard Sumner's through a vocoder. John dipped her a second time, and a third. Then he raised her up, the water sucking at her arms and legs, back into the light.

Still nothing new.

Dum, dum, dum, dum, dum, dum, da-da-da-da-da-da-da—

It's exciting, living inside the song. And she gets inside, even as, inevitably, almost immediately, the thump of her foot on the pedal falls out of synch with the stuttering drum machine.

The failure, the gap. Somehow, that's her connection to the song. An emotional robot; a machine with a body.

How does Tracey feel? By pretending not to feel. Until she can't stop it pulsing through her hands, gushing out between her fingers, swirling into her ear.

Dum, dum— Click. Enough.

If she can find some place in herself, in her past, that's outside God, then maybe she can prick a hole in the barrier between her and Him – and let Him back in.

She puts her gloves back on and claps her hands to encourage the blood to keep moving. Muffled: the wool absorbs the sound. 'God, help me today to find the right words,' she says, and that sound is heavy and clear, like glass.

Bing; … *bong.* Twenty minutes later, she's back next door and Robert's ringing her bell. It's obviously him, because he waits several seconds after the *bing* before he lets go of the button. It's a game they play. Tracey waits by her front door, and tries to swing it open before he releases the *bong.*

They walk to school every day, but they usually separate where Greenhill Road meets Heath Road. New Heys Comprehensive is spread over three sites. The lower school used to be a boys' secondary modern, and it shares playing fields with the custom-built middle-school building, where Robert spends most of his time. Most days, Tracey walks on alone from the middle school, past the lower and on to the upper, which used to be a girls' grammar. Her birthday's at the end of October, and Robert's is at the beginning, but she's a year older, so she's in fifth form and he's in fourth. Today's different: because of the assembly, they both have to report to the upper-school staff room.

In the porch, Robert's wearing his snorkel parka, zipped all the way up, so she can't see his face, just the flash of the orange lining. He's still looking at the doorbell. She says, 'Auntie Rose told me I can't practise in the garage any more.'

The parka funnel swivels towards her. 'Why?'

'You tell me. Something to do with Uncle Edward.'

Robert taps his red nylon mittens against his blue parka pockets. 'I can ask her. But if she's made up her mind, it won't do any good.'

They set off. It's been overcast or drizzling the past couple of days, but it's clear and bright today. Robert falls silent, and Tracey doesn't speak either. Two prisoners heading towards the scaffold. At the top of Ravenstone Road, they cross over Brodie Avenue, before turning right and continuing along towards Greenhill Road.

Robert says, 'I had a dream.'

'Oh?' Other people's dreams are usually boring, like other people's illnesses.

'I was on a game show on telly, like that Japanese one, *Endurance*, where they have to eat cockroaches, or carry weights hanging from their goolies.' She can't see Robert's mouth, and the sound has to make its way out of the parka funnel into the cold air, like his head's one of those old gramophones with a horn instead of a loudspeaker.

'Were you reading poetry?' Dear God, please don't do that in the assembly.

He shifts his backpack up on his shoulders and says, 'I was eating myself.'

'Eating?'

'They had me tied up. On a cross.'

'Like Jesus?'

'No nails, just ropes; and laid out flat on the ground.'

'And they were filming you?'

'There was a chef with one of those white hats, holding a cleaver. He started to cut things off me.'

'Things?'

'Just toes and bits of fingers – to start with,' Robert says. 'And he had a big cauldron, with gravy and vegetables, bubbling on a fire.'

'A pot of Scouse.'

'He threw the fingers and toes in. Splash, plop. Then the cauldron would rumble, like a stomach.'

'Did the chef say anything?'

'I couldn't understand him.'

'Was he Swedish?' Tracey asks. 'Bork bork bork!'

'He filled a bowl, and I had to eat a few mouthfuls.'

'I thought you were a fussy eater,' Tracey says. When he stayed with her, he used to have dried bread and water.

'I had to keep it down,' Robert says, 'and if I did, the presenter asked me if I wanted to keep going, on to the next round. Big microphone. I had to speak as loud as I could. "Yes, I want to continue."'

'So you could understand what he said?'

'No. But there was a translator.'

Tracey shuffles through the remains of the winter mush on Brodie Avenue, sliding her feet along the ground so her shoes push it up into a ridge in front of her as she goes. 'Were there any other contestants?'

'Two. One on either side of me.'

'Of course.'

'But behind me, so I couldn't see them properly. I couldn't turn my head because of the ropes.'

'You had ropes around your head too?'

'Forehead,' Robert says. 'So I was worried. Maybe the other two weren't really playing, and it was all a trick. When it was their turn, they were just cutting bits off a dead pig, and making slurping noises. "Ha ha! You divvy. There's no prize either!"'

'Do we have to talk about this? Shouldn't we go over what we're going to do in the assembly?'

'They started with fingers and toes; then they moved up my arms and legs.'

'Weren't you bleeding?'

'They moved the ropes as well, for a tourniquet.'

'Robert, this is really disgusting.'

The funnel points down at the floor. 'I have to tell you. I don't want to.'

'Okay. But hurry up, because we'll be at Kevin and Paul soon.'

Over the last couple of weeks, they've all started to meet up at the junction where Brodie Avenue turns into Greenhill Road, by the lollipop lady. Kevin lives down in Cressington but comes up by Whitehedge Road; Paul lives farther along Long Lane, on the council estate near the church. She can already see the two of them in the distance: shoulders hunched, hands in pockets, not looking at one another. Kevin waves when he sees her.

'When they get to my elbows and knees,' Robert continues, 'they stop. And they move the knife up to my face. The presenter's in front of me; someone's holding my mouth open. The presenter says, "Do you want to continue?" A knife in my mouth; they're going to cut my tongue out. What am I going to do then? How am I going to keep playing? And then the presenter's gone, and Jesus is there. They're crucifying Him properly, so he's up in the air in front of me. And until then, I feel sick, but I'm not scared. But now I'm trapped. And just before the knife cuts into my mouth, I shout, "Do it to Him! Do it to Him instead!"'

Robert's still looking at the floor. He slows down to step over a puddle.

'It's only a dream,' Tracey says. 'Don't you remember what Mark said? We're not responsible for our dreams. It's not a sin.' The funnel turns towards her and she can see Robert's furrowed eyebrows inside.

Ah, right. Mark was talking about boys having wet dreams. He didn't say so, but he had a nudge nudge, wink wink tone in his voice. And Kevin blushed. She says, 'I think dreams are just our brain sorting through stuff.'

'Not in the Bible,' Robert says. 'Dreams are about the future, not the past.'

'Some dreams. The ones from God. I don't think this one's from God.'

Robert's slowed to a crawl; even so, he can't put off the rendez-vous with Kevin and Paul forever. They're both in full uniform, but they belong to different armies. Kevin's is simpler: a leather biker jacket with zips and studs. Paul's is more elaborate: a white Fred Perry tennis shirt, a cashmere Pringle V-neck, drainpipe Farah trousers. His tie is done up backwards so the thin part is at the front, with only a few inches visible and the rest of it tucked away inside the tennis shirt. Over all this, he's wearing a fishtail Merton parka, with a giant Who target on the back and badges on the lapel for The Jam and The Specials.

Robert has a badge too: it says, 'Jesus Saves'.

There are a few other rockers in school, so Kevin's got a tribe outside of church friends, but Paul's the only remaining mod, which is why he makes the effort.

Kevin asks Robert, 'What are you going to do? In the assembly.' He's in the lower sixth with Paul, so they don't have to go, but they're going to sit at the back today to show their support.

'He doesn't want to talk about it,' Tracey says.

'No rehearsals,' Robert says.

'Ah, I forgot,' Kevin says.

'BUT WHEN THEY SHALL LEAD YOU, AND DELIVER YOU UP,' Robert says, 'TAKE NO THOUGHT BEFOREHAND WHAT YE SHALL SPEAK, NEITHER DO YE PREMEDITATE.'

'Do you memorize this stuff?' Paul asks.

'Yes.'

'Isn't that kind of like rehearsing?'

Kevin laughs, but Robert doesn't join in. Instead, he holds up a mittened hand to forbid any further questions.

'He's going first,' Tracey says, 'then me.' That way she can do damage control if Robert flips out.

'How did you get the teachers to agree?' Paul asks.

'Are you kidding?' Tracey says. 'They love it. Kids doing their jobs for them. They hate assembly too.'

Kevin says, 'Just so you know, we might not walk in with you tomorrow. Depends how it goes.'

'You're assuming the Rapture won't take place before then,' Tracey says.

'Yes,' Kevin says. 'I am.'

These are her friends, but they're going to disappear in the assembly hall. They're already wearing camouflage. How does it feel? Like all the instruments are being recorded separately, and she's beating out the missing rhythms on her own body.

Dum, dum, da-da-da-da-da-da-da—

'Where do you practise your guitar?' she asks Kevin.

'At home, in the attic.'

'The attic?' She imagines a ladder leading up to a trapdoor in the ceiling.

'It's like another level. The stereo's up there too.'

'Don't your mum and dad mind the noise?'

'They're two floors down with the telly turned up,' Kevin says.

'Do you think I could keep my drums at yours? I need to move them. I can't play at mine.' She glances at Robert, who says nothing.

'Fine by me,' Kevin says. 'We could practise together. I'll ask my dad.'

5
ROBERT

A sea of faces: rising, falling; surging, breaking apart. The advancing and receding hiss, the murmur and the chatter. Robert lets this sea swallow him: Jonah in the belly of the whale. And like the whale, all those empty mouths will vomit him out.

He puts his hands over his ears. There's a sea inside him too: his head is a conch shell. Concentrate. There's something else, trapped with him deep in the belly of the whale; something scuttling out from inside the conch, unfolding itself.

Damn and bloody. Shit, fuck.

A finger of Fudge is just enough to give your kids a treat.

It can't get out if he drowns it in babble. It can't come in if he doesn't leave any space for it to enter. The problem is, there's no space for him to think either. He swallows, tries to swallow again with a dry mouth.

Jesus is shit. Fuck Jesus.

A finger of Fudge is just enough, Until it's time to eat.

He told Tracey about his dream, but he didn't tell her everything. As the knife went into his mouth, words gushed out in a mixture of blood and water. Terrible words whose monstrous shapes lurk now, waiting to form themselves again and take possession of his tongue.

He's sitting next to Tracey, behind a table on the assembly stage, waiting while the fifth form files in and arranges itself cross-legged in rows on the floor of the hall below. Robert fiddles with the zip on his parka, which he's still wearing, although he's pulled the hood down. The assistant head, Miss Murphy, is on the stage too. She stands to one side and just behind them with her arms crossed, daring anyone in the audience to question this arrangement.

Robert comes to the upper school for PE, but today it feels different. He even got to go inside before the bell rang and look at the staffroom. On the way in, the crowds broke around them, and Kevin and Paul disappeared somewhere behind in the churning foam.

Now he's inside the sea; and it's inside him.

I worship the Devil. Satan is God.

It's full of Cadbury goodness, But very small and neat.

Mark said we're not responsible for our dreams. Or stray thoughts that come in. Radio waves; our mind flickers along the dial. It's only sinful if we tune in. But it's exhausting, trying to keep them out.

'Quiet, everyone!' says Miss Murphy. 'Today, two of your fellow pupils have asked to share something with you. They're going to tell you what their faith means to them. Now, this isn't a church school. Our assemblies are non-denominational.' Robert's eyes zero in on the sneering face of Tommo Donnelly, cock of the school. Wouldn't it be amazing if he converted after hearing today's assembly?

Wouldn't it be amazing if he kissed Satan on the mouth?

A finger of Fudge is just enough to give your kids a treat.

Miss Murphy continues, 'But we thought it would be good for you to learn about each other's beliefs. Most of you know Tracey, from 51G. And this is her friend Robert, who's in the fourth year.'

Does the presence put these thoughts in his mind? No. Because it arrives now. Its skin has hardened but it's still translucent: like a fingernail. Its body is suspended in mid-air, between Robert and the audience. The tips of its toes touch the edge of the stage, where the lip falls away to the floor of the hall. If it slid forward a few inches it'd be standing on the apron, with no need to defy gravity, but it doesn't seem to care about that.

The cone expands out of its head and surrounds Robert, as if he's the one moving forward – as if he's falling into a tunnel. There's no disc inside it. Instead, there's a red jet, like a fountain, which gurgles out from where the disc used to be. As if the disc was a plug which has now been removed.

Out of the same mouth proceedeth blessing and cursing. My brethren, these things ought not so to be. Doth a fountain send forth at the same place sweet water and bitter?

Robert prays to himself: Sanctify my speech, Lord.

He stands up and opens his arms. He wants to gather the crowded hall to himself, but he can't see anyone from inside the cone. The red jet waves its way towards him, twisting over itself to stop its shape from falling apart.

Robert shouts, 'What do you want with me, Jesus, Son of the Most High God? I beg you, don't torture me!'

Miss Murphy takes a step back from the table, and someone behind and beyond the cone, to Robert's left, shouts back, 'Jesus isn't here!'

'Yes he is,' Robert says, hoping the audience can see him, even if he can't see them.

Someone to his right blows a raspberry, but it's just a sound, without a mouth. There's nothing solid in front of him: only the presence.

He had some idea of role playing an episode from the gospels. He doesn't mind seeing himself through invisible eyes, or Miss Murphy's, or even through whatever the presence perceives him with. But Tracey's rigid next to him with her eyes closed, and he can't stand that.

The hall's still there, behind the cone. People can hear him. Does he trust God or not? He empties his mind.

Lord, fill me with your signal. Let me receive You, loud and clear.

'U2,' he says. Tracey opens her eyes.

'Most of you probably know them from "New Year's Day". Off their third album, *War*. I like the second one, *October*. Ugly cover. Picture of the band outside, shivering. They look like they're thinking, "What are we doing here?" Kind of like Tracey looks now.'

Robert smiles at her, and a few people in the hall laugh. The sound ripples through the cone as a kind of liquid interference. 'What are we doing here?' he says again, pointing to himself and Tracey.

'When they were doing *October*, U2 were trying to understand what it means to be a Christian. Living and praying together, part of a church group called Shalom. Everyone in Shalom had a voice; some said they had to give up the band. Others said no, use your music for God. Meanwhile, they had to record an album, but Bono lost all his lyrics. He didn't know what to sing.

'So he went to the microphone, with nothing. That's all we ever have to offer God. He hears us anyway. Bono sang about not knowing how to sing. It's in the song titles: "I Fall Down", "Is That All?" Please help me. Get back on my feet, find the words to praise You. Make my life a sacrifice.

'The best song on *October* is called "Tomorrow". It's the first on side two, which just goes to show: never too late to start again. To be born again. Bono's asking Jesus, "When will you return? Will it be tomorrow? I want to be ready." But it's about his mum too. He says he didn't know that, when he started singing. Only afterwards.

'A knock at the door.' Robert raps on the table. He skins a knuckle on its edge, but he doesn't wince. 'Jesus. But Bono's mum died, and it's the day of her funeral, and that's the knock too. Black car waiting at the kerb. Don't answer the door. I have to; I must. Open it to eternal life; open it to death. Because Jesus is coming, but his mum's gone forever.

'I'm like Bono. I found Jesus after my mum died,' Robert says. He's not sure anyone in the assembly even knows about his mum.

A voice from the hall says, 'Didn't know He was lost!'

'No,' Robert says, 'but I was.'

And now he's lost again, up here on the stage. He sucks the cut on his hand. He opens his mouth, but nothing comes out.

The red stream from the presence leans in to kiss him. First it tastes like cherry liquorice – and then it tastes of coins, like his bloody knuckle. A hard finger, forcing its way down his throat. He can't spit it out. It's already part of him, and it's leaking out of his mouth.

It's no use. He's failed. The school won't vomit him out, and there's no room in their mouths for God. No room in Robert's mouth either; he can swallow and swallow, but he can't keep God down.

'Robert, have you finished?' Miss Murphy asks.

He's trapped. The presence is trapped too – their tongues are joined together by a red rope. Now it speaks: 'I prayed I'd last until you came home.' The words are a transmission. They travel up the rope, where they hum against his teeth. 'I didn't want Robert to be alone.'

He's not alone. Tracey's with him.

He turns his head to signal to her, but she's not looking at him. She stands up and grabs the table to keep her hands still. 'The church we go to, I grew up in it,' she says, and then frowns. 'I think it's okay to go to other churches too. It's more important to know God.' She pauses. 'Love your neighbour as yourself. I used to think that meant the people in my church. But it means everyone else too.'

Robert moves his hand over her jittering fingers – and now

she's connected. They're both connected – plugged in to the presence.

Tracey says, 'I'm not going to tell you about God. I'm here to learn about Him – from all of you.' She turns to Robert. 'But I agree with everything my friend said.'

And now the words come in a gulping rush. They pulse out from his mouth back up the red stream towards the presence, and the cone vibrates to their rhythm. Robert speaks of the power of the risen Christ in his life. He speaks into darkness, but the cone amplifies his words, and the school hears him. Tracey hears him.

'God isn't cool,' he says. 'He doesn't care what clothes you wear, how popular you are. He doesn't care what music you listen to. He chooses weak people, sick people, to show His strength. He chose me.'

The cone disappears, and Robert is naked and afraid. Someone out in the hall on his left sniggers. But someone on his right whistles: loud, the kind where you have to put two fingers in your mouth. Robert can tell it's meant to be supportive: Paul.

Now the presence is gone, and Robert's looking out at teachers, kids, the lines on the floor of the hall marking out a netball court, gym bars over the windows.

Interference; patterns.

Miss Murphy raises her arm to usher Robert and Tracey off the stage. On the way out, the maths teacher, Miss Baker, grabs Robert's arm. 'Thank you,' she says. 'I wish more Christians would do the same.' She shakes his hand.

He takes it back, but it doesn't stay empty for long. Somebody worms little fingers through his. A hot hand, reaching up. He looks down.

A girl. Naked. Hair shaved, skull too big for her head. Visible bones, bloated belly. 'Hello,' she says. There are crescents of blood where her teeth meet her gums; the same around the fingernails biting into the palm of his hand.

'Don't stay here,' she says, squeezing his fingers. 'Come with me.' When he shakes her off, she laughs and says, 'I wish more Christians would do the same.' No one else reacts to her.

'Robert, you can go back to the middle school now,' Miss Murphy says as they reach the foyer, 'they know you're going to be late. I hope that all went okay for you. It wasn't quite … what I was expecting. But it was fine.'

'Are you okay?' Tracey asks – she's looking at something behind him. Robert turns, expecting to see the presence, but it's only Kevin and Paul, filing out with the crowd. Kevin pulls his jacket open on one side and uses it to screen his hand, with which he makes a thumbs-up gesture at Tracey. Paul grins.

'Yes,' Robert says. The naked girl's now skipping a couple of steps ahead of him. 'I'll see you after school.'

'I've got to move my drums,' she says. 'I'll ask Kevin: he's got a car. But I'll stop in and say hello.'

Outside the foyer, the girl leads him onwards. Now they're alone, he calls after her: 'Did God send you too?'

'You sent me.'

He zips up his hood and says, 'Aren't you cold?'

'I'm used to it,' she says, shivering, while she waits for him to catch up.

He watches her tremble for a moment, and says, 'Do you acknowledge Jesus Christ as the Son of God?'

'Sure,' she says. 'Why not?'

He sniffs. 'You don't smell,' he says. 'You *look* like you smell.' The presence reminds Robert of things turning from one state to another: of transformation. The girl looks more like a bleached bone.

She says, 'Have you got anything to eat? I'm hungry.'

He rummages in his parka pocket and pulls out a squashed

Club biscuit, which looks as though it's been there for a while. The outer wrapper's missing, but it's still covered in silver foil. He holds it out to her.

She looks at it for a second, then grabs his hand instead. The chocolate falls to the floor with a silver wink. Before he understands what's happening, she brings his scabbed knuckle up to her lips and licks the coagulated blood. He snatches his hand back.

She says, 'I wish more Christians would do the same.'

Robert thinks of the unforgivable sin: He that shall blaspheme against the Holy Ghost hath never forgiveness. Mark thinks it means accepting Christ, then denying Him; or saying His miracles come from the Devil. But if you're worried about the unforgivable sin, it means you haven't committed it.

Robert's not convinced. Maybe it isn't something you say. Because he can fight against words forming in his head, but there's something below the words, biting and tearing and chewing.

6

ROBERT

Wings, eyes, wheels. Multiplying faces. That's what angels are made of.

Some angels: the ones in dreams and visions. But when they appear in person to deliver a message, they're anonymous, man-shaped outlines. Not tall or short, thin or fat. No distinguishing features at all, except shining clothes, or a drawn sword.

Robert is kneeling on the floor by the side of his bed, with both his Bibles – the King James and the NIV – plus a concordance, all laid out on the duvet in front of him. It's not a comfortable position. The bed has storage drawers in the bottom part, which means it's quite tall, so he has his elbows propped up on the duvet at chest height. He holds his wrists together, as if they're tied. He'd prefer to keep his palms pressed flat against one another, but it's impossible to turn the pages that way, so wrists are the next best thing.

His hands hover like flapping wings.

In some stories, the angels are invisible, or they don't seem to have a body at all. They speak out of nowhere, and their words alone constitute their presence: or rather, God's words. A messenger, but also the medium through which the message travels. If angel lips, teeth and tongue congeal around God's words, then flesh doesn't shape speech; speech shapes flesh.

Robert looks up at the bare light bulb and out towards the black windows, which, because of his position close to the floor, only reflect the bulb and ceiling back at him. Curtains open, no lampshade: he doesn't like to block light. Or darkness.

He's at the centre of the room, under the hanging cord of the bulb, his rigid back parallel to its plumb line. Around the walls are a bookcase, a wardrobe and, near the door, an old kitchen table with Airfix aeroplanes in various states of assembly. There's a bench tucked under the table: the only place to sit other than the bed.

He stands, and reaches up to tap the bulb. It swings back and forth, casting shadows.

Robert's King James Bible is bound in black. The leatherette cover has lines and seams. If his hands are sweating, his palms stick to its surface and he has to peel the book off his skin.

Inside the King James the pages are thin, almost translucent, and in the text, whenever Jesus speaks, the words are printed in red. The New International Version is different: a flimsy card cover with an abstract, colour pattern, but the pages are thicker than the King James, so the book's harder to carry in his hand. The concordance is Mark's: an oversize hardback that falls open wherever you want it to and stays that way; whereas the Bibles clam shut unless he bends the pages back, so they're splayed face down on the bed.

He rubs a fold of the duvet cover between his fingers. A recent innovation for Auntie Rose, who still has piles of blankets in the chest on the landing, just in case. Robert doesn't like the way the Bibles sink down into the puffy quilt. Like the bed is trying to digest them.

He flicks through the KJV to Isaiah, in which the seraphim, who sit around the throne of God, have six wings: two to cover their faces, two to cover their feet, two to fly with. Are they angels too?

Outside the bedroom door, Uncle Edward is huffing and puffing up the stairs, giving plenty of warning of his arrival.

From Isaiah, Robert flips to the back of the Bible, and the four LIVING CREATURES in Revelation. They also have six wings, and their song of praise to God is the same one that the seraphim sing. But they have eyes all over their heads, bodies, wings – like chickenpox.

Uncle Edward pauses for a few seconds at the turning of the stairs, where there's a small landing, and gathers himself for the final steps. He stops again on the larger landing at the top, breathing through his mouth. As if he's about to knock on Robert's door. But he goes into the bog instead.

The pages whirr through Robert's fingers as he moves from book to book in the Bible: backwards, forwards; up, down and across the twin columns of words.

Ezekiel has creatures with wings and eyes too. But they have multiple faces, and – even more bafflingly – a wheel made of topaz. Maybe this is how angels appear in heaven, and when they come down to earth, they adopt the form of a man.

In the bog, Uncle Edward sits down. The tiled walls act as an amplifier. *Thppthph. Ththppbh. Pfft. Pbpp. Pht.*

The bulb has stopped moving above Robert, and as he leans over the Bible pages, his shadow falls on them. He closes his eyes and rubs his wrists together. He can't imagine what any of the biblical creatures look like. He can see isolated details but the bodies won't come into focus as a unified whole, which means they can't move in his imagination. He can't articulate their various parts.

Pwrpp. Pfb. A splash, a groan. The toilet seat creaks.

The creatures in Isaiah, Ezekiel and Revelation all seem to have similar components. An empty torso. Rummage around in a box of assorted wings, heads, wheels. Pick up a sticker sheet of eyes. Peel them on and off.

The toilet flushes.

The presence has no wings, no eyes, no wheels. No face

either. It does have a human shape – like the angels who deliver messages. But its body changes every time it appears, like the creatures in the visions.

As for the girl, Robert doesn't want to remember her naked body. He avoids looking at it. If he had wings, he'd cover his eyes.

Uncle Edward's in the bathroom now, slippers slapping the lino.

When angels come in person to deliver a message, the message is personal too, for that individual alone. But when they appear to prophets in visions, it's for the church, or the nation of Israel. Is the message from the presence just for Robert, or is he supposed to pass it on to Tracey and Mark and Jenny too?

Uncle Edward puts the plug in the sink. The radiator gurgles as the taps gush. The water'll be hot now, because the central heating only went off an hour ago. Robert has a bath every Monday and Friday night; Auntie Rose has hers on Thursday, the day before her weekly hairdresser's appointment. Uncle Edward doesn't have a regular slot.

Ezekiel eats the words of God. He chews a scroll, which tastes sweet as honey, even though it's full of LAMENTATIONS, AND MOURNING, AND WOE. In Revelation, John eats another honeyed scroll, but, he says, AS SOON AS I HAD EATEN IT, MY BELLY WAS BITTER.

We eat God, but we can't digest Him. We eat God's words, and spew them back out onto the page.

Grunt, splash. Furious rubbing.

Robert gets his Walkman and puts the headphones on. The tape is the new Simple Minds album, which came out a couple of weeks ago: *Sparkle in the Rain*. He presses play, but tries not to listen. He doesn't want music; he wants noise.

The sink swallows dirty water. It belches.

Change me, Lord Jesus. Sound me, as Your lyre and tambourine. Pluck me; beat me.

Robert's read the entire Old Testament and New Testament twice (once in the KJV, and once in the NIV), so what's it to him if theologians say that angels are purely spiritual beings, who never change? Isaiah, Ezekiel and Revelation don't agree. Not exactly. Robert knows what to do with tradition, with priestly vestments and stained-glass windows and departures from Scripture.

Strip; smash; burn.

The Bible speaks for itself; he just has to tune in to its wavelength. But he could ask for help. God can speak through other people too.

He pulls the earphones off. Uncle Edward's still in the bathroom. The direction of the sound's changed though, so he must be standing in front of the mirror.

Robert grabs his coat and bounces downstairs, two steps at a time. He opens the door to the television room. 'I'm going to see Jenny,' he says.

Auntie Rose prunes her mouth. 'Well, you have to be back by ten thirty.'

'I know.' Once, he got home at ten forty-five, and had to ring the bell for ten minutes before Auntie Rose undid the bolts, quivering with anger. She didn't shout; she kept her mouth closed. She'd already taken her teeth out.

In the hallway, Robert can hear Auntie Rose pushing the insulation snake back against the bottom of the door. He hurries to the front door, to get there before he has to speak to Uncle Edward; he pulls it shut behind him.

It's a half-hour walk to Jenny's, in the opposite direction to school. South Mossley Hill Road is a monotonous procession of semi-detached houses, one pair after another. Then Robert crosses several junctions around where Mark lives, before he turns onto Mossley Hill Road.

Jenny has a degree in theology. Robert's suspicious of this – every time you ask her a question, it's 'On the one hand, this; on the other, that' – but he's not in the mood for Mark, who seems determined to interrogate him every time they meet.

There actually is a hill on Mossley Hill Road, which runs alongside empty fields on both sides as it comes up over the summit. There are hardly any street lights, and it almost feels like you're in the country. He stops walking when he gets to the top of the hill. The moon's barely there, a thin sliver, but the sky's clear, so he can see across the fields down towards Mark's house.

There's a horse in the field. It doesn't move; it's probably asleep. He should bring an apple next time. When he stayed in Harmon House after his mum died, he had to feed the chickens.

Jenny lives in a dilapidated mansion, which is split into bed-sits. It's near the university halls of residence, and Jenny's been here since she was a student; she likes her neighbours. Or she likes complaining about them.

South Mossley Hill Road; Mossley Hill Road; then Jenny's flat on North Mossley Hill Road. Robert likes the symmetry of this route.

He waits for a few seconds at the gateway to Jenny's house, to let his eyesight adjust, because there's no outside light and all the curtains are closed in the rooms facing the street. Next to the front door, there's a dozen buttons on little black boxes for the different flats, arranged haphazardly. Some buzzers have scribbled names; others, numbers; one or two have no identifying marks at all. Lucky dip.

Spinks.

As he pushes, there's a buzz deep inside the house. He imagines Jenny strapped to a machine, which gives her an electric shock: Aagh! He presses two more times: Aagh, aagh! There's no intercom, and it always takes her a couple of minutes to get to the door.

Robert never phones people, because he has to ask for permission from Auntie Rose or else go round the corner to a phone box. Anyway, Jenny's house only has a shared payphone on the stairs, which no one ever answers.

She doesn't want to see him. Why would she? If she's not home, it's God's will.

Jenny opens the door. She usually wears a dress to church, but tonight she's in green dungarees. Robert says, 'I can come back another time, if you're busy.'

'No, it's fine. I was just finishing marking.' He follows the backs of her bare feet up the stairs. Her soles are dirty; so is the carpet. It's loose, and it slips under the runners if you move too fast.

'I finished *The Odyssey*,' he says when they're inside her room. Jenny bought the Penguin translation as a present for his last birthday.

'Did you like it?'

'Gods and goddesses. What do I do with that?'

'Good to think with. Like *Lord of the Rings*.'

It's a large room, with a sofa and a double bed. The sofa is covered in a paisley throw. There are several bookshelves, but also piles of paperbacks on the floor. The heap nearest his foot has a dog-eared copy of *Militant* newspaper on top. The headline reads 'Liverpool Council … Stop Tory attacks!' Robert still has his hands in his coat pockets; he lifts one leg off the floor and pokes the front page with the toe of his Dunlop Green Flash. 'Were you on strike today?'

'Half-term. Not much point.'

'But you would be, if school was on.'

Jenny folds her arms. 'Yes.'

'Our MP's David Alton,' Robert says. 'He's a Catholic.' Which makes him the enemy, sometimes. But not compared to Derek Hatton, the public face of the council. Robert studies the photo on the front page of *Militant*. 'He looks like a spiv.'

'Do you know many spivs?' Jenny turns the newspaper over, so the photo's not showing. 'Do you want a cup of tea?'

'Four sugars please. No, hang on. None.'

'On a diet, are we?'

'Something like that.'

While Jenny's gone to the shared kitchen, Robert looks at the poster on the wall above the gas fire. It shows a woman's face, floating in front of a watery background. It's for a film called *Nostalghia*. He takes off his coat and sits down on the edge of the sofa. He rolls a pinch of the nylon throw between his finger and thumb. What's Jenny hiding under here?

She comes back with two grubby mugs: the sink in the kitchen's usually full of unwashed plates. As she places their drinks down, her neighbour knocks. 'Phone for you,' he says in an accent. As Jenny passes him on the way out, he adds, 'Dave.' That's Jenny's boyfriend. They both work at St. Margaret's – an Anglican school. The neighbour smirks at Robert, and says to Jenny, 'I covered for you. This time.'

While she's gone, Robert sips his tea, which tastes bitter without the sugar. He gets up to have a flick through her LP collection, which is stacked to the left of the fire. Mark's the same age as Jenny, and his music's all from yonks ago: Pink Floyd, Genesis. But Jenny's is all over the place: Marvin Gaye and The Clash; Joni Mitchell and The Raincoats; albums with hippies on the cover, like Fairport Convention, and others with abstract shapes and patterns, like Brian Eno.

When she comes back, he asks, 'Why isn't it alphabetical?'

'I like surprises,' she says. Then she adds, 'I think that's the first time Eduardo's ever answered the phone.' She takes off her Lennon glasses and scowls as she polishes the lenses. '"I covered for you." I don't know what he imagines I'm doing in here with a schoolboy.'

Robert looks at the double bed. 'Angels don't marry,' he says.

'What?'

'Jesus says.'

'Right. Well, nor do I. Not at the moment.'

'Have you ever seen one?'

'An angel?' She laughs. 'No. Have you?'

Robert waits for a second, and says, 'When the apostle John sees a vision, or Ezekiel, *where* is that?'

'Oh, okay. We're being serious.'

'I'm always serious. The seraphim sing God's praises. In heaven.'

'So one assumes.'

'Then there's the Whore of Babylon, drunk on the blood of the saints, riding a beast with ten horns and seven heads. She doesn't sit in God's presence. So where's she?'

'Symbols. Of Rome, empires. Avatars.'

'What does that mean?'

'In Hinduism, it's a manifestation of a god on earth.'

Robert says, 'I don't see how that's relevant.'

'Or in Catholicism, Mary appears in different aspects. Our Lady of Sorrows.'

'Again, not relevant.'

Jenny laughs again.

'Why do you keep laughing? What's so funny?'

'Sorry. Nothing.' She straightens her face before continuing. 'It's relevant because this is the same but in reverse. The manifestation of an earthly reality in heaven. Like a projection. I always imagine John in a darkened cinema, eating popcorn. Armies, battles. Goodies and baddies. Big budget, widescreen. An angel sitting next to him, explaining everything.'

'So it's not real?' Robert asks.

'It's an allegory.'

'But the angel explaining it's real.'

Jenny says, 'Christ has avatars too. In Revelation, He has

stars in his hand, a sword coming out of his mouth. And medieval people prayed to His wounds.'

'His wounds?' Robert can't process this, so he returns to the previous point. 'Jesus left His earthly body behind, after the Resurrection. So He can appear how He wants. Can angels do that too?'

Jenny rubs her forehead. 'Maybe they put different bodies on, like a set of clothes.'

'But when an angel appears in a vision, it's really somewhere else, not there with you?'

'Or it takes you up to heaven. Then *you're* the avatar.'

'Angels can be there in person too. So how do you know it's actually there, physically there?'

Jenny shakes her head.

He puts his mug down and picks up his coat. 'I'm going to go home now.'

'You don't have to. If you want to talk more.'

He looks at the poster on the wall. The water behind the floating head reminds him of the presence and the assembly. He says, 'I have to be back by ten thirty.'

He should have asked Jenny about THE ANGEL OF THE LORD. It stops Abraham from killing Isaac, but then suddenly God's there instead, speaking in His own voice. When Tracey pointed that out, Robert borrowed Mark's concordance and found other appearances by the same angel. For example, to Moses in a burning bush. But when the bush speaks, it says, I AM THE GOD OF YOUR FATHER, THE GOD OF ABRAHAM, THE GOD OF ISAAC AND THE GOD OF JACOB.

Unlike Gabriel or Raphael, the Angel of the Lord has no name: only a title. Whenever it appears, it also disappears, but the disappearance happens when no one's looking, in-between the words on the page. A scratch and skip on the record. And the angel is the record. But it's also the living presence of God. Like listening to Annie Nightingale on the radio – then, suddenly, she's in the room with you.

At the summit of Mossley Hill Road, Robert extends his arms like the wings of a plane. He runs down the hill, and as the gradient increases, he loses the rhythm of his steps, until he can feel the impact of the pavement all the way up to his knees. He stops again near the bottom of the hill, doubled over, gasping. Acid breath.

He's near Mark's house on Aigburth Hall Avenue, so he takes that route home. Mark's curtains are open, and he's standing with his back to the window. A dumbbell in each hand: up, down; up, down.

Robert starts moving again. Back to a fast walk.

Jacob wrestles an angel. Hours and hours. No progress: blocked. It can't win, so it dislocates Jacob's hip, but he won't let go. Finally, the angel gives him a blessing, and after it leaves, Jacob says, I HAVE SEEN GOD FACE TO FACE, AND MY LIFE IS PRE-SERVED. Was that the Angel of the Lord too?

The presence has spoken to Robert, but what do its words mean? He has to make it explain. Step inside the vision; put his hands around its throat. Take the blessing; smear it on his face – like the Passover blood on the doorpost.

He doesn't know what he's supposed to do about the girl.

7
ROBERT / TRACEY / ROBERT

Pickets and police on the six o'clock news: the miners' strike. Robert doesn't think much of the pushing and shoving, the beer bellies and pasty faces. He's on the side of the man alone, walking into work through a hail of jeers. Always the individual; never the group.

Except in church. Except in Mark's home group. Except in heaven.

Why don't the miners just take the redundancy pay; get a different job? Leave. Never come back.

At New Heys, ninety per cent of the kids stop after O levels and CSEs. But Mr Higgins the art teacher, who lets Robert draw robot animals alone in the classroom when everyone else does PE on Wednesday afternoons, told him he could stay on and then go to art college. Robert's dad joined the merchant navy at sixteen and worked his way up from able seaman. He doesn't think much of students. An engineer might be okay; a lawyer. But art?

Uncle Edward, looking at the television, says, 'You're nothing, if you don't stand by your mates.'

Robert and Auntie Rose both turn to him. What mates?

The phone rings in the morning room. Normally, Auntie Rose won't answer in the evening, but it keeps going. After a minute, she says to Robert, 'Are you expecting anyone?'

'No,' he says, his eyes now fixed deliberately on the screen. She tuts and goes through. Robert can hear her clear her throat and pause before she picks up the receiver, to put on her phone voice. 'Hellloo?' Silence for a few seconds. 'Mmm,' she says, then, 'I didn't get a cheque.' More silence, before she calls out, 'Robert! It's your dad!'

He stands up, but pauses to adjust the antimacassar on the back of the sofa. It falls off otherwise. He keeps looking at the screen as he sidles towards the door. He's not that interested in the miners' strike –it's just a way to stay calm; keep his mind elsewhere.

In the morning room, Auntie Rose hands him the phone. Robert squashes the receiver between his cheek and shoulder and presses his stomach against the edge of the sideboard, as hard as he can. 'Hello?'

'Son,' his dad says, then falls silent. Breathing down the line. 'How are you?'

Pause. 'I'm watching the news.'

His dad speaks over him. 'I'm fine.' The voice sounds tiny: a homunculus inside the phone.

'I've got to go next door in a minute, to watch a film. With Tracey.'

'Is she your girlfriend?'

'No. I told you that before.'

'Did you? Sorry.' A long pause.

'Hello?'

'Yes.'

'Where are you?' Robert asks.

'I'm … on holiday. I'll see you soon.'

'Alright.'

His dad says, 'I love you.'

Robert holds the phone away from his ear, as if his dad's shouting. He waits until he can hear the distant dial tone, then puts the receiver down.

70

In Tracey's front room, Kevin stands in front of her, holding a videocassette in each hand. '*Time Bandits*, or *The Thing*?'

'*The Thing*,' Paul says.

'*Time Bandits*,' Tracey says. 'Because it's my dad next door who's going to walk in at the worst possible moment.' Kevin's being clever. Obviously they're not going to watch *The Thing*, which has an 18 certificate.

Paul has a bass guitar, so Kevin asked him to join in for their Friday-night practice sessions. For the last two weeks they've watched a video at Kevin's afterwards, but Tracey's feeling guilty about leaving Robert out, so tonight they've come back to her house and Robert's joined them. They're all crammed on the sofa in the front room. Paul on the left, then Tracey, Kevin – and Robert on the right.

Kevin pushes the cassette into the VCR. 'Trailers?'

'No,' Paul says.

Tracey's about to say 'Yes', but Kevin's already hit fast-forward.

Crackly white slashes speed across the screen, and then people jerk like frenzied puppets. When the picture goes black again just before the main film starts, Kevin switches back to play and sits down.

On the television, a boy lies down in bed and closes his eyes. His wardrobe rattles. 'There's a lion and a witch in there,' Kevin says. The wardrobe door creaks ajar. The boy's eyes open as a dwarf in a pilot's helmet with a monocle steps out, followed by a succession of other dwarves, like a conjuror pulling coloured scarves out of a hat.

A whoosh and a crack of thunder: low-budget, tinsel magnificence. A giant, disembodied head follows the dwarves out of the wardrobe, and starts complaining in a creepy, booming voice about a stolen map.

'Wait, wait,' Robert says, moving off the sofa and placing himself in front of the television.

Kevin cups his hands around his mouth and copies the voice from the floating head on the screen. 'Return the remote control!'

'It's right by you,' Tracey says.

Robert waves both palms out in front of him like someone flagging down a car. 'Was that supposed to be God?'

Kevin pushes pause on the remote control, but he can't get the film to stop because Robert's in the way. On the screen, the boy and the dwarves have used the stolen magical map to escape through a trapdoor in the sky. Kevin sticks his arm out to bounce the signal around Robert, and the dwarves freeze, flickering in mid-air.

'Was that supposed to be God?' Robert asks again.

'Sort of,' Kevin says.

'I don't like it. You can't do that.'

'It's not really God.'

'Like Brian isn't really the Messiah?' Tracey suggests.

'Have you even seen *Life of Brian*?' Kevin asks. 'They're at the Sermon on the Mount, standing at the back. They can't hear what Jesus says. It's not about God. It's about how the message gets distorted.'

'We're not watching *Life of Brian*,' Tracey says, although she was the one who brought it up.

'But *that* was God,' Robert says, pointing at the television.

'Not our God,' Kevin says. 'Not the God in the Bible.'

Tracey says, '*What if* there was a world with a God like this?'

Robert says, 'You can imagine other worlds outside this one. That's fine. But there's nothing outside God.'

'Deep,' Paul says.

'You can't imagine Him different than He is, because that denies His perfection.'

'How does the film deny His perfection?' Kevin says.

'It's cheap.'

'So if there was a bigger special-effects budget, that'd be okay?'

Robert says, 'They want it to be cheap. It's part of the joke.'

'What does everyone else think?'

'I don't think God minds a joke,' Tracey says. 'And I think it's my house.' She looks at Kevin's fingers, caressing buttons. 'My remote control too.'

'Oh sorry – do you want to—?'

'No, you're alright.'

Robert signals his surrender by sliding his palms across each other. Wiping the responsibility off his hands, like Pontius Pilate. He sits down again. The sofa cushions humph in protest.

Play. The tape grinds and crinkles across the VCR heads. Tracey can hear the spools squeak as they turn.

The boy in the film's called Kevin too. 'Is that why you like it?' Paul asks. 'Because he's got the same name as you?'

Film Kevin and the dwarves are in Napoleonic Italy, where they meet the emperor, who utters the first swearword of the film, a 'bloody'. Tracey once watched a film with Mark, who has a very strict policy. More than three 'shits' or 'fucks': turn it off. 'For God's sake' more than twice, and that's it. The worst is 'Jesus Christ!': no second chances at all. But this is a children's film, so it should be okay.

The dwarf with the monocle explains to Film Kevin that God created everything important – the stars and planets, human beings, right and wrong – but left the small stuff to the dwarves.

Robert says, 'So the dwarves are angels?'

'Shh,' says Real Kevin.

'No.' Robert corrects himself. 'Angels only deliver messages. They don't create things.'

The dwarves got sacked for incompetence and sent down to the repairs department, where they stole a map showing all the holes in the universe. Now they're using it to travel through time and space to rob people.

'You've seen this before?' Robert says to Kevin.

'Yes.'

'And you're asking me what I object to?'

Paul says, 'Can we just watch the film?'

Robert stands up again. 'I'm not staying in here.'

'Okay,' Tracey says. 'Can you make us a cup of tea?' But then she remembers: her dad's working next door, and who knows what Robert will say to him? 'No, I'll do it. Can you stop the film?'

'Oh, for goodness' sake,' Kevin says. A nice Christian expletive.

'Can I go and read in your room?' Robert asks.

'If you want,' Tracey says. Behind Robert's back, Paul taps the side of his head and moves his finger in a circle.

In the dining area by the kitchen, her dad is marking a set of written exercises from his students. They're covered in red pen. He teaches quantity surveying at the Poly, and he looks the part, even on his days off. Brown cords, grey shirt, knitted tie. He doesn't like to stand out: it's immodest.

'Everything okay?' he asks. He looks naked without his glasses, embarrassed to be caught blinking.

'Yeah.' She flicks on the kettle in the kitchen. 'We're watching *Time Bandits*.'

Her dad crosses out a set of figures on someone's homework. 'Oh?' He smells of coal tar soap: a big improvement on the front room, where she's trapped on the sofa between Old Spice and Hai Karate.

She looks down at her feet. 'It's about a group of dwarves who steal a map of creation, and travel through the holes.'

'Sounds … colourful.'

'God's in it. As a character.'

'Right.' Her dad places his pen down and puts on his glasses.

'Is that okay?' Why's she telling him this? She might as well have sent Robert through.

'We're not Jewish. We don't have a law against depicting God.'

'I don't know how I feel about it.'

'You can make up your own mind.'

When her mum was alive, her dad was worse than Mark. No television at all, except the news and nature documentaries. But since she died, he doesn't seem to care. Or he cares about other things. Last Christmas, they even watched James Bond. Whenever there was a bedroom scene, her dad went outside and stood in the garden.

Now he smooths his tie down. Even at home, he keeps it pulled tight, with the top button of his shirt done up. At least it's not black. Plain, but still blue.

Tracey's out of mourning too. She looks down at her purple woollen tights while she's waiting for the kettle to shudder to a halt. School rules say grey or black; nobody cares, so long as the rest of your uniform's regulation. She remembers her dad's socks on the morning of the funeral, and she wiggles her toes. 'Robert's upstairs,' she says.

'Okay. Don't leave him by himself up there.'

'I won't.'

For a second, she hates her dad. Because there's never any excuse to close the door, shut him out.

When she gets back, Robert's hovering in the downstairs hallway, pretending to read a book from her room: *The Screwtape Letters*, by C. S. Lewis. He comes back into the front room to pick up his tea. 'No sugars, right?'

'I put four in.'

He scowls. 'Fine.' He sits down in the middle of the sofa between her and Kevin.

'There's no room,' Kevin protests – but Robert's all pointy and sharp: a knife, cutting her and Kevin apart. Tracey looks at him more closely: he has a baggy T-shirt and an even baggier pink shirt over that, so it's hard to make out his shape.

In the Fortress of Ultimate Darkness, Evil watches the dwarves via a magic pool of water. He's imprisoned, and he needs the map to escape. Robert holds C. S. Lewis up between himself and the screen so he can't behold Evil.

The dwarves flee to Ancient Greece, where Film Kevin gets separated from everyone else. He arrives in the middle of a fight between a warrior and a guy wearing a cow head. Wait, no. A Minotaur. But the fight's out in the open. Where's the labyrinth?

Later, in the final battle, God turns Evil to charcoal.

'See,' says Kevin. 'It's a theologically orthodox conclusion.'

God reveals Himself to be a posh Englishman in a white suit.

'Typical,' Paul says. 'Why can't God have a Scouse accent?'

Robert tuts. 'He's not *from* anywhere.'

This is all much worse than the beginning of the film, but it seems pointless to turn it off now, ten minutes from the end.

Robert turns a page of C. S. Lewis and sniffs. 'So there's no hell in this universe?'

'Isn't this hell?' Tracey says, pointing at the screen. 'The Fortress of Ultimate Darkness?' She doesn't know what she believes about hell. She doesn't think Robert knows either.

'I love this film,' Kevin says.

Robert puts his book down.

Tracey doesn't want them to argue, so she says, 'We had a good practice tonight.'

'It was okay,' Paul says.

'He barely plays,' Kevin says to Robert. 'Lets us do all the work, then adds a note or two.'

Paul pats his permed hair. 'But it makes all the difference.'

'Does anyone sing?' Robert asks.

This question falls into a hole of silence, until Tracey says,

'We're just messing about. Cover versions and that. We don't need a singer.'

In his room, Robert gets into bed and turns out the light. His wardrobe door creaks open. He scrunches his eyes tight as fists – he doesn't need to look. The quilt flips back. Breath on the back of his neck. In the bed next to him, a hand snakes across his stomach. No smell, no body heat: an absence. But around this absence, he imagines fleas, lice, mites – creeping across the sheets. The plagues of Egypt.

The headboard of the bed is made up of a metal frame with struts. He reaches up and wraps his hands around two of them, then braces his feet against the frame at the bottom. He pushes his body backwards across the mattress, until he forces her off the edge.

A bony thud on the floor.

He sits up, still with his back to her. The light switch dangles down from a cord in the ceiling above the bed; he turns it on. Uncle Edward's in the master bedroom next door; Auntie Rose is in the box room at the end of the landing. He listens: nothing from either of them.

The girl sucks her teeth and says from the floor, 'That wasn't very nice.'

'It's *my* bed.' He's trying to whisper loudly.

'No it's not.' She stands up. She hisses, 'Goldilocks.'

He can't take it any longer. He turns around.

White skin; red between her legs. A wound. Livid, raw.

'Stop looking,' she says, covering it with her hand. 'You fucking pervert.'

Smears on the rumpled bed. The sheet, his pyjama waistband, his stomach. How's he going to explain this? The few times he's had a wet dream, he wiped the bed down with a sponge and said he peed himself. But blood?

IF ONE OF YOUR MEN IS UNCLEAN BECAUSE OF A NOCTURNAL EMISSION, HE IS TO GO OUTSIDE THE CAMP AND STAY THERE.

AND IF A WOMAN HAVE AN ISSUE, AND HER ISSUE IN HER FLESH BE BLOOD, SHE SHALL BE PUT APART SEVEN DAYS: AND WHO-SOEVER TOUCHES HER SHALL BE UNCLEAN UNTIL THE EVENING.

'Where's your mum?' the girl says.

'She's dead. What's it to you?'

'Yes, but *where* is she?'

'I don't know.'

'I do. And it's your fault.'

Robert turns the light off again; he doesn't want to see her any more. But she's still there.

She laughs, and says, 'Everyone likes picking scabs.'

8
TRACEY / ROBERT

The Lord's Supper. When Tracey was little, the name used
to confuse her, because it's the morning meeting. For church
members only: the gospel service is in the evening. There used
to be two different songbooks: the *Believers Hymn Book* for the
Lord's Supper; *Redemption Songs* for the gospel. But since last
year they have used *Carry the Message* for both: a compilation of
songs put together as part of the preparations for a forthcoming
UK mission by the American evangelist Henry Prince.

Prince is famous. Tracey's seen him on the news, during a
visit to the White House. But he's not the one organizing the
Carry the Message campaign, which covers the whole country. She's not sure how the idea started, or when Prince got
involved –Garston Chapel had a meeting about it six months
ago.

Tracey doesn't know who compiled the book either: it's a
mixture of familiar hymns and newer, shorter, choruses – more
like pop songs.

Her dad gets to the morning meeting early every week, to
help set up. For the Lord's Supper, the pews are arranged in
four sections, parallel to the four walls of the hall, and around
the sides of the table with the bread and wine in the centre of
the room. Tracey sits at the back of the hall on the side farthest
from the entrance, so no one's behind her and she can see
people arrive.

Jenny Spinks is early too. She goes over to the piano. In

the gospel meeting, there's a guitar and tambourines; for the Lord's Supper, it used to be unaccompanied singing. But now you can ask for piano if you want: another recent innovation. Jenny plays a few notes to reassure herself it's in tune. Then she disappears through the double doors on the other side of the hall, out towards the entrance. Waiting for her parents to arrive.

Mrs Evans sits down alone on the front row in the section opposite Tracey, mumbling to herself. She has a hat with peacock feathers; other women wear a beret or a kerchief. Another reason for Tracey to sit on the back row: because otherwise she imagines disapproving stares boring into the back of her naked head.

John Cooper sits down next to Mrs Evans and says something. She adjusts her hat in response. John moves around the room before he settles down. He talks to anyone who's sitting alone – except for Tracey.

The room's getting noisy, people catching up on the week's news before the service starts. Kevin slides in next to her. 'Didn't you come with your dad?' she asks.

'Yeah, but I went to get a KitKat,' he says, patting his coat pocket.

'Robert didn't knock for a lift, so he'll probably be late,' she says.

'Uh huh.'

'Where's Paul?'

'Derby game yesterday, so we went out.'

'Who won?' she asks, to be polite.

'1–1, but that's a good result – for Everton.' Kevin sniffs. 'I didn't stay on in the pub.' He lifts an imaginary glass, and tilts it back towards his open mouth.

'You were drinking?' Tracey wrinkles her nose.

Kevin holds up a single finger, then points it towards himself.

'I was a good boy, unlike some I could mention.'

Mark arrives with Sandy and Liz. They all sit in the section to Tracey's left, near to her cousin Sally, who waves when Tracey looks in her direction. Sally should be in Sunday school, with her brother Richard, but she likes to do whatever her big cousin does. Tracey doesn't want her to come over, so she puts her palms together and nods towards the table at the centre of the room. It's covered with a plain white cloth. A plate with a couple of slices of white bread from a Morrisons loaf, and a jug of red table wine next to an empty brass goblet.

Her dad's sitting in the section to her right, next to Trevor Jenkins, who became an elder last year. Her dad put his name forward.

The church is full now. When everyone's quiet, Trevor stands and says, 'Lord, in this time of strife, we ask you to heal the wounds of our city and our nation. We meet today to remember your death and celebrate your resurrection. We are not divided. We share a spirit of fellowship and brotherhood because we share in your sacrifice. Help us to be the instrument of Your healing in the world around us. Amen.'

As the congregation chants the last word, Paul and Robert slip in through the doors at the back of the hall. Paul looks grey; Robert looks at his shoes. They don't acknowledge each other.

Mark stands up and says, 'I'd like us to sing number 13.'

Tracey flicks through *Carry the Message*: 'As we are gathered, Jesus is here'. Only five lines long. Which means they'll sing it through twice. Mark starts, because he chose the song.

God leads the morning meeting. The only fixed point is the sharing of the bread and wine, about fifteen minutes before the end. Otherwise, no one's in charge; no one prepares; anyone can participate, as the Spirit moves them. Anyone male, that is. Women can ask for a song or read a Bible passage – but they can't presume to let God speak through them.

Silence falls again.

A cough, a sniff, a creaking pew. Jane Gibbon's baby burbles at the back, and Jane makes a soothing noise. A gust of sleet spatters against the window to the courtyard. Sally swings her feet against the underside of the pew in front. Thud, thud. Aunt Maggie taps her on the knee, and Sally makes a theatrical sigh. Mrs Evans blows her nose. Jane Gibbon stands up and takes her baby outside.

Not music; not noise. Part of the silence.

Mark stands up again. There's no rule about multiple contributions, but it's not common. Easier to justify if the first one was only a song request. He opens his Bible and reads, 'COME OUT FROM THEM AND BE SEPARATE, SAYS THE LORD.

'This is a fallen world. We're called to be a light on a hill, to shine in the darkness. The light is not part of the darkness; where there is light, there can be no darkness. When we come to Christ, we leave our old lives behind. We leave the world.

'The apostle Paul tells us we must obey the secular authorities. He doesn't tell us what to do when there are two authorities, in conflict with one another.' Mark closes his eyes.

'What's he talking about?' Kevin whispers.

Tracey thinks for a second. 'Maybe Hatton and Thatcher?'

'Ha! *He's* not an authority.'

Mark opens his eyes and looks around the room, as if he's surprised to find himself here. 'I've been in a war,' he says.

'Yeah, we know,' Kevin mutters.

'Now I contend with THRONES AND PRINCIPALITIES in the heavenly realm. Christ won the victory for us by His death on the Cross. Our struggle is to take hold of that victory and apply it in our own lives.' Mark sometimes misjudges the mood in the morning service. He forgets he's not speaking to a bunch of teenagers. But not today.

He sits down. Quiet again – it won't last. People can't stand it for longer than a minute. How can you hear God, if you don't shut up and listen?

Paul stands up. Tracey's never heard him speak in the morning meeting before. He says, 'I'm not as good a Christian as you lot.' He leans on the back of the pew in front. 'In junior school, we used to say the Lord's Prayer every morning. HALLOWED BE THY NAME. What be thy name? FORGIVE US OUR TRESPASSES. Forgive us our what?' He runs his hand over his forehead, as if he's dizzy. 'Chew the words, over and over, until you can't taste them any more. Like school dinners.'

Tracey looks at Robert, who's looking at Paul.

'I didn't even know the Lord's Prayer came from the Bible,' Paul continues. 'Where is it?' He looks around the room, and it takes Tracey a couple of seconds to realize the question isn't rhetorical.

Her dad says, 'Matthew 6.'

Paul opens his Bible. It takes him a while to find Matthew, but everyone waits. Tracey can hear him turning the pages. That's part of the silence too.

Paul moves his finger over the words. 'It's different here. MAY YOUR HOLY NAME BE HONOURED. MAY YOUR WILL BE DONE ON EARTH AS IT IS IN HEAVEN. *On earth*. What does that mean? I honestly want to know.'

He sits down.

John Cooper says, 'THE KINGDOM OF GOD IS WITHIN YOU. There'll come a time when Jesus returns, and then He'll rule on earth. Until then, we watch and wait.' He doesn't bother standing up for this.

Jenny says, '1 Corinthians 12:25–7.' She doesn't stand up either. She reads, 'THERE SHOULD BE NO DIVISION IN THE BODY, BUT ITS PARTS SHOULD HAVE EQUAL CONCERN FOR EACH OTHER. IF ONE PART SUFFERS, EVERY PART SUFFERS WITH IT; IF ONE PART IS HONOURED, EVERY PART REJOICES WITH IT. NOW YOU ARE THE BODY

OF CHRIST, AND EACH ONE OF YOU IS A PART OF IT.' Then she breaks the rules by saying, 'I'm part of this church. I'm also part of this city. This country.'

Tracey wants to sit and listen for God's voice, but she can't, knowing that someone else will break the silence for her. So she might as well do it herself. She says, '1 Kings 19:11–12: AFTER THE WIND THERE WAS AN EARTHQUAKE, BUT THE LORD WAS NOT IN THE EARTHQUAKE. AFTER THE EARTHQUAKE CAME A FIRE, BUT THE LORD WAS NOT IN THE FIRE. AND AFTER THE FIRE CAME A GENTLE WHISPER.'

Her dad's looking at her. She hides in the pages of her Bible, but she can't stay there forever. When she raises her eyes again, he nods.

He stands up. He holds out his copy of *Carry the Message* and says, 'Do you remember when we got this?' He looks around and smiles. 'Quite a mix-up.' People smile back. 'Lots of us liked the old hymn books. Why change?

'It's not long now till Henry Prince comes to speak at Anfield, in July. This book was created for that; for any church that wants to take part. We made a decision. It was difficult; we talked about it. God is going to speak to our nation through Henry Prince, and we want Him to speak through us too.

'We examined our hearts.'

And watched a video too: her dad had to bring the VCR machine from home. Henry Prince travels all over the world – even to Russia – but the video looked like it was recorded ten years ago in an underground bunker. Prince alone at a desk in a windowless room: sideburns, glasses with gold rims; one of those shirts where the main part is stripy but the collar and cuffs are plain white. He spoke so quietly they had to turn the volume up to hear him. He thanked everyone watching, taking their involvement for granted.

'This is a Brethren church,' Tracey's dad says. 'We don't go on about it, because the name's never been important. It's what the apostle Paul calls the early Christians. It used to be the case, years ago, that if you wanted to take Communion, and we didn't know you, you had to bring a letter from your home church. A recommendation, from the elders, to show you were in good standing.

'We don't do that any more. I'm glad.

'I examine *my* heart. Not the heart of the man sitting next to me.' He looks at Jenny. 'The woman. We could say: well, okay, you don't need a letter, but there has to be a rule. Only baptized Christians. Who am I to deny someone fellowship with Christ, just because he hasn't been baptized yet? We're not *against* anyone.

'But I got caught up in tradition. And because I held on too tight, God told me to let go. So this isn't a Brethren church any more. Not for me.'

John Cooper frowns.

'And then I discovered something: my faith's strong enough to survive without that label. Strong enough to join with all the other Christians singing from this book today: in Liverpool; in England.

'Not the letter of the law. The spirit.'

He continues. 'Carry the Message is at Anfield. I've never been there.'

'You're not missing much,' Paul says. Quiet, but loud enough that everyone can hear.

Her dad smiles. 'We all know how important football is in this city. Bill Shankly said Anfield's a shrine; people go there to worship.

'Carry the Message. It's an interesting name, isn't it? Because we think of a mission as something for *them*, out there.' He waves in the direction of the entrance. 'But it's a command addressed to us: it lays the responsibility on us, not Henry Prince.

'We don't sit waiting for the world to come to us. It won't. We go out, and we take the gospel into the beating heart of our city. To enthrone God, where God is not.'

He sits down.

Jane Gibbon asks for number 137: 'Let there be love shared among us', which has a line about God sweeping the nation. 'With the piano, please.'

While Jenny goes over to the piano and turns pages on the music stand, Kevin unwraps his KitKat. 'Thought your dad didn't like giving sermons.'

'He doesn't.'

'Sounded like one to me.' He snaps the KitKat in half and takes a bite. While he chews, everyone else opens their mouth to sing.

At the end of the song, Trevor Jenkins moves to the table at the centre of the room and picks up the plate with the bread for Communion. He hands it to Mrs Evans on the front row. She tears off a small piece, pops it in her mouth, and hands the plate along.

Silence again.

When you look at the surface of an LP, there are thin bands between each song. The whole record's black, but the bands seem to be even darker. Because the grooves are empty.

The hiss of the needle.

Robert stands up. He trembles. He says, 'BUT, BEHOLD, THE HAND OF HIM THAT BETRAYETH ME IS WITH ME ON THE TABLE. AND TRULY THE SON OF MAN GOETH, AS IT WAS DETERMINED: BUT WOE UNTO THAT MAN BY WHOM HE IS BETRAYED!'

Her dad says, 'Robert, this isn't the time to speak. You need to be quiet during this part of the service.'

Robert hiccups. He gets down on his knees behind the pew in front of him, which means he's lower than everyone else, and his head disappears, but Tracey can hear when he knocks his forehead against the wooden seat back. Deliberately: one, two.

He's crying.

That's not part of the silence.

When the bread comes round to Paul, he takes a piece and hesitates before handing the plate down to Robert. Tracey can't see what happens next, but it's a long time before the plate reappears.

When the bread reaches her section, Kevin swallows a mouthful of KitKat before he plucks a morsel off. Jenny's the last to take the plate, and she returns it to the table.

Trevor tries to ignore Robert sniffling. He reads, 'AND LIKEWISE THE CUP AFTER SUPPER, SAYING, "THIS CUP WHICH IS POURED OUT FOR YOU IS THE NEW COVENANT IN MY BLOOD."' He fills the goblet and hands it to Mrs Evans, together with a folded cloth napkin. She takes a sip and passes both items along. The napkin accompanies the goblet around the room every week, but no one ever uses it.

Germs fester on the rim of the cup; drooly spit dilutes the wine. But isn't it worth the risk of getting sick?

Robert's still down on the floor; he's quieter now. When the cup reaches him, there's another pause. Murmuring encouragement from Jenny's parents, who are next to him, on the other side from Paul. Tracey imagines them holding the goblet to his lips. Drink up; take your medicine.

Banging knees and elbows; copies of *Carry the Message* fall to the floor. Robert flounders through the door out towards the entrance hall. Everyone exhales. Thank goodness.

Paul waves to get Tracey's attention. He tilts his head back towards the door, rolling his eyes upwards to follow. She gives him a thumbs up, and he slips out after Robert.

She presses her knees together under her pleated skirt and moves the soles of her feet up and down, as if she's walking. But she's not going anywhere – at least until the cup reaches her. Robert's not her responsibility – not *just* hers. He belongs to everyone here.

In the toilet cubicle, Robert's leaning over the bowl, but nothing comes up. No breakfast today: he wanted to keep his stomach ready for the Lord's Supper.

The bread wasn't bread. It moved. Tried to speak.

Killing Christ over again. Stretching and tearing His body, which remained whole, even on the Cross; even in the tomb. But not on the plate. Robert put the bread in his mouth. He tried to speak with it, to become its body, but no words formed. Only mewling sounds.

He retches over the toilet.

He lifted the goblet to his mouth. Tilted his head back, as if he had a nosebleed. The wine pulsed down the groove of his throat. A circuit closed. A chain of hands, passing the cup along, linking him to Tracey on the other side of the room. Plugged in. Then the circuit broke. The hands let go.

Robert's a blockage, an impasse. A clot. His throat tightens; he can't breathe. Get it out.

A knock on the cubicle door. Paul says, 'Are you okay? Do you need any help?'

Not from you.

A red jet: not from his stomach; from the root of his tongue. No muscles clenching: free-flowing. Unquenchable, renewing itself miraculously.

Robert's left the cubicle door unlocked, so Paul opens it. The red stream disappears. 'No!' Robert says.

'Okay. I'll wait outside.' Paul retreats past the urinals and out of the bathroom altogether.

Robert gets up off the floor and leans his forehead on the cubicle door frame. Behind him, the girl sits on the shelf below the frosted window and swings her legs back and forth, kicking the side of the cubicle. When she gets bored with that, she squeezes past him into the bathroom, where she peers at the bleeding cake of disinfectant at the bottom of the urinal, then pokes it.

She waddles round the bathroom, puffing out her cheeks, massaging her distended belly: holding it in front of her, as if it's a bowling ball. She says, 'BLESSED ART THOU AMONG WOMEN, AND BLESSED IS THE FRUIT OF THY WOMB.'

'Who's the father?'

She presses a finger against each cheek to fart out the air in her mouth. 'The Holy Spirit.'

Robert steps back inside the cubicle and kneels down in prayer. The water at the bottom of the toilet bowl blinks like the wine at the bottom of the goblet. He presses the flush.

This is wrong. Why is it happening? He looks at the girl.

'Never a good idea,' she says, 'alcohol on an empty stomach.'

9
ROBERT / TRACEY

Friday is gammon, green beans and powdered mashed potatoes. Robert doesn't mind mixing food in his mouth, but it has to be separate on the plate. He cuts the meat up into little cubes which he pushes to one side, away from the white ooze of the potato. Then he attacks the beans, but he can't get through the stringiness.

The knife slips, and squeals across the plate. Chew, chew, swallow. Chew. Swallow. Chew, chew, chew. Swallow.

Breakfast is easy: a few mouthfuls of cornflakes. Lunch is even easier: he takes ham or cheese sarnies to school and throws them away. He even asks for an extra round, so he can say he's full at teatime. It doesn't work. Come five o'clock, he still has to finish everything on his plate, or he's not allowed to leave the table. The only space left for his will is to refuse dessert.

Butterscotch Angel Delight. Fondant fancies. Strawberry Supermousse.

He can hurt the girl, if he's willing to hurt himself. AND IF THINE EYE OFFEND THEE, PLUCK IT OUT, AND CAST IT FROM THEE: IT IS BETTER FOR THEE TO ENTER INTO LIFE WITH ONE EYE, RATHER THAN HAVING TWO EYES TO BE CAST INTO HELL FIRE.

She's a tapeworm. Starve her out. It's not working though. Neglect only makes her stronger. Hunger makes her belly swell.

When he falls asleep that night, he dreams the phone's ringing. But it's the girl on the other end, so he won't answer. He wakes up; throws the covers back and drums his fingers against his stomach. Suck it in; let go. Not much difference.

He's thirsty as well as hungry, but that's easy to fix. On his way to the kitchen, he stops on the landing at the turn of the stairs. In an alcove, below the stained-glass window, there's a ceramic statue, about a foot high. A woman, in medieval armour, with a pageboy haircut. Kneeling in prayer, with her sword held upright in front of her like a cross.

Joan of Arc. Auntie Rose and Uncle Edward brought her back from their honeymoon in France. Her hands fuse together in a fingerless blob, with a circular hole drilled through the centre. Maybe somebody had that job in the factory, for all the Joan of Arcs. Moving the drill, down and up, down and up.

Her letter-opener sword's separate, and made of metal. It hangs down through the hole in her hands, held in place by the cross guard. A loose fit. He jiggles the pommel, then pulls the blade out. Cheap alloy: about six inches long. He holds the blade in front of his face, with the point towards him. He opens his mouth and presses the flat against his tongue. He supports the sword grip with his right thumb and taps the pommel with his left index finger, slowly. Farther back, into his mouth, until the point touches the back of his throat, and he gags.

Shush.

He pulls the sword out of his mouth and walks downstairs, where he unlocks the door into the morning room. He steps inside and lets it drift closed behind him. Moves the sword to his right hand, and feels for the light switch with his left.

He can't find the wall.

No moonlight, because the morning room has no windows. He's always been puzzled by this: how can it be a morning room, if you can't tell it's morning? He turns around to face where he came in, looking for the outline of the door. He steps forward with his left hand held out in front of him.

No door.

Dizzy. Stop; calm down. Try the kitchen door on the opposite wall of the room. He turns around again and steps forward. His hand pats the air to his left, where the table should be, because he doesn't want to walk into it. Forward: one, two, three strides.

No table. No door, no wall. He closes his eyes, then opens them again, but it makes no difference. Just keep going forward until you hit the kitchen door, as long as it takes. Another stride. Another. Then his nerve fails.

He trips on nothing. Expects to bang his head but tumbles across the floor, the sword skittering away. It doesn't hit the door or the wall.

The floor. Concentrate on that. Hands and feet on the lino. It should be sticky, peeling off the soles of his feet; he should be able to feel the lines of the pattern through his skin. He tries to visualize the pattern, but in his mind there's only disintegrating inkblots. In the dark, it's difficult to remember yellow, green. He leans as far forward as he can, like a Muslim praying. He sticks his tongue out, so the tip touches the floor.

Cool. Dry and smooth. Not lino: more like a pane of glass.

Find the sword. Blunt, soft, but still a weapon. He crawls forward, palms down, sweeping around his path: windscreen wipers.

There. Thank God.

He stands up again. Turns to his left, then, thinking about it, back to his right. Looking for the sideboard. Not looking; feeling. In the dark, you have to fall over what you're trying to find.

He wants the telephone. Nine-nine-nine. I'm lost, in my own house. Come and get me. How can he even be sure which direction he's facing? Like someone's spun him round in a blindfold.

Don't shout. There might be something in here with him. Assuming he is inside. Maybe he's not trapped; maybe he's locked out. Of God's love. And this is hell.

He wants to run, but where would he run to? If he gets stuck here, he's going to starve, and he's not ready for that kind of hunger. Not yet. They're going to find his skeleton under the morning-room table, and they won't understand what happened. It won't *mean* anything.

What if he needs to go the bog?

Breathing. Fast, shallow. Shouldn't empty space be full of air, even if there's nothing else? Unless he's in a bell jar, suffocating.

Please God, help me. Say it. 'Please God, help me.' Let me be alone.

A yellow light pricks his eyes. He blinks back tears.

A colour, a shape: far away. Coming into focus as his vision clears. Shapes, plural. He can't see the light source. Wherever it's coming from, it's shining on a wall, an arch, a table.

Stupid to look away from the light, but it's still there when he looks back. He walks towards it. Moves the sword back to his left hand and holds it out in front of him. He daren't run, because he can't feel the floor. But it must be there, otherwise he'd be falling.

One minute, two. Before the light came, it could have been an hour, a day. In the dark, time's as meaningless as space. The shapes are larger; he can see chairs round the table, a sideboard to one side, a grey window behind. There's carpet under his feet now and he stops, flexing his toes. Like he's standing on a beach in the sand, letting the sea swirl in and out round his ankles. A fixed horizon in front, near and far in their proper places.

Tracey's house, downstairs at the back. But he's coming into it out of nothing, through the wall. From the space between the houses. And it's all wrong.

To get to the kitchen in Robert's house, he has to go through a locked door into the morning room, then another on its opposite side, and that whole section of the house is separated from the television room by the hall. In Tracey's house, there's a single, open-plan area at the back, with empty arches. And she has different names for the rooms: lounge, dining area, then kitchen.

Robert's standing in her lounge, so the dining area's straight ahead, but the door out to the entrance hall is on the right side of the room, instead of the left; and the kitchen turns off to the left, not the right. A mirror image of itself. The two houses still unfold in opposite directions from their common wall, but they've swapped places.

He steps through the arch into the dining area, then turns into the kitchen, where there's a night light on the countertop. He steps up to the sink and turns the cold tap on. Puts his mouth underneath, gulps and slurps. Burps air between swallows.

He looks at the window. Black outside, nothing visible: not even his reflection. Probably just as well. What if the moon and stars were reversed?

He walks through to the entrance hall behind the front door. He could get home from here – but he'd have to go outside, into the dark. Barefoot in the frost. And won't his house be reversed too?

There's a long mirror at the bottom of the stairs. He keeps his eyes fixed on Tracey's puffa jacket, which hangs from the knob on top of the newel post. He turns the inside edge of the hood out and presses his face into it. Mint shampoo.

This is where he belongs, where he wants to be. Not next door. But he doesn't want it like this, with everything wrong.

One of Tracey's hairs sticks to his lip. He picks it off with his finger and thumb, like he's threading it through his mouth with a needle.

Up the stairs. Stained glass, but no Joan of Arc. Then onto the landing at the top. Three bedroom doors. Tracey's, directly in front of him, echoing his own; replacing his own. Far left, at the end of the upstairs hallway, the spare room where no one sleeps; where Auntie Rose sleeps. In-between, Bill's room; Uncle Edward's room.

Ip dip doo.

The spare room's wide open, Tracey's old teddies piled on the bed – she can't bring herself to throw them away. Her bedroom door's ajar: her name in rainbow stickers, half-picked off. The letters are the right way round, as is the prancing-pony sticker. So not everything's reversed.

Bill's door is closed, but there's a sound coming through the crack at the bottom. Not breathing. A continuous click, reset, click. A halo of crackle: expanding, contracting. A needle in the terminal groove of a record, thrown back against itself. Scoring a channel into flesh; deeper, deeper.

Robert turns the handle on Bill's door and pushes it open. Inside, the room's dark, but not black. Grey shapes. He steps through the door and turns to his right; finds himself facing the wall. The paper's smooth, with coloured stripes; the paper's textured, with paisley shapes. The wall's vibrating. He places his palm against it. Stretched taut, like a drum skin. He's at the centre of the labyrinth, inside the ear of the house.

He turns around. The girl's sitting on the edge of the bed. She opens her mouth, and the needle hiss comes out. He holds the sword up in front of him. She nods, then does it again. Her neck flops down and snaps back, following the rhythm of the hiss.

The sword is the needle. No longer blunt and soft. Piercing.

The girl lies down on the bed and beckons him closer. He asks, 'How do I get back?'

She snatches at the sword. But she's not trying to take it away, so he relaxes. She makes a fist around the blade, then slides her hand up over the grip; hooks her fingers between his; spread-eagles her thumbs over his thumbs. Their hands move the sword together, like the pointer on a Ouija board – across her swollen belly, into her navel.

She pushes down; blood wells up.

The rhythm of the sound accelerates. Narrowing space between the click and the hiss; narrowing time between the point and its sheath of blood.

She pulls the blade along the taut surface of her stomach. Lips opening to speak. Light spills like a pile of guts. Flickers over the shivering walls. Her mouth closes, but something moves inside her belly: a white tongue, trying to speak.

She lets go of his hands. The sound slows to a heartbeat. She reaches inside herself and cups her palms around something. Lifts, and it sucks away from the lining of her stomach. She manoeuvres it through the lips of the wound and holds it up to him.

The presence.

Or is it? He's not sure, because it's about a foot long, the same size as Joan of Arc. Covered in jelly and brawn, but smooth and white underneath. He can't see how there was room for it inside the girl. Maybe it was pressed up against her lungs. Maybe she's hollow, has no organs.

A liquid cord joins her to the presence. It twists out of her middle, turning over and back on itself, and it disappears into the hole at the centre of the smooth, white head of the presence. But this stream isn't red: it's an angry purple, as if it's choking on its own coils.

The girl hugs the presence to her chest and rocks it back and forth. She sings, 'My Aunt Nellie had a hole in her belly, And a hole in the biscuit tin. She was sitting on the grass, With her finger up her ass, And her tits going ding-a-ling-a-ling.'

'It's not yours,' Robert says.

She turns her upper body to move the presence away from him. 'It is mine. I swallowed it.'

'I don't believe you.'

The girl doesn't respond.

He asks again, 'How do I get back?'

The girl shakes her head. 'No going back. You don't want to go back. You want to stay here.'

'No. Not like this.'

The girl holds the presence up to him. 'You take it then. Cut the cord.'

Robert shifts his grip on the sword and takes a step back. 'No.'

'Too much responsibility? You're all the same. You want to know what the presence means – its message. I'll show you.'

'What?'

'Close your eyes.' He doesn't seem to have any choice in the matter: a black curtain descends over his vision. When it lifts again, the girl's standing by the side of the bed. She's not holding the presence any more. There's a coffin on the bed, its weight distorting the shape of the mattress underneath. He recognizes it – from the funeral parlour, three and a half years ago – except the hinged panel at its head is now open.

The girl tries to stand on tiptoe, so she can see inside. She totters a step to the right, then drops flat-footed and tuts. She beckons to Robert. 'You have to say goodbye. This is the only chance you'll get. You have to.'

'I don't want to see.'

'It's okay. It's just your mum. She wants to say goodbye too.'

The girl takes his hand and pulls him forwards. Another step. 'You're here now,' she says, squeezing his fingers.

He opens his eyes. A head, on a satin pillow. Sealed inside a plastic bag. Tied at the neck, sucked in tight over the face.

She won't be able to breathe: he tears at the plastic. It thins and blisters. A finger through. Two. Inside: the presence.

The bag's not covering its face. The bag's its skin, and its head is collapsing. Dissolving, a dirty halo seeping into the sodden pillow underneath. But the cone inside the head stays intact and upright, balanced on its truncated point – like the gramophone horn in the HMV logo. There's no red stream this time. The disc inside the cone begins to blink on and off: red, black.

A noise comes out, slow and stretched. Then it jerks forward into a scratchy voice. 'Dearest Frank,' it says, apparently addressing his dad.

'What's that?' the girl says, leaning in against the coffin and cupping her ear. 'I can't hear you.'

The voice continues: 'You remember when I had to bring you home. The last time I told you what I thought was wrong with me. Well, it's true. It's started again, only it's worse. How you will hate me. No one hates me more than myself.' The cone quivers and the red disc flashes to the rhythm of the words.

'Speak up!' the girl says.

'My heart aches for you both. If only you knew how sorry I am.'

'No,' Robert says. 'It's not true.'

'It is true,' the girl says.

The disc flickers. 'Please be strong, for Robert's sake. He's going to need you so much. Try and keep calm. I'm sure Rose will help you.'

Robert turns to the girl. 'I don't want *this* message,' he says. 'Make it stop.'

'Me? I'm not the one sending it.'

The voice drops into a slur, before correcting itself and concluding at a normal speed, 'I beg your forgiveness. I'll miss you so much.' The last words are barely audible, lost in a sea of crackle, as if the speaker's moving away from the microphone.

The girl nudges him with her elbow. 'It's your fault,' she says. 'You did this.'

'What?'

'You know it's your fault. That's why you're being punished. First Harmon House, then buried alive with the dead people next door. You're in prison – you've been there since your mum died.'

'No. Jesus set me free.'

'Your mum's in prison too. But it's not too late. I can stop her suffering – if you do something for me in return. If I let her go, someone else has to take her place. A sacrifice.'

'What?'

'You know what I want. Because you remember Abraham and Isaac. The person you can't bear to lose.'

'I don't know who that is.' He's lying: he does know.

'Tracey. She's the sacrifice. And you're going to give her to me.'

Whump-ump, ump-whump, whump-ump. On Tracey's Walkman, it sounds like two drums are hitting the same beat at once. But sluggish, exhausted. Tom-toms: no cymbals. A knife runs up and down a guitar string. Then there's a distorted moan, replaced by a chant: *Hai, hai, hai, hai, hai, hai, hai, hai*!

The song was recorded with two microphones: one close to the drum kit, the other farther away to capture the echo in the room. The sound from the drum lasts about half a second; the echo has a longer half-life as it bounces around the walls. A machine called a noise gate shuts off the room mic when the volume on the close mic drops below a certain threshold. So the sound's multiplied, but there's no natural decay: the echo's chopped off.

Gated reverb. An effect invented for this song: 'Intruder' by Peter Gabriel.

Tracey presses stop on her Walkman. The fluorescent numbers on the alarm clock say eleven thirty. She's supposed to be asleep by now. She swallows, struggles to do it a second time, coughs. A drink of water would be nice.

She swings her feet over the edge of the bed. The room shifts with her. A fireplace instead of the walk-in wardrobe; a table with model aeroplanes. Blink. She's not even thinking about Robert.

A thud on the wall. Another.

From behind the sliding mirrored doors of the wardrobe, in front of the wall connecting her to next door. Where Robert knocks for her, when he's in his bedroom. It's nearly midnight! He's going to wake her dad up.

Thud, thud. Thud, thud. Speeding up. *Hai, hai, hai, hai, hai, hai, hai, hai.*

The sound stops, but her heart keeps on echoing the beat. She goes to the side panel of the bay window, peeks round the edge of the curtain – there's no sign of Robert and his room is dark.

Thud, thud.

She slides a mirrored panel to one side and steps inside the wardrobe. Something rough and staticky brushes her face, and she jerks away. Black polyester fabric swings on a hanger in front of her face: the dress suit her dad bought her from M&S for her mum's funeral. She deliberately chose the cheapest, ugliest one: like wearing sackcloth. She only wore it the once, but it has bobbles sticking to it like burrs. What's it doing here, in front of her school clothes on the hanger rail?

Thud, thud.

The whole wall's vibrating now. She pushes the dress suit aside and reaches forward to press herself against the bare brick, where the X is written in black marker. Maybe Robert will be able to hear her voice that way, telling him to stop.

Her hands meet nothing and she stumbles, falls forward.

She jerks awake.

'I can do you tea,' Robert says, standing at her side, 'but we've only got powdered milk.'

What? Where is she? Next door: Robert's house. Sitting at the table in his dingy morning room. But that doesn't make sense. How did she get here? 'No thanks,' she says to him, as if this is all normal.

'Squash?'

'Okay.' His voice is higher than it should be. He's smaller too; fleshier. Like he used to be when he first moved here.

He takes a glass from the compartment inside the end of the dresser and unlocks the kitchen door. In the kitchen, he opens the fridge, pours an inch of Robinsons Barley Water into the glass and turns the tap on at the sink. Then he comes back into the morning room and places the glass on the table in front of her. He closes the kitchen door and locks it again, following Auntie Rose's rule.

Dull, ordinary. Maybe everything's okay here, whatever this is. But Tracey still feels a moment of panic at being cut off from the daylight. There are no shadows under the fluorescent light. It's a finger poking at her eye.

The glass is chunky. Thick, stippled. Wide at the top, then thinner, then widening out again. Uncle Edward does the washing-up, and inside at the base, beyond the narrow waist, where it's probably difficult to get your fingers in with a cloth, Tracey can see a line of brownish stuff under the yellow squash. The glass is only semi-transparent, so it's hard to make out, but it looks like dried blood.

Robert sits down at the other end of the table and says, 'You're wondering what the smell is.'

'What?' she says, a second before it hits her. She gags.

'It's your mum,' he says, 'in her coffin. Good job they kept it closed. The drunk driver made quite a mess.'

This is very wrong.

'Or maybe it's God. His body. The one you eat every week.' Robert smiles. His teeth are too large, the gums drawn back. Crescents of blood.

It's only now she notices: the morning room's the wrong way round. Like she's looking at it in a mirror. The fluorescent light stutters, and strobes the space into semi-darkness for a couple of seconds.

'Do you remember what your Aunt Rachel said to you, two weeks after the funeral?' Robert asks.

Tracey closes her eyes.

'She took you to a cafe on Lark Lane. The first time you had a cappuccino. You fiddled about with a spoon, trying to scoop the foam off.'

'I don't want to think about that. I want to go home now. Back to my bedroom.'

'She asked your dad to put your pocket money up by a pound. So you could buy tampons. Because obviously *he* wasn't going to get them. He tries. With his Delia Smith and his apron. But Sundays are better, because then it's Aunt Maggie in the kitchen – or Rachel. You said to her, "I don't use tampons." Of course. Because you have to stick them inside you, don't you?'

'You're not Robert. He wouldn't say any of this.'

'But Aunt Rachel explained how it works, and your face was so red. It was sweet. She did a better job than your mum. "Eve's curse", for God's sake. And the story about the woman with the ISSUE OF BLOOD.'

Robert picks up the glass of squash from in front of Tracey and takes a gulp. When he puts it down on the table, there's a suspended sliver of red, expanding into the murky liquid around. Disappearing, hiding.

He continues, 'And you said, to Rachel, "I won't need a pound a week," which wasn't true, but you felt guilty. Not about the money though.'

Robert picks his teeth with his fingernail and sucks air through the gap between the front two. 'And Rachel said, "Get some more cappuccinos then." I like her. Did you know she fucks her boyfriend? He's not a Christian. You all know. You just pretend.'

'Stop it!'

'I will, if you swear at me. Go on. Just say fuck. Not even that. Shit'll do, if you can't manage a fuck. Why don't you have any girlfriends at school? Do you remember when Becca Donnelly and her gang got you in the loos? Held you down and put a compass point to your ear? Said they were going to pierce it for you – unless you swore. What a brave girl you were. Because you didn't say anything, did you? Not even when they asked you, "Do you love Jesus? Is He your boyfriend?"'

Tracey slaps herself in the face. 'Wake up!'

'That's not going to do you any good.'

'What's happening? What is this?'

'Do you ever imagine your mum fucking your dad?'

Tracey puts her hands over her ears. She says, 'This isn't real. It's not real.'

'They must have done it. But probably only once. Or maybe your dad had a wet dream, and your mum just happened to be in the right place.'

Robert picks up the telephone handset from the dresser and dings the little black circuit breakers in the cradle. Tracey can hear the dialling tone cutting in and out. Then Robert drops the telephone handset with a clatter. 'People talk about hell being the absence of God,' he says. 'That won't work. Because if He's not there, He's not omnipresent. And if He's not omnipresent, He's not God.'

Tracey prays silently to herself: God, I don't know what's happening, but I want to go home. Please take me home. She gets up from the table. There's daylight in the kitchen beyond the locked door, but Robert's in the way, and there's no way to get home from there, so she fumbles behind her for the door back into the hall. She keeps her body facing towards him but turns her head so she can look back through the door. Is the hall going to be back to front as well?

The space beyond the door is black. Not even a space. No dimensions or directions. No end – but it has a beginning. An entrance; a threshold. Blood on the doorpost. The Angel of Death outside. Or inside, with her.

'You lot,' Robert says, 'always going on about blood. His precious blood. Magic.'

'It's not magic. It's faith.'

The florescent light spasms again, and goes out.

Robert says, 'Abracadabra,' as Tracey steps out into nothing.

And finds herself back in her wardrobe in her nightie, her dress suit back on the hanger, the fabric tickling her nose; Walkman headphones covering her ears, tape hiss like the sound of rain falling outside.

10
ROBERT

Robert's in the front room at Auntie Rose's, looking out the window, watching his dad stagger out of a taxi and up the driveway. His dad hasn't changed much since the funeral three years ago – except now his shirt is untucked, buttons in the wrong holes. His trousers sag, and he holds them up as he walks. His bare ankles flash white with each step.

Bing; bong. A downward lurch between the two chimes.

Auntie Rose has been expecting the taxi since the phone rang two hours ago. She answers the door and walks out in her dressing gown and slippers to pay the driver. Robert's dad slumps in the porch until she returns and shoos him inside.

The lights are off, and no one knows Robert's in here. As the taxi pulls away, he turns on his pencil torch and shines it onto the open page of the KJV on his lap. He wishes he could read by touch.

THEN WAS JESUS LED UP OF THE SPIRIT INTO THE WILDERNESS TO BE TEMPTED OF THE DEVIL. AND WHEN HE HAD FASTED FORTY DAYS AND FORTY NIGHTS, HE WAS AFTERWARD AN HUNGRED.

Robert fingers the empty holes on the left side of his belt buckle: one, two, three; prong in the fourth hole. He undoes the belt and cinches it tighter, until he can get the prong in the fifth hole. Too tight, cutting into his guts. Maybe next week.

Satan takes Jesus up to the top of a high mountain and shows him ALL THE KINGDOMS OF THE WORLD. And says, 'You can have it all. Just bow down and worship me.'

The first Christmas after his mum died, Robert bought his own presents, with money his dad gave him. Anything he wanted: an Airfix Lancaster bomber; the spaceship from *Battlestar Galactica*. And a black-and-gold Raleigh Super Grifter. He was already bored of it all by Christmas Eve.

No wrapping paper; no surprises. On Christmas Day, he ate a box of Milk Tray for tea. His dad stayed in bed all day. Robert saved him the coffee creams.

GET THEE HENCE, SATAN: FOR IT IS WRITTEN, THOU SHALT WORSHIP THE LORD THY GOD, AND HIM ONLY SHALT THOU SERVE.

'Robert!' Auntie Rose calls from the hallway up the stairs, thinking he's in his room. 'Come down! Your dad's here.'

He turns the torch off, closes his Bible, stands up. When he steps out into the hall, Auntie Rose is still staring up the stairs. He clears his throat; she twitches and gasps. He's always catching her by surprise. Sometimes he whistles a tune, just so she can hear where he is. He steps closer to her, so he can whisper. 'How long's he been back from Kuwait?'

'I don't know,' Auntie Rose says.

'Did they send him home again?' Robert doesn't want his dad to get the sack, because then he won't be able to send money to Auntie Rose. Robert doesn't want to go back to where he stayed before he moved here. He doesn't want to go back to Harmon House.

You'll have to borrow the airbed from next door,' Auntie Rose says.

'Why? Why does he have to go in my room?' She could move back into the main bedroom with Uncle Edward instead, leaving the front bedroom free.

'I thought you'd want to see him.'

They both go through to the television room. Robert's dad points to Auntie Rose as they enter. 'Her,' he says. 'She's a good sister to me.' He raises trembling fists, as if he might need to violently defend this statement.

'I know.' Robert stays in the doorway. No Uncle Edward: gone to bed early. His drinking record's not exactly spotless, so he probably thought it wise to avoid a conversation on the subject. His dad's in the seat Auntie Rose normally occupies, the *Radio Times* crumpled underneath him. Auntie Rose is standing in front of him in the centre of the room, her hands holding her dressing gown closed. Robert squeezes past her and sits down in his usual seat, at the far end of the sofa.

'I'll make some tea,' Auntie Rose says, and goes through to the kitchen.

'What's on telly?' Robert asks, pointing at the half-hidden *Radio Times*.

'Talk to me,' his dad says, wiping his palms on his trousers, staring at the electric flames in the fireplace.

'What about?'

'I don't know.'

His dad hasn't shaved, and there's grey in the stubble. His fingers move over his scalp like a spider. He prods at his hair-line, where there's a scab.

'How did you get that?' Robert asks.

'I fell over.'

'Okay.'

'I've got the DTs.' He holds his hands up, so Robert can see them shaking. 'I haven't had anything to drink since yesterday morning.'

Big wow. Gold star for you.

'Come closer,' his dad says.

'This is where I normally sit.'

'Please.'

Robert has to honour his father: it's one of the Ten Commandments. He looks at the middle sofa cushion, which is riding up, and fusses it back down into place. It'll give way; there's a gaping pit underneath. But he takes a deep breath and shuffles along anyway. He lowers himself into the middle of the sofa, keeping his weight pressed down on his rigid right arm, which is still on the edge of the cushion where he normally sits.

His dad's head drops, so Robert's looking at the cropped hairline at the back of his neck. He always goes to the same barber in Liverpool town centre – Jack the Snipper – where he gets a crew cut. Robert doesn't like barbers. He goes to the hairdresser on Brodie Avenue.

His dad says, 'Why did she do it? Why?'

'Who?'

His dad turns to look at Robert. 'Your mum.'

Why's he asking that? Robert jiggles his knee. The accepted fiction is still a heart attack. He can't even keep his lies straight any more. It's pathetic. 'I don't know,' Robert says.

His dad's shoulders shake, but he doesn't make a sound. Auntie Rose has left a box of tissues on the pouffe, so Robert reaches forward to take one. He hands it to his dad, who crumples it in his fist and wipes his nose with the back of his hand.

Robert feels the next words stick in his throat; he grinds them out of his mouth anyway. 'I love you.' His voice sounds like a robot.

Do it. Do it now. He raises his arm, inch by inch, reaches it over his dad's hunched back, leaves it hovering in the air for a few seconds, and finally rests his open palm on his dad's left shoulder.

'That arm means more to me than anything.'

Robert burns, as if his dad has heaped coals of fire on his head.

'When I was your age,' his dad continues, 'I was at sea.'

'I'm only fifteen.'

'Close enough. I was in a ship off Vancouver.' His voice has changed. 'We got hit by a Japanese submarine.' When Robert was younger, he was proud his dad had been in the war. But now he just sees the stiffness in his movements, the loose flesh round his jaw.

'We had an Oerlikon gun,' his dad continues. 'They put one

on a lot of merchant ships. And we had time to fight, before we went down. But I couldn't load and aim and fire all by myself, and no one would help. I asked the captain. He was already in the lifeboat; he said, "No, we don't want to provoke them." So I gave up, and I got in too.'

'Was it cold?' Is Robert supposed to leave his hand on his dad's shoulder all night? When is it okay to take it back? He tries to squeeze near the neck, but there's too much bone and not enough flesh.

'You could feel the fog sticking to your face, and the snot freezing on your upper lip. Then a searchlight came, floating above the water. Looking for survivors.'

'Were they going to sink the lifeboat too?' Robert's read comics about the Japanese.

'They wanted prisoners,' his dad says. 'They didn't have room for everyone, but they always took the officers.' He closes his eyes. 'The captain, he was next to the wireless op, who had a busted arm, so he was in shock, shivering.'

His dad's shivering too. Robert holds on tighter.

'And the captain: "There, there." Took off his jacket; draped it over the op's shoulders. I didn't understand at first, and then I did. The epaulettes.' His dad twists his mouth in disgust. 'The op had a wife and two kids.'

'Didn't anyone say?' Robert asks.

'The first mate tried – the Japs didn't believe him. They took him too.'

'What happened after?'

'He was still the captain. But no one spoke to him.'

'Were you in the lifeboat long?'

'The coastguard came.' His dad unfolds the tissue screwed up in his hand and folds it smooth on his knee, before blowing his nose and scrunching it back up again. He looks at Robert. 'I'm sorry,' he says.

The door opens, and Robert snatches his arm away. Auntie Rose puts the tea tray down on the pouffe. 'I have to go get the airbed from next door,' Robert says.

When he's collected it, he drops it in the porch. Before it's blown up, it could be anything: a swimming pool, an inflatable dinghy – a life raft. He steps outside, closes the porch door, and starts walking towards Mark's.

Mark says, 'You've missed the last few Tuesday nights.'

They're in his bedroom. Robert's sitting on one of the wooden chairs, near the open door. Hands in the pockets of his parka. He ignores Mark's implied question and says, 'My dad's turned up. I needed to get away.'

'Does he visit often?' Mark asks.

'He works overseas. On the seas. First mate on an oil tanker.'

'We had merchant guys in the Falklands. From the reserves.'

'He's only here because he's been drinking.'

People tense up when Robert mentions stuff like this; Mark stays loose. 'I'm sorry to hear that. But I don't think it's what you want to talk to me about.'

'I don't have time to explain,' Robert says. He doesn't have the words either.

'You can make a start.'

Sandy and Liz are in the kitchen. Talking about bedpans; making retching noises. Robert lowers his voice, so they can't hear. 'You know the story of Legion, the possessed man?'

Mark, who's sitting on the edge of his bed, leans forward. 'I do,' he says.

'He lives among the tombs, in the mountains. He won't behave. Everyone tries to tie him up in chains and irons, but he breaks free. Cries out, and cuts himself with stones.' Robert's always been jealous of Legion. He can do whatever he wants and blame it on the demons.

He continues, 'Then Jesus comes, and the man falls down and worships him. WHAT HAVE I TO DO WITH THEE, JESUS, THOU SON OF THE MOST HIGH GOD? I ADJURE THEE BY GOD, THAT THOU TORMENT ME NOT.'

'That's the demons speaking,' Mark says.

'So Jesus asks who He's talking to, and the man says, MY NAME IS LEGION: FOR WE ARE MANY.'

Mark picks up the story. 'And the demons beg Jesus, "Don't send us away. Put us in that herd of pigs." So Jesus agrees, and the whole herd runs into the sea, and drowns itself.'

'What are demons?' Robert asks. 'No one ever explains.'

'The Bible calls them unclean spirits.'

'And how do you know if someone's possessed?'

'You mean, if they don't live among the tombs and cry out and cut themselves?'

'Yes.'

'You don't,' Mark says. 'But most people are.'

Robert takes his hands out of his pockets and presses the heels into his eye sockets, feeling the shape of the bone. He stays like that for a second, then takes his hands away. He doesn't say anything, but what he feels is relief. Gratitude. Because Mark's going to tell him what everything means.

'You probably have a demon of alcoholism, a demon of suicide. "Possessed" is the wrong word though.' Mark picks up his mug and takes a sip of boiled water, waiting for Robert to reply.

Robert lifts his legs and feet up off the floor and places the heels of his trainers on the front edge of the chair seat. He wraps his arms around his lower legs, pulling them together. 'Why is it wrong?'

'The Greek is "demonized": "with a demon"; "in a demon" would be better. Like "in love". Or "in drink".'

'Inside a demon?'

'More like the demon's surrounding you,' Mark says. 'A filter. Messing up how you see things. Like drinking does. Or love.'

'I wouldn't know.'

Mark laughs. 'The point is: demons are everywhere. We're all "in" them, and they're in us.'

'How's that different to possession?'

'Because the demon doesn't own you. It's hitching a ride, trespassing, because you're under the protection of Christ's blood. You need to stick up for your rights: throw it out. With the power of the Holy Spirit.'

Robert thinks. 'We're "in" the Holy Spirit too. Like the water of baptism.'

Mark frowns. 'Yes,' he says, after a moment.

Robert goes quiet as Sandy and Liz pass the bedroom door. When they've reached the top of the stairs, Mark says, 'We're soldiers in God's army; we have to fight the enemy. Hand to hand. No point saying, "I command you, in Jesus' name," if you don't make His victory real in your life. So I never try deliverance, unless I know you really want it.'

'Deliverance?'

'Throwing demons out.'

'Have you ever spoken to one?' Robert asks.

'Yes. They're not very interesting,' Mark says. 'And the only thing I need to know is their name.'

'Like Legion?'

'It's usually the sin they're in charge of. Fear, anger, lust. And there's always a leader: the "strong man".'

'Why do you need to know their name?' It's better to keep asking questions. Otherwise Mark will come up with some of his own.

'Demons don't play fair,' Mark says. 'They take advantage.'

'I thought you had to invite them in.' Robert can't remember inviting the girl – but she acts like he did.

'If there's a crack for sin to get in,' Mark says, 'a demon can get in too. When you throw them out, that's when they get legalistic. They won't obey unless you use their name. Unless you identify the sin, and repent.'

What sin has Robert committed? Against his aunt, his uncle – his dad. His mum. 'Do you think people who commit suicide are in hell?' he asks.

Mark sighs. 'I think it's not up to me to place limits on God's mercy. But let's not change the subject. Do you think demons are attacking you?'

Robert hums a tune to himself. It's been in his head all day. He picks up Mark's interlinear Greek Bible and flicks through the pages.

Mark puts his mug down and says again, 'Do you?'

The tune won't tell him its name, but Mark's waiting, and eventually he has no choice. 'Yes,' he says. 'But there's only one.'

'No,' Mark says. 'They always hunt in packs. One comes, and invites others. Like I said, addiction's demonic. And suicide.'

Robert fidgets. 'I don't want to drink. Or kill myself.' What does it mean, this resistance? Is it the demons in him, resisting the truth?

'It's an opening, for the spirits to enter.' Mark reaches over and takes his Bible back; he places it on his lap. 'I don't want to upset you. But I'd like you to be free. God wants everyone to be free.'

'I want to be free too,' Robert says. Then adds, 'I don't want to be his son.'

'God's?'

'My dad.' That's the real temptation. Take another name: Legion, for example. Or Forester. What if Bill was his dad, and Tracey was his sister? But doesn't that mean abandoning his mum too?

'Think about it,' Mark says, ignoring Robert's last comment. 'Pray. If you're willing to work, we can throw the demons out.'

Robert's not so sure. None of this sounds *wrong* exactly, but it doesn't sound right either. Is he 'in' the girl? Is she 'in' him? What about the presence? He wonders if he summoned it. It comes when he puts his mind somewhere else: between the misaligned edges of the wallpaper, or the stage and the floor of the assembly hall. And the girl's getting in the way. Interfering. Is she changing its message? If he summoned her, he didn't mean to.

'It doesn't have to be the two of us,' Mark says. 'I can ask Tracey.'

'No.'

'Why not?'

'It's not safe.' And that's true. But it's not the only reason. All this: it's Robert's secret, not Tracey's. He doesn't even want to tell Mark. Not *everything*.

'You don't need to worry,' Mark says. 'God will protect her. You have to have faith.'

And Robert has no answer for that. 'Okay,' he says, because he wants to overcome his lack of faith.

On the way home, Robert can see the blue ambulance light from halfway up South Mossley Hill Road. When he gets closer, Auntie Rose waves to him from the back of the ambulance. His dad's lying on a stretcher inside, groaning – a wet patch on the front of his trousers.

'He had a seizure,' Auntie Rose says. She's got her coat on over her dressing gown.

Robert looks around, trying to see if any of the neighbours are peering through their curtains. Tracey's house is dark.

The ambulancemen are wearing blue uniforms. Their jackets have silver buttons up the front, and on the pocket flaps. No epaulettes, but they do have insignia crests on each shoulder.

Robert's dad stayed on a sinking ship: tried to fight the enemy. Robert has to fight too – but all he needs to do right now is climb into an ambulance. He looks inside: a prison cell. No escape.

Auntie Rose pulls her coat tighter. 'Are you going to go with him?'

'Okay,' Robert says. 'Yes.'

After the forty days in the desert, Satan never comes back to tempt Jesus again. If only it were that simple. The problem for Robert is that he has to keep facing the same temptation, over and over. The Devil won't take no for an answer. Maybe it's that way for his dad too.

What if Mark does cast the girl out? Will the presence go too? Maybe that wouldn't be such a bad idea. He thinks of the sodden coffin, and the words floating up towards him.

No more visitors. He'll be alone. Who's he going to be then?

11

Tracey / Robert / Tracey

'What's on at the Odeon?' Tracey asks.

'A load of rubbish,' Kevin says, without even looking at the copy of the *Echo* he's holding. He's obviously made his decision already.

'What's the review?'

Kevin reads the summary of a film called *Footloose*: 'Kevin Bacon takes the leading role as the hip Chicago teenager who takes his big-city ways to small-town America and preaches the virtues of Rock 'n' Roll. Lori Singer, of *Fame* fame, plays the hell-raising vicar's daughter who teams up with him.'

'Sounds like it's taking the mickey.'

Kevin flicks the newspaper flat and folds it over. 'No more than usual,' he says. 'I tune it out.'

'Maybe you shouldn't.' Paul couldn't make the practice session tonight, and Kevin suggested going to the pictures. Tracey hasn't felt right since the weird dream about her mum's funeral two weeks ago. She normally forgets dreams as soon as she wakes up, but every time she thinks about this one, there it is again: too vivid, too close – like a broken vial of ammonia under her nose.

So she said yes to Kevin, because she wanted to do something normal, something everyone else does. Now she's not sure what she's agreed to. She wishes they had American-style 'dating' in Liverpool, which, as far she can tell, allows you to go out with someone without officially going out with them. She thinks of

Rebecca Miller, who gets asked out all the time, and says, 'I've prayed about it, and I don't think it's God's will.'

Kevin's just passed his driving test, and he got an M-reg Allegro as a present. He wrestles with the gearstick and stalls the engine before getting the car off the pavement onto South Mossley Hill Road. He starts in second gear, and the car lurches forward, bouncing Tracey backwards and forwards against the seat belt.

'Oops,' he says.

'Lights.'

He flicks the windscreen wipers on and off before he finds the right lever.

'Are you sure you passed?'

'You should see my three-point turn.'

Kevin's not tall, so he's hunched over the wheel like Mr Magoo. Maybe he has to stretch to reach the pedals. She peeks over and looks down. There is a hole in the bottom of the car. He follows her glance. 'Don't mind that,' he says. 'Free air conditioning.'

'How did it pass the MOT?'

'It probably won't, next year.'

After getting out of Booker Avenue and onto the dual carriageway on Brodie, Kevin accelerates. 'Did you go into town yesterday?' Tracey asks. There'd been a one-day strike. The teachers didn't come out, but the jannies did, so New Heys was shut.

'No. Did you?'

'Yes.' That was an attempt to get her mind off the dream too. There'd been a march and a demonstration, then a council meeting at the town hall. The plan was to pass an illegal budget in defiance of government cuts, and local unions gathered to show their support.

'Weren't the buses on strike?' Kevin asks.

'There were trains.' Tracey got off at Central and joined the march there. If you listened to the whole crowd walking, no consistent rhythm. But if you focused on the people around you, everyone was marching in step. No Jericho trumpets, but banners and chants, and politicians at the front with squawking megaphones.

Labour council, Labour council, We'll support you ever more!

'What was it like?' Kevin asks.

'Heaving.' From a distance, she could see women dotted through the crowd; up close it was all hairy arms and necks. She got caught up in the crush in front of the police lines round the town hall on Castle Street, and someone behind pinched her bum. Then laughed.

Maggie, Maggie, Maggie! Out, out, out! Maggie! Out! Maggie! Out! Maggie, Maggie, Maggie! Out, out, out!

'I think Paul went too,' Kevin says. 'Did you see him?'

Tracey laughs. 'No.'

'He was in Manchester the day before, at the Cup replay.'

'How did he manage that?'

'He sagged off.'

There were football colours and banners in the crowd on the march: 'Everton supporters support the City council'. Football chants too: *They all laugh at us, They all mock us, They all say our days are numbered. Born to be a Scouse, Victorious are we.*

She says to Kevin, 'How are you two such good friends, if you don't mind me asking?'

'He's not like you and me.'

'You and me?' Kevin's house in Cressington isn't much bigger than Tracey's, but it's set back from a tree-lined street with speed bumps, and it has sandstone gateposts flanking a driveway up to the front door. A man comes to mow the grass and clip the hedges.

Kevin thinks about what to say, and finally offers, 'His uncle's on the council.'

'Really?'

'St Mary's.'

'What's that?'

Kevin shifts gear. 'Council ward: like a constituency for an MP. Paul knows the boundaries, because he had to do the leaflets in the election last year.'

'Are we in St Mary's as well?'

'No. We're over the border,' Kevin says. 'Grassendale. Conservative. Enemy territory.'

At the demonstration, Tracey left after the speeches. Today's *Echo* said the meeting went on for eight hours and they couldn't get the budget through, because some of the Labour councillors broke ranks and voted with the Conservatives and Liberals.

Kevin continues, 'I don't care, but Paul does. It's easy to wind him up.'

Tracey smooths her denim skirt flat. 'The city's going to go bankrupt.'

'How would you tell? It's not like anyone collects the bins now.'

'The school'll shut down.'

'Well, it's not going to happen before summer.'

They say cut back, We say fight back!

She wipes the condensation off the car window as they drive through Toxteth. She remembers, during the riots, playing tennis in the public courts down on Otterspool Promenade and seeing the pall of smoke hanging over the city centre. She was younger then and she thought it was CS gas, because the news had shown the police firing canisters.

We love you Maggie, we do! We love you Maggie, we do! Do we fuck, do we shite! We stick up for our own, right!

Kevin parks the car in the Mount Pleasant multistorey, on only his second attempt, and they walk along to the ABC. She lets her hand dangle, but he doesn't take it. At the ticket booth by the entrance, Kevin says to the clerk, 'Two kids for *Footloose*, please.'

Tracey frowns. 'No,' she says, 'I'm sixteen.' Should she buy her own ticket? Will he get offended?

'So,' the clerk says, 'that's one adult' – she looks at Kevin, who's obviously older than Tracey – 'and one child.'

'Oh, is it under sixteen?' Kevin asks. 'I thought it was eighteen.'

The clerk pops her bubblegum.

'Two adults then.'

'Smoking or non-smoking?'

'Non.'

'Four pounds forty,' the clerk says.

Kevin hands over a five-pound note.

When they're farther away from the booth, Tracey says, 'Sorry, I don't like lying.'

'You're right. I just object to the prices.'

'I can pay. I brought the money with me.'

'You can buy the popcorn.'

They're in Screen One, up on the balcony. Tracey loves the ABC. There's an organ, and an arch framing the screen, with two sets of curtains. The outer set, in red velvet, swish aside to reveal a translucent canopy, like the screen has a petticoat, all gathered in ruches, which rises up into the ceiling when the film starts.

In the film, Tracey's supposed to identify with the minister's daughter, Ariel, who explains the reason for the town's ban on rock music: her brother was killed in a car crash after a night of drinking and dancing. Tracey's more interested in the minister.

In films and books, no one ever believes something simply because it's true. There's always a secret, personal reason. Righteousness is hypocrisy; conviction is prejudice. God is a mask to hide behind. And the story strips the mask away. Reveals the secret that explains who you are. But the minister's trying to be a good person.

It takes Kevin an hour to get his arm up over the back of her chair, where it wriggles its way over her shoulders, like a caterpillar. She can feel her heart bumping and she's angry with her body, because there's nothing to get excited or worried about. She resists the urge to scratch her inflamed neck, and tries to concentrate on *Footloose*.

In the film, the kids of the local town are pure and clean. They don't have any secrets. They don't have doubts either. It's the minister who changes his mind. He even fights the rest of the town council when they start burning books.

We don't hide from ourselves in God. *He's* the secret that explains who we are.

Maybe Kevin's arm's gone dead, because he removes it from her chair and flexes his fingers. He takes some popcorn from the bucket she's holding squeezed between her thighs. Has a good rummage around first.

She's got to wait for him to do things: ask her out; touch her. Why?

When the film's finished, they walk down to Topshop on Church Street, because a Burger King's opened on the first floor above, and Kevin wants to try it out. 'I don't think it's going to be like the diner in the film,' Tracey says.

'Anyway.'

They're still not holding hands.

Inside the Burger King, Kevin looks up at the menu, which is on the wall above the till. Backlit, glowing: radioactive. 'What's good?' he asks the girl on the till, who's wearing goth eye make-up. Her little hat sits awkwardly on her dyed black hair, which is backcombed underneath it.

'It's all the same,' the girl replies. Her uniform's not that different from the girl in the ticket booth at the ABC. But no fake marble or plush seats here. Everything is plastic and fluorescent.

'Okay, I'll have, um, a Whopper,' Kevin says. He looks at the girl to check he's doing it correctly, and when she says nothing, he adds, 'And fries; and a Pepsi.' He turns to Tracey. 'Do you want anything?'

'A strawberry milkshake.'

Although Burger King and the new Topshop have been here for a couple of weeks, they only had the official opening earlier today, with a visit from the new Miss World – apparently Miss England won this year. Tracey picks up a signed photo from a pile by the till and holds it up. 'First prize: a trip to Liverpool and a burger. What was she like?'

'Nice hair,' the girl says, scooping fries into a cardboard container. 'Just like the photo. Exactly like the photo. Which was weird.'

Tracey and Kevin sit down at a little table with bucket seats bolted to the floor. 'What did you think of the film?' he asks.

'I didn't think the minister was the villain.'

'I don't think he was supposed to be. The music was *last*.'

'Good to dance to. But you wouldn't know about that.'

Kevin grins. He jerks his head up and down and shakes it from side to side.

'That isn't dancing.' She takes one of his fries. 'How's the burger?'

'Okay. Lettuce and so on.' He puts it down on the waxed-paper wrapper and picks at it with his finger. Slides out something soggy and greenish from the compacted mass. 'What's that?' he asks.

Tracey cranes forward, and they examine it together. 'I think it's a pickle.'

'Oh.' Kevin sounds disappointed.

'The milkshake's thick. Super cold. Like sucking ice cream.'

He says, 'The girl in the film reminded me of you.'

'Kevin Bacon didn't remind me of you at all.'

'Doesn't it get you down,' he asks, 'being an elder's kid?'

'I don't mind.'

'I hate it,' Kevin says.

'Have you been baptised?' She can't remember.

'Yeah. Got it over with quick as I could.'

He talks like he was trying to lose his virginity. 'You're not wearing a band T-shirt tonight.'

Under his coat, Kevin has a red-and-blue striped shirt, and a dark blue blazer with a missing button. He's also clean-shaven, although his hair's still down to his shoulders. 'I borrowed this off Paul,' he says, fingering the remaining gold button on the blazer. There's a wisp of stray thread where the other should be.

'I figured,' Tracey says, pointing at the badge for The Specials on the lapel. 'Why do you like heavy metal? Don't the lyrics bother you?'

'I don't listen to them.'

'I don't believe you.'

Kevin shrugs, then says, 'It's like reading a story. You pretend to believe it, because it's bigger than real life. You don't carry it out of the song.'

'Pretend? You mean be a hypocrite?'

'I'm not explaining it properly. You can try something out, see how it feels. But then you turn it off.'

'Like dating,' Tracey says.

'What?'

'Never mind.' She gurgles up her milkshake through her straw.

Kevin looks out the window, down at the people in the pedestrian zone on Church Street. 'I don't have anything against God. I just don't like the people who claim to speak on His behalf.'

'But you believe in Jesus?'

'Not the same way my dad does.'

'How do you know you've been saved?' Tracey says. 'How can you be sure?'

'Does that worry you?' Kevin asks.

'It's more, what's supposed to come after? What am I supposed to become?'

WE WILL NOT ALL SLEEP, BUT WE WILL ALL BE CHANGED — IN A FLASH, IN THE TWINKLING OF AN EYE, AT THE LAST TRUMPET. 'Do you ever think about heaven?' she asks.

Kevin wipes his fingers on the burger wrapper, avoiding his discarded pickle. 'When we went to Tenerife last year, there was a swimming pool in the hotel. Every day, bobbing. Boiling sun, peeling shoulders.'

'Lucky you. We go walking in the Lake District. Bed and breakfast.'

'But the chlorine gets in your sinuses,' Kevin continues, 'and your skin gets wrinkly, so you have to get out, and by the end of the fortnight, I was desperate to get home.' He looks up at the ceiling. 'What actually *happens*, in heaven? You can only say, "Holy, holy, holy" so many times.'

'An eternity of choruses.'

'You asked me before, why I'm friends with Paul. Why are you friends with Robert?'

'I don't know if I am any more. He's stopped calling for me.' She can't help feeling that has something to do with the weird dream too, since Robert was in it with her. Or something that looked like him. When she woke up the morning after, she showered three times, until there were spots of blood on the towel.

Kevin waves his hand in front of her unfocused eyes. 'You don't seem to have much in common with him.'

'We like the same music, mostly,' Tracey says. 'Don't you have someone you grew up with? I'm responsible, whether I like it or not.'

'I thought he only moved here a couple of years ago.'

'He used to visit Auntie Rose. It's easier to connect when you're seven. Nothing to disagree over. Even now, if you make the effort, you can find things in common.'

'I'm jealous,' Kevin says.

Tracey laughs. 'Don't be.' But he doesn't mean that kind of jealous. 'Why?' she asks.

'He doesn't have any doubts.'

'I don't know about that.' She tries to think of someone who doesn't have doubts, and says, 'He's not like Mark. But I think God speaks to him.'

'Speaks?'

'You know what I mean.' How can Kevin know, when she's not sure herself?

What does Robert *do* all day, when he's not with her? What's his life like, alone in that house? It's impossible to imagine *him* on a date. What if God said, 'You can swap places for a day'? She twitches away from that thought, like it's ammonia too. Because she knows what that would be like. It would be like living inside her dream.

Does she want God to speak to her, or not? Because He might do it through Robert, but He's definitely not going to do it through Kevin.

'I had a nice time tonight,' he says.

'Me too.'

'Do you want to do it again some time?' Kevin asks, fingering his missing moustache. 'Next week maybe?'

I've prayed about it, and I don't think it's God's will.

She says, 'I've got to revise for O levels. I'll see you next Friday at practice.'

Robert's not sure where his dad is. After the ambulance took him to hospital, they transferred him to a detox ward in

Clatterbridge on the Wirral, but when Robert went to visit him there, he'd already discharged himself. And every time he phones Neston, there's no answer.

The 488 bus goes to Neston from Whitechapel in the city centre. Robert sits downstairs at the back. He can feel the vibrations of the engine up the inside of his thighs, like he's inside its throat. As the bus passes the shadow line at the entrance to the Queensway tunnel, it enters a fog of exhaust fumes, which seep through the windows. Robert breathes deep. In, out; in, out. Then holds it.

In the twilight, he can still read the sticker on the side window. It used to warn vandals that

> The executive will press for
> heaviest penalties against offenders,

but someone's changed it to

> The executive will press
> h   i s pen   i s against offenders.

Robert's heart is a fist, clenched tighter and tighter as the seconds tick by. A minute; a minute and a half. He tries to push the feeling back down his throat, but he can't keep it in any longer. He sucks the grubby air.

He runs his fingers over the graffiti scratched into the glass around the defaced sticker: LFC, IRA, UDF. Eventually, the bus emerges back into daylight in Birkenhead. But even though he's on the Wirral, he's still inside Liverpool. The bus carries the city with it.

Once they get past Clatterbridge Hospital, they're in the countryside. Miles between the bus stops, and nothing around them. The smell of manure. He'd rather breathe the fumes in the tunnel.

He puts his headphones on and plays an album Mark copied for him: *Nebraska*, by Bruce Springsteen. Folk songs. Mark says Springsteen recorded them at home. They were only supposed to be demos, but when the band tried to rerecord them in the studio, Springsteen decided he preferred the original versions. An acoustic guitar chug-chugs along like the bus engine throbbing under Robert's thighs. The voice is echoey: maybe Springsteen's house has really big rooms, but it sounds more like he's playing in an empty church hall. You can hear when he breathes in; the smack of his lips shaping the words around the microphone.

They're not soppy songs, which Robert likes. They're about brothers and fathers and people who've forgotten how to love each other but keep trying anyway. Mark says love is a choice, not a feeling. You have to keep chug-chugging along – towards a destination you don't even want to reach.

Robert gets off the bus at the bottom of Talbot Avenue and walks up. It's not so different to South Mossley Hill Road: rows of semi-detached houses. Then overgrown thickets of green start appearing between the houses. Then a garden with a chicken coop; Land Rovers with spattered mudflaps. Woollyback land. Harmon House's not far from here – he's not going back there.

It starts raining. A dog barks from inside a house; flings itself at the front door. The letterbox rattles.

His dad's house is by itself on the corner at the top of Talbot Avenue. He blinks the drizzle out of his eyes and climbs up onto the bars of the old farm gate. He can feel the cold of the metal through his damp cords. His Peter Storm cagoule sticks to his ribs.

He gets down off the gate. It's fifteen feet wide, heavy, so he only pushes it wide enough to slip through then lets it clang back against the post. He steps over the cattle grid and grinds gravel until he reaches the front door.

They moved in here six years ago. His dad got the house cheap because it was almost derelict, and it's not that much better now. The buildings are arranged in an L shape, with the farmhouse in the centre and the deserted stable and cowshed on either side. Different parts of the house were built at different times, and they don't really fit together. The core has three floors, but other sections have two, and the stable and cowshed only have one, so the grey slate roofs aren't in line, as if parts of the building are subsiding.

He rings the bell. *Brrrrrring.* No answer. There's a bunch of folded fliers stuck between the brushes in the letterbox. He pushes them through and uses his fingers to flatten the brushes so he can see through the slot. There's a pile of mail behind the door. He stands up again and pushes the door: locked. He rings the bell again. The sound's all alone, nothing to touch in there except the walls – but a fly comes to answer. He can hear it buzzing and see its shadow bumping against the frosted-glass panel in the door.

Wherever his dad is, he's not here.

On the bus home, Robert thinks about demons and unclean spirits. He still doesn't know where the girl fits in. Maybe he doesn't need to. He just needs to be empty – have faith. Let Mark figure it out.

Except that's not how it's supposed to be. Robert's the one who God speaks to.

Tracey's staring at a Get Well Soon card. A cartoon of a man in a hospital bed. He's wearing striped pyjamas, sheet pulled up to his chest. A cartoon of a man – cross-eyed, sticking out his tongue, which is covered in red spots – in a hospital bed. He's wearing striped pyjamas, sheet pulled up to his chest. Inside the card, a printed message says, 'Hope you're back to your old self soon!'

She found the envelope on the porch floor when she came home from school. She nudged it with her foot and stared at it for a minute, because she thought it might be a love letter from Kevin. When she picked it up, she tore the flap open fast – like pulling off a plaster.

From Robert, not Kevin: 'You are hereby invited to my deliverance, at Mark's house. But you can't ask me any questions.' After she read the message, she ripped the card in half and crumpled up the envelope, but now she's put the two halves next to one another on the coffee table in the front room.

Bing; bong. Surely that's not Robert? He wouldn't dare.

Her dad's in the back room with the church accounts, and when the chimes sound again, she hears him go to answer the door. He sighs loudly when he passes the front room. She tenses her shoulders when he opens the front door; then she hears Mark's voice in the porch. They're probably talking about money.

She stares at the divided card. Her house – and Robert's. Joined at the seam – ripped in half.

Her dad sticks his head round the door. 'Mark's here to see you.'

'Me?' She stands up. 'About what?'

'I don't know. He can tell you.'

'I didn't ask him here,' she says, even though Mark can hear.

'Thanks, Bill,' Mark says, squeezing past him through the doorway. 'No need for tea or anything.'

'You don't drink tea,' Tracey says.

'I'll be in the back if you need me,' her dad says, to no one in particular.

Mark looks spiffy: white jeans and a denim shirt under a darker double-breasted pea coat. Is that for her benefit?

He moves over to the sofa. He grimaces as he sits, favouring his injured arm, even though it's not touching anything.

Tracey waits until he's settled, then sits down again. She leans forward and puts her palm over the two halves of the card.

'Robert came to see me,' Mark says.

She touches one of the ragged edges of the card. 'So I gather.'

'I thought that's what you wanted.'

'Well, he's stopped talking to me since then.'

'He's only next door.'

'That's not how it works. He comes here.' Is that true? It didn't used to be. Then she moved her drums, and suddenly there was no reason for her to step over the fence. 'He sent me a card,' she says to Mark, holding the two pieces up, one in each hand.

'Maybe that's his way of asking for help.'

Tracey laughs. She hands the pieces over.

Mark puts them back together on the table. 'Have you been ill?'

'I get "Deepest condolences for your loss" on my birthdays. What's deliverance?'

Mark stares at the card. 'Remember when we did the study on spiritual warfare, from Ephesians?'

'Yes.' Tracey didn't enjoy it. Talking to God in prayer makes her feel more real, more present to herself. But imagining demons overhearing that conversation, broadcasting thoughts of their own to interfere – she doesn't know how to feel about that.

'It's part of my ministry,' Mark says, tapping the bottom half of the card. 'I don't go on about it, but it's important.'

'What is?' Tracey asks, but she already knows.

'Deliverance. Casting demons out.'

'What's that got to do with Robert?' She knows that too. Or at least, she knows what Mark's going to say.

He leans forward. 'He's oppressed by demons.'

'Maybe he's oppressed by God.' She gets up and steps over to the television. She touches the dead screen and gets a pinprick static shock.

'Do you believe in the Bible?' Mark asks.

Tracey's not looking at him, but she can see a curved version of his face stretched across the glass of the television screen, like an expanding soap bubble. She moves her palm across the milky image and wipes off the clinging film of static. Electronic dust. 'Of course.'

'So you believe the Devil's real too.'

She shakes her head, but she means yes.

Mark continues, 'And you believe in angels and demons.'

She feels like she's lying face down on the carpet, with his knee in her back, her arm twisted up behind.

'Well?' he says.

'Why does it matter what I believe? Why do I need to be there?'

'I need your help. Robert needs your help.'

'He's got a funny way of asking for it.'

Mark shakes his head. 'He doesn't know any better.'

Tracey's neck stiffens, as if someone's standing behind her. She leans forward and lowers her voice. 'Does my dad know about any of this?'

'That's up to you. It's you I'm asking, not him.'

But who's *really* asking? Mark, or God speaking through him?

12

'Stop looking at my boobs!' Someone's taken a biro and coloured in all the nymph nipples on Mark's art poster. Added little tassels, so they look like stripper pasties.

Tracey's in his bedroom with Robert and Jenny. She walks around the edge of his bed and sits down on its corner, near where Mark's cleared his weights away to make a space in front of the bay window. He's also brought in some fold-up wooden chairs, which he's arranged in a circle. Now he comes back through from the kitchen and places a plastic bucket in the middle of the circle.

'What's that for?' Robert asks. He's standing behind one of the chairs. Still in his school uniform, though he's taken the tie off. Tracey's shocked at the change in him. He looks like his flesh has been boiled away: like he's on the point of disappearing. When was the last time she saw him eat?

'Demons come out through the mouth,' Mark says.

'So you puke them up?' Robert already looks queasy.

'Not quite.' Mark's wearing black wool trousers with a crease and an ironed white shirt with a button-down collar. It's the first time Tracey's seen him in proper church clothes. She remembers him saying he used to write the word Satan with a small *s*, until God told him, 'No, he's dangerous. You have to treat him with respect.'

'Why the mouth?' she says.

'Because they're spirit, breath,' Jenny suggests. She's already sitting in one of the fold-up chairs. Judging by his reaction when she arrived, Mark wasn't expecting her to be here. So Robert must have asked her. Maybe he sent out a whole lot of invitations but Tracey and Jenny were the only ones who showed up. Jenny's still in her work clothes: a cream silk blouse with puffy sleeves and tight cuffs, a grey pencil skirt. Knees tight together. Tracey's in jeans and a sweatshirt. No one told her there was a dress code for exorcisms.

'Look, this isn't difficult,' Mark says. 'Jesus did it all the time. But it only works if everyone in the room believes.' He leans back against the windowsill.

'Believes what, exactly?' Jenny asks.

'That the power of Jesus is available here, right now.'

Tracey also understands what he doesn't say: it's only going to work if everyone agrees that Robert's really oppressed by a demon. Tracey wants to believe this – if it'll help Robert – but she's taking it on faith, because Mark hasn't offered any proof.

Jenny says, 'What's your biblical warrant for this?'

'The authority of Jesus' ministry. Proved by my own experience, and the experience of people I trust.'

Jenny can't compete with that. She says, 'I don't see how you can justify the idea that demons are sins.'

'Common sense,' Mark says. 'Demons want us to sin.'

'But the idea of each one bound to a sin, taking its name, its purpose – its whole identity?' She shakes her head.

'Why not?'

'People are more complicated than that. So demons have to be too.'

'Why?' Mark asks again.

'Because God created them,' Jenny says.

'He created worms and cockroaches too. Who knows what demons were like, originally? It's what they've *become* that matters.'

'I thought they were fallen angels,' Tracey says.

'They don't behave like angels,' Jenny says.

'You mean they don't carry messages?' Robert says.

'Angels can make bodies. Demons have to take over someone else's.'

'So if something has a body of its own,' Robert says, 'then that could be a fallen angel?'

'I don't know,' Jenny says. 'I don't know a lot of things, because the Bible doesn't say. It's important to know what it doesn't say.'

'I know exactly what I need to know,' Mark says. He draws the curtains; closes the bedroom door. Everyone's locked in now. No escape.

Robert sits down in one of the chairs: Tracey moves to the one opposite him, with Jenny in-between. Mark stands behind Robert and puts his hand on the top of his head. 'Repeat after me,' he says. 'Lord Jesus, I know you are the Way, the Truth and the Life.'

Robert says the words.

'Like you mean it,' Mark says.

Like he means it. What does that sound like?

Robert says the words again.

Mark moves to the empty chair and sits down. He continues, 'You died for my sins on the Cross, and rose again, so that I can be forgiven and receive eternal life.'

Robert leans forward and says the words – into the bucket. There's an echo, like it's a wishing well. Then he raises his head again. 'She's here.'

Mark frowns.

Tracey beams her attention out at the room. Has the temperature dropped? Is there a bad smell? She's not sure anything's changed, but her skin prickles in anticipation. Is she frightened? Is she … excited? It feels like doing a sketch with Robert: like speaking at the assembly.

'Where is it?' Mark says to Robert.

It? Robert said *she*. Do demons have a sex?

'She's sitting cross-legged on the bed,' Robert says. 'Where Tracey was.'

Everyone turns.

Mark looks annoyed, as if the demon's not sticking to the script. He tweaks the creases on his trousers into sharper peaks. 'Everyone hold hands and pray together. When I say a line, you all join in with "Amen".'

Tracey and Jenny shuffle their chairs towards Mark. Robert does the same, pausing after each lurch to push the bucket ahead of him with his foot.

Tracey looks from side to side. She has her left hand in Mark's; her right in Jenny's: she's not directly connected to Robert, but he's in the chain too. Mark prays, 'Lord Jesus, I'm nothing without your strength, your power. Your righteousness. Amen.'

Everyone repeats, 'Amen.' Tracey moves her eyes along the line of their joined hands. Up, down: like a wave.

Mark continues, 'I can't hide from you. You know the thing that binds me, torments me – defiles me.'

'Makes me unclean,' Robert says.

'Amen,' Jenny and Tracey say.

Mark says, 'So I confess to you now …'

Robert leans forward again, his mouth hanging open. Jenny shifts her grip on Tracey's hand. Does everyone have to join in for this? Is there something Tracey can say? A *little* secret: one she won't miss too much.

'Robert?' Mark says.

'What?'

'Do you have anything to confess? Anything holding you back from God?'

Robert cocks his head to one side, as if he's listening to someone speak. 'I don't like sex,' he says, after a moment. 'Why does everyone always want to talk about that? You can't make me.'

Tracey laughs, then clears her throat and starts saying the Lord's Prayer under her breath.

'Are you talking to it?' Mark says to Robert. 'Don't.'

Tracey looks at the bed – there's no imprint there. Then she looks at Jenny, who shakes her head in response, but only slightly, so Mark can't see. With the curtains closed and their hands all joined, it feels more like a seance than an exorcism.

Mark asks Robert, 'What about masturbation?'

Tracey prays a little louder.

'I don't do that,' Robert says.

'Never?'

'No.' He pulls away from Mark and Jenny and crosses his arms over his chest, with his hands slipped under his armpits. 'I tried once; it didn't work.' He nudges the bucket away with his foot, moving it up onto its edge. It wobbles, then settles down again.

'Alright,' Mark says. Since the circle's already broken, he takes his other hand back from Tracey. She watches it withdraw, and leaves her own hanging in the air for a few seconds. 'Let's go on,' Mark says, continuing his prayer. 'I want to be free, so I forgive others, Lord Jesus. Anyone who's ever harmed me, I offer them all to you.'

Tracey and Jenny say, 'Amen.'

'No more resentment,' Mark says. 'No more anger. No more hatred. Specifically, I forgive—'

'No one,' Robert says. 'There's no one I need to forgive.'

'What about your dad?' Mark says.

Robert shakes his head.

'What about your mum?' Mark says.

Robert raises his voice. 'No.'

'You don't forgive her?'

'I don't need to.'

'You do.'

Robert makes his hands into fists. 'What did she ever do to me?' he says.

'Say it anyway,' Mark suggests. 'I forgive—'

'My dad,' Robert says.

'What for? You have to be specific.'

Tracey keeps muttering the Lord's Prayer. Jenny reaches over and tugs at Robert's left hand, and Mark takes his right again. They keep him crucified between them. Helpless, forsaken.

Robert takes a deep breath and says, 'I forgive my dad for going to bed, when he got home from Kuwait. And not getting up until the evening, even though I woke him, to tell him she hadn't come back from shopping. I forgive him for not calling the police until the following day.'

'Good.' Mark shoves the plastic bucket back closer to Robert.

'I forgive him for not telling me.'

'Telling you what?'

'How she died.'

'How did she die?'

'You know that.'

'Tell me again. Tell all of us.'

'She killed herself.'

Tracey stops praying. Did she know this? Perhaps she did – but she's never heard Robert say it.

Jenny squeezes Robert's hand tighter and moves forward on her seat in his direction.

'What else?' Mark says to Robert.

'I forgive him for leaving me there.'

'Where?'

'Where I was,' Robert says, 'before I came to Liverpool.'

'Where was that?'

'Harmon House. A children's home.'

'You never told me that,' Tracey says. 'Was that before you stayed with us?'

'Before Auntie Rose agreed to have me.'

'Maybe you need to forgive her too,' Mark says. 'For not agreeing sooner.'

'Okay.' Robert shrugs. 'I forgive her.'

'What for?'

He pushes out a long breath – as if it's an unclean spirit, starting to leave his body. 'For not being my mum,' he says.

'I'm sure it was horrible,' Jenny says, 'but they were probably doing their best.'

'Is there anyone from Harmon House you need to forgive?' Mark asks.

'No one in particular.'

'Say it anyway.'

'I forgive *everyone* in Harmon House,' Robert says.

'And now your mum,' Mark says.

Robert snatches his hands back again. 'I don't ...,' he says, with his fingers over his mouth, as if he's trying not to be sick.

Mark rubs his injured arm. 'You forgive her.'

'It's not fair. What for?'

'For leaving you alone.'

Robert stares.

'There it is,' Mark says. 'That's the demon.'

'No it isn't,' Robert says, and points towards the bed. 'She's over there.'

Tracey's blood beats faster in her ears – but it's not as loud as the silence in the room. The bed's still empty – does the emptiness have a shape?

Mark's palm goes up again, like a policeman directing traffic. 'I'm speaking to Robert now,' he says. 'Let him speak, in the name of Jesus.'

'It is me. I am speaking.'

'Forgive your mum,' Mark says.

'Why do you keep saying that?'

'Because you haven't done it yet.'

Robert presses his hands over his ears and raises his voice to a shout. 'I forgive her.'

Jenny and Tracey flinch, but Mark doesn't move. 'Now I'm going to speak to any demon who torments Robert. Reveal yourself. You cannot hide. I command you in the name of Jesus to step into the light of God and say your name.'

'My name is Azazel,' the girl says to Robert from the bed. Since no one else can see or hear her, he copies the sounds for everyone else's benefit. 'Az-a-zel.'

'What does that mean?' Mark says.

'Ask Jenny,' the girl says. 'She knows.'

Robert repeats, 'Jenny knows what it means.'

'Me? I'm not—' Everyone looks at Jenny. 'Fine,' she says. 'It's from Leviticus. The ritual for the Day of Atonement. It might not even be a name.'

'It's my name,' the girl says. Robert doesn't bother passing that on.

'We don't have theological discussions with demons,' Mark says. 'They've got nothing to teach us about God.'

Jenny pulls her bag out from under the chair and gets her Bible out. She places it on her lap.

'It's hardly the right moment for a Bible study,' Mark says.

'It's the ideal moment,' the girl says. But Robert's scared Mark will tell him off again if he acknowledges her interruptions.

Jenny says, 'Maybe it's something Robert needs to tell us.'

'Well, there's no harm in reading from God's Word,' Mark says.

'Take your time,' the girl says. 'Talk it over.'

'On the Day of Atonement,' Jenny says, 'the High Priest stood before the Ark, in the presence of God. But first he had to make a special sacrifice.'

'Nothing to do with demons,' Mark says.

'So he took two goats, and he cast lots between them. One goat for God; the other ... for Azazel.'

'It doesn't say that.' Mark gives in and goes to get his Bible from the top of the dresser on the other side of the room. He gives the bed a wide berth.

'You won't find it in the NIV,' Jenny says. 'Or the King James. They all translate it. But they're guessing, because no one knows what it means.'

'I know,' the girl says.

'In Hebrew,' Jenny continues, 'it's something like "sent away"; "removed".'

'Exorcised,' Robert suggests.

'The Latin Bible calls the goat for Azazel *caper emissarius*. Messenger. Scout, spy.'

'Angel,' Robert says.

Jenny flicks through her Bible to Leviticus. 'In English, it's usually *scapegoat*, but Tyndale invented that word in 1530 for his translation, and everyone else copied him. Except the RSV.' She reads, 'THE GOAT ON WHICH THE LOT FELL FOR AZAZEL SHALL BE PRESENTED ALIVE BEFORE THE LORD TO MAKE ATONEMENT OVER IT, THAT IT MAY BE SENT AWAY INTO THE WILDERNESS TO AZAZEL. Which could just be a place in the desert. Or a demon who lives there.'

'Both,' the girl says.

'Jesus,' Mark says. 'He's the scapegoat. And He wasn't sacrificed to a demon.'

'But they don't kill the scapegoat,' Tracey says. She hooks her feet around the front legs of her chair and looks down again.

'Right,' Jenny says. 'Literally, "the goat who escapes". Because it doesn't matter what happens to it, after they send it away.' She closes her Bible but keeps her finger inside it to mark her place. 'Why Azazel, Robert?' she says, as if he chose the name. 'Did you hear it in a sermon?'

Robert tuts. 'No.'

'In the desert, outside the camp.' Jenny taps her Bible against her knee. 'The Greek word for hell is *Gehenna*. Which was a place outside Jerusalem where people sacrificed their children.'

'Maybe Abraham went there to kill Isaac,' the girl says, drawing patterns on the quilt with her finger.

'In Jesus' day, it was abandoned, cursed. A rubbish dump.'

'So Azazel is hell?' Robert says, thinking of Jesus in the wilderness, tempted by Satan. Maybe that was Gehenna too.

'I don't know,' Jenny says.

'If Azazel eats the goat, does that mean it's eating sin?'

'What else would a demon eat?' Mark says.

Jenny says, 'In medieval paintings, the entrance to hell is a mouth. So when Jesus dies, it tries to eat Him. But He's too pure; it can't digest Him. So it spits Him out.'

The girl burps.

'We don't need to know this,' Mark says. 'It's not relevant.'

'Yes it is,' the girl says.

'Enough.' Mark gets up and stands in front of Jenny. He takes her Bible and puts it with his own under his chair. He turns back to Robert. 'I'm speaking now to any demon that is present. I command you in the name of Jesus to speak to me directly now.'

The room recedes, as if Robert's falling away from it, or sinking underwater.

Tracey looks at her friend. Something shifts in his face, like his bones are moving under his skin. He grows gaunter, his teeth sharper. He nudges Tracey's foot with his own, runs the edge of his trainer along her bare ankle. *'Your dream,'* he says. Is his voice different? Not harsher, or deeper: higher, like it hasn't broken yet. *'It wasn't a dream,'* the voice says. *'It was me. I took you there.'*

144

This isn't exciting any more. She feels like her body's shrinking. She's suddenly back in Robert's empty house, trapped in the morning room. Jenny holds out her hand again, and Tracey takes it. Holds on tightly.

'Is that a demon speaking now?' Mark asks.

'*Maybe.*'

The bottom drops out of Tracey's stomach, but Mark doesn't seem concerned. She holds on to that too. 'What brought you to this child of God?' he asks Robert.

'*He's got something I want. Someone.*' Robert looks at Tracey and grins. She wishes she could hide behind Mark.

'Are you a demon of suicide?' Mark's using a much louder voice now, as if the demon's hard of hearing.

'*Sometimes.*'

'Demon of suicide, you have no power over this redeemed soul. The blood of Jesus covers him. In the name of Jesus, I cast you out.' A pause – no one says anything, but Tracey can hear Robert breathing. Mark says, 'Is there another demon there?'

'*I don't like sharing.*'

'Are you a demon of alcoholism?' Mark asks.

'*I can be, if you want.*'

'This body is the temple of the Holy Spirit. You don't belong. You're trespassing. Get out! The blood of Jesus washes you away!'

Robert leans over the bucket, and a thick trail of drool starts leaking out of his nose and mouth. It's almost transparent. Not quite: A hint of pink. It gushes darker and darker out of his face, until it's thick scarlet. He tries to hold his nostrils closed in case the overflow sprays over the edge of the bucket, but Mark bats his fingers away. 'Let it out!'

Out it comes.

Tracey looks at Jenny, whose face is now damp with sweat. She's wearing too much foundation, so it looks like her skin's melting. Her hand is shaking in Tracey's. Tracey brings her other hand across and places it on top of Jenny's, to try and stop herself from shaking too.

Robert wipes his face on his sleeve. He examines the contents of the bucket, sloshes them around a little. '*Where did all that come from?*' He sits upright. '*Why are you here?*' he says to Tracey in his piping, childish voice. '*You're useless. You don't know anything. God's never going to speak to you.*'

When she gets control of her breathing, she says, 'You're my friend. *He's* my friend.'

'Who am I speaking to now?' Mark says. 'Is that Azazel? Are you the one in charge – the strongman?'

'*What do you think? Am I the one in charge?*'

Mark says, 'In Jesus' name, tell us your hold over Robert. Why are you tormenting him?'

'*I'm not tormenting him. I'm here to help him – if he gives me what I want.*'

'Say who you are, in Jesus' name.'

'*Azazel.*'

Mark puffs himself up, and the burnt skin on his neck flushes. He says, 'Come out from Robert now, by the power of Jesus!'

'*Oh dear,*' Robert says. '*This isn't going how you thought it would, is it?*' He mushes his mouth with his hand and pulls at the skin on his cheeks, as if he's pinching them to get colour in. '*Do you remember your bunk-mate on HMS Sheffield? How he died?*'

Mark collapses back into himself.

'*His life jacket shrivelled like a crisp packet on a bonfire. You couldn't even recognize him. Only his smile. The shape of his teeth as the lips bubbled away.*' Robert grins. '*Then you were burning too. You wiped your skin off on him.*

'"*Mummy, mummy, help me." He couldn't even say it, with his black tongue. And then you. "He's done for. But I'm alive. Take him, not me." God heard your prayer.*'

Mark slaps Robert's face, then looks in horror at his burnt hand. Tracey stands up with him. Her legs are unsteady, but when she and Jenny join hands together with Mark again, she feels stronger.

'Leave now,' Mark says. 'Go back to where you came from.'

'*No.*'

'Yes.'

Robert says, '*I have permission to be here.*'

'No you don't.'

'*Remember the apostle Paul? He was tormented too.* Lest I should be exalted above measure, there was given to me a thorn in the flesh, the messenger of Satan to buffet me.'

'Go!' Mark says.

'Amen,' Jenny says.

'I besought the Lord thrice, that it might depart from me.'

'Go!'

'Amen,' Jenny and Tracey say.

'And he said unto me, My grace is sufficient for thee: for my strength is made perfect in weakness.'

'I'm a servant of Jesus,' Mark says, 'and I have His authority. In my name they will drive out demons.'

'*Ah, the Great Commission,*' Robert says. '*But it's not in the earliest manuscripts. You should be like Jenny: check the footnotes.*'

'I've got nothing to do with you,' Jenny says.

'*Me?*' Robert says. '*What if there's no demon?*'

'But there is,' Mark says. 'It's speaking now.'

'*What if it's just Robert saying all this?*'

'Then I'll forgive him,' Jenny says.

'*Good for you.*' Robert's head turns towards Tracey. '*What about you?*'

'Don't speak to it,' Mark says.

'*Shall I tell you why you're here?*'

Mark's face is a safe place to look. Tracey keeps her eyes anchored there.

'Because this is the proof you've been waiting for. It doesn't come from God. He wouldn't lift a finger. But He created me, so He must be real. That's my gift to you. My existence.'

'You're going back where you came from,' Mark says.

Into the pit that's opening up beneath Tracey's feet.

'Robert doesn't want me to go.'

'I'm speaking to Robert now. I command you to let him speak.'

Robert doesn't answer. Then his face goes slack, and he jerks, like he's just woken up. 'What do you mean?' he says, looking around. 'It is me.' His voice is deeper again, but it still sounds wrong somehow – as if it's not quite at home in his mouth any more.

'Do you renounce Azazel?'

'I don't know what that means.'

'Say after me: I renounce Satan, and every part of his kingdom. There is no path to the truth except the one revealed by you, Lord Jesus.'

'Wait,' Robert says.

'Yes,' the girl says to Robert. 'Wait.' She steps down off the bed and comes closer.

The room is getting darker again. He can't make out the others or hear Mark – as if someone's turned the lights and volume down and they've disappeared into the shadows. 'You remember,' the girl continues, 'in Harmon House, you used to feed the chickens?'

'What does that have to do with anything?' But he can't take his eyes off her, and he feels like he has to answer. As if she's hypnotized him. 'The buckets were heavy,' he says. He can feel them now, dragging his arms down. 'I couldn't lift them away from my legs, so they slopped on my shoes.'

'You hated the chickens when you arrived.'

'Mindless mouths, stepping over one another.'

'But you listened.'

'Not just *cluck, cluck. Bawk bawk bawk, bak awk!* when the hens were laying. And when they saw me coming with the buckets, they puffed themselves up: *quooark, quooark.*'

'One of the older boys caught you copying them.'

Robert says nothing.

'"What the fuck are you doing?" He didn't understand, did he? They were your friends.'

Now the girl seems to be walking ahead of him, leading the way along a path. 'Where are we going?' Robert asks.

'Don't you want to see your other friend?' And he doesn't seem to have any choice but to follow her: through a doorway, into Harmon House, and up to the threshold of the staff flat, which stands alone, like a set on a darkened stage. A home within the home.

A cracked leather sofa, a television with a portable aerial on top – the nutrition poster by the kitchen listing all the different food groups. That's all familiar. But something's out of place: a life-size dummy on the sofa. It belongs to the local fire brigade and normally it stays in a cupboard; once a month the kids hide it somewhere in the house, and then the firemen arrive. 'Someone's trapped in the smoke! You have to find him!'

The television flickers, but the sound's turned off. The girl walks inside the flat and flops down on the sofa next to the dummy. It has a sculpted face and hair, but the body's covered in clammy rubber skin under the jumble-sale shirt and half-mast trousers, with a seam at the bottom of its neck. The girl sidles up to it, pokes it with her shoulder so it moves closer to an upright position on the sofa, then lifts one of its arms up – moves it back and forth, as if it's waving to Robert. 'Hello!' she says out the corner of her mouth, as if it's the dummy speaking. 'I've missed our little chats! How are you?'

Robert doesn't reply – stays in the doorway.

'What's my name again? I've forgotten.'

Robert says nothing.

'Come on. What's my name?'

'Guy,' he finally admits.

'Why did you leave me behind? All alone.' She makes a crying sound, then says, 'There, there' in her normal voice and pretends to wipe tears from the dummy's eyes. She turns back to Robert. 'But that's what you do, isn't it? Leave people alone. Do you want to hear your mum again? I can play the tape too. I can do anything the presence can do.'

She opens her mouth and tilts her head back, like a bird waiting for food. But nothing goes into her empty mouth, and his mum's voice comes out: '*I have to go. I'm going blind. I can feel my brain going. I don't want my son to see a madwoman.*'

'Why didn't Mark ask God to forgive *you*? Because you're the one who really needs it. It's your fault she's dead.'

'No,' Robert says – but he doesn't believe his denial.

'Didn't you ever ask her why there was no one from her side of the family? No grannie, granddad; uncles, aunties, cousins? Where do you think she grew up?'

'I don't know. She never said.'

'You never listened. She grew up here.'

'Here? That doesn't make any sense. It hasn't even been here that long.'

'Here. Outside the camp, in the wilderness.' The girl closes her mouth and swallows air. Opens it again and tilts her head back. '*I beg your forgiveness. I prayed I'd last until you came home. I didn't want Robert to be alone.*'

She burps.

'You could've asked where she came from. You could've helped her, but you didn't even notice anything was wrong. Now you know what it was like, living here. They let *you* go,

150

even though you didn't deserve it. Imagine staying for years – no hope of escape. Imagine staying forever.

'She's still here. And it's always the same.'

Now it's Tracey sitting on the sofa with the girl's voice coming out of her mouth. 'It's not too late – you can still save your mum. But if I let her go, someone has to take her place. You heard Jenny: a goat for Azazel.'

'No.'

'Guy here's no good.' She picks up the dummy's arm and waves it again. 'He wouldn't be much of a sacrifice. Abraham was willing to give up his only son – I want your best friend. Tracey. That's my price for saving your mum.'

'You can't save anyone,' Robert says, 'and you can't have Tracey. Mark's going to cast you out.'

The dummy suddenly sits up by itself. It turns towards Robert – and Mark's voice floats out of its frozen mouth. 'Say after me: I renounce Satan, and every part of his kingdom. There is no path to the truth except the one revealed by you, Lord Jesus.'

'Wait,' Robert says.

'No,' Mark says. 'We can't wait. There's no time. You have to choose. Do you renounce Azazel?'

'Yes,' Robert says, with tears in his eyes. 'I renounce her.'

He renounces his mum. He renounces his dad. He renounces everyone.

13
TRACEY / ROBERT

It's been three months since the deliverance. Nobody's asked Tracey about it, not even her dad – but people at church whisper now when Robert or Mark walk past. Even if the rest of the world seems determined to carry on as normal, shouldn't Tracey be different now?

Everything's faded, even the dream of her mum's funeral, and it's hard to keep a grip on the reality of that cruel, childish voice, speaking to her out of Robert's mouth. *Why are you here? God's never going to speak to you.* If demons are the only proof of God's existence, what does that say about God?

Now that Tracey's exams are over, Jenny's asked her round to watch an old black-and-white film: *The Trial of Joan of Arc.* Tracey picks up the VHS cassette cover. 'You didn't tell me it has subtitles.'

'Aren't you doing French?' Jenny asks.

'I stopped after third year,' Tracey says, handing the film back. 'The teacher looks like Cruella de Vil.' The French textbook had a character called Jean-Paul. In Tracey's copy, someone had changed it to 'Jean-Paul, George and Ringo'. Every single time. It must have taken hours. It couldn't have been Robert, because he's in the year below her.

'Which O levels did you do then?' Jenny says.

Did: past tense. Tracey has to get used to that. She goes into a skipping-rope rhythm. 'Physics, Chemistry, Biology, Maths, Further Maths, Geography, English. And Home Economics, but that's a CSE. I want to be a doctor. If I get the grades.' She crosses her fingers as she says this. Behind her back, so Jenny can't see, because it's superstitious.

'Cautiously confident?'

'Not *confident*, no.' But she did come top of the class in Physics, Chemistry and Biology for the last two years.

Jenny swirls a herbal teabag around in her cup, dips it twice, then dribbles it out over the edge of the cup onto the saucer. Even though the windows are open, the bedsit still smells of hippies. What is it – patchouli? Tracey's never had herbal tea before, so she copies Jenny's movements with her own cup. They're both sitting on the sofa, in front of the television.

'I wanted to get this film a couple of months ago, but I couldn't find a copy,' Jenny says. She and Tracey haven't talked since the deliverance. She asks, 'How's Robert doing?' Then adds, 'At school.' Because that's a safer question.

Tracey shrugs. 'He's in the top band.'

'There are no bands in Liverpool comprehensives since Labour took over. Everyone's equal.'

Tracey laughs. 'Right. Well, they keep him there because he'd get beaten up lower down, but he doesn't do well in exams. He won't answer the questions; he just writes whatever he feels like.' She hasn't seen Robert much, because of revision. Well, that's the story she's got ready, if anyone asks. He seems better, as far as she can tell. But he still looks hollowed out, and his skin is taut and shiny. She's scared of him.

'How have you been?' Jenny asks.

'I haven't stopped to think about it,' she lies.

'Joan of Arc heard voices,' Jenny says. 'St Catherine, St Margaret.'

Tracey frowns. 'Dead people? Spirits?'

'Saints. Virgin martyrs.' Jenny fiddles with the top button of her blouse. 'Killed because they wouldn't marry pagans.'

'Nothing about saints in the Bible.'

'Especially Catherine and Margaret,' Jenny says. 'Because they never existed.'

'So it was demons, speaking to Joan?'

'Well, she heard St Michael too. The archangel Michael.'

'How can an angel be a saint?' Tracey sips her peppermint tea. It's murky brown. She licks the back of her teeth. Shouldn't peppermint make them feel cleaner?

'Not "holy person". "Someone who intercedes in heaven".' Jenny puts her cup down on the floor. She puzzles over the VCR, which is new. 'Joan's a saint now too. But only since the First World War.'

'You have to tune the telly,' Tracey says, 'like you tune it to BBC1.'

'I've done that.' The picture resolves. 'There we are.'

A courtroom. Joan's chained hands, joined at the wrist, descend like a dove on a copy of the Bible. She swears to tell the truth. It reminds Tracey of her exams.

You should have a question paper on your desk. Do not open it until I tell you to. You are now under exam conditions.

In the courtroom: rows of priests, all the same. One of them asks Joan, 'How do you know if your visions are men or women?'

'I don't even know if they have a body.'

'How can they speak without a body?'

'I trust God. The voice is soft and speaks the language of France.'

'Who cares what language they speak?' Tracey asks.

'What language do angels normally speak?' Jenny waits, like she's expecting Tracey to put her hand up.

'So they translate?'

'Everything's a translation. Joan spoke in French, but the trial record's Latin. So the dialogue here's translated back into French. And then English for the subtitles.'

'It's weird. Someone's mouth moves, but the sounds aren't connected to the words. I have to keep looking up and down.'

A quill scratches. Joan complains they're not recording all her words. 'If it's from the trial record, then how do we know what they *didn't* write down?' Tracey says.

If you have a question, raise your hand and wait. Invigilators cannot answer any questions about the content of the exam.

'There was a second trial,' Jenny says, 'years after Joan's death, to clear her name.'

'French, Latin, English,' Tracey says. 'It doesn't matter. I still feel like she's talking *to me*.'

Now the priests are interrogating Joan in her cell. Tracey imagines them coming into her bedroom in South Mossley Hill Road; or waking up with her bed in the middle of the upper-school assembly hall. Her whole life under exam conditions. Will the Day of Judgement be like that? But Tracey won't be alone then. Jesus will stand by her side.

You have three hours to complete this exam. You may open your papers and begin.

All the different exams are blurred into one now. Chair legs shuddering across the gym floor. Zips opening and closing on pencil cases. Becca Donnelly at the desk in front, sighing loudly, rattling a biro tube against her teeth, with blue lips from chewing the ink tube.

The priests take turns to interrogate Joan, but she stands alone, with no one on her side of the room. She doesn't look at anyone in particular when she speaks. And she's never surprised, never stuck. As if she knows all the questions in advance. As if she's reading from the trial record, repeating what she's already said.

'Why do they keep asking her about clothes and haircuts?' Tracey asks.

'Because angels have no sex. But Joan does. And she dresses like a man.'

Jenny's in dungarees; Tracey's in jeans. She thinks back to the church revue show. 'John Cooper wouldn't mind. He likes wearing women's clothes.'

The interrogation continues. 'Aren't you subject to God's church on Earth, and to its churchmen?'

'God must be served first,' Joan replies.

Jenny says, 'Mark was asking Robert to submit to *his* authority.'

'Not Mark's,' Tracey replies. 'God's.'

'Who gets to say if it's a demon or an angel?'

'I don't think it was an angel.'

'No.'

'Anyway, our church isn't like that,' Tracey says. 'No one's in charge. Only the Bible.'

'You don't really believe that.'

A priest reads out the sentence against Joan. Others walk out in protest.

'You think it's impossible,' Jenny says, 'to stand up for what's right. You think you're the only one in the room. But it's not impossible.' She wipes her eyes.

Tracey reaches out to touch her arm, and nods at the screen. 'Who do you think was speaking to Joan?'

'What if it was God?'

'He doesn't pretend to be someone else.'

'What if He created Catherine and Margaret? Young girls believed in them, prayed to them. Hundreds of years. What if *that* was the answer to all those prayers?'

That's my gift to you. My existence. My afterlife too. My continued existence. Because now Tracey's waiting for that voice to come back. Keeps expecting to hear it in Robert's mouth. Maybe he'll be the one by her side, on the Day of Judgement. Smiling, with blood on his teeth. Listing everything she's ever done wrong.

You have five minutes left until the end of the exam.

Joan's execution pyre catches fire. A priest holds up a cross on a pole so she can see it, but he's driven back by the heat and smoke. He squints as the sweat runs into his eyes. The smoke clears, and the stake's empty.

'Like when Darth Vader kills Obi-Wan Kenobi,' Tracey says. *Stop writing and put your pens down.*

Tracey walks up Rose Lane to Mather Avenue, to catch the 86 bus home; the signalmen are out in support of the miners, so the train station's closed. The sky's overcast, so the summer twilight's grey, apart from the yellow windows of Chris's chippy. She likes coming here on a Friday in term time when the students are here – escaping from the canteen food at the Carnatic Halls – because she can imagine what it's like to be one of them. But the chippy's still full, even in July. She only wants chips tonight, so Chris waves her to the front of the queue. As he wraps her portion, he gives her a wink and calls her a 'little lady'.

The chips are just out the fryer: so hot she has to juggle them round her mouth with her tongue, eating with her mouth open so she can blow cold air in and out at the same time. She's got an ulcer, and the salt and vinegar sting.

The beer garden in The Rose is full: someone gives her a wolf whistle. She keeps her eyes down on the pavement. The British Legion's safer: toothless men on the benches outside with pints of mild. Quarry Bank school is on the other side of Rose Lane at the top. They're rivals with New Heys, but no one cares about school sports, so it just means lads fighting. Not serious. Twos and threes: no gangs. Fists and stones: no bricks or bottles.

She crosses over Mather Avenue and walks past the fire station to the bus stop. Crumples up her chip paper and throws it in the bin before she gets on. Shows her Saveaway ticket with the day and the month scratched off.

She sits at the front on the top deck, level with the orange street lights, which strobe down the line of windows as the bus accelerates. There's a group of scallies at the back. She can see them in the round mirror above the stairwell. Legs spread-eagled, and when they speak, they all shout over each other. She puts on her Walkman and keeps her shoulders hunched.

The top of the bus swings and lurches as the wheels run over potholes. She rests her face against the window, which squashes her left headphone and vibrates against her cheekbone. Her temple shudders down the glass, so she has to keep moving it back up, but she likes the rhythm of it.

She brought *Architecture and Morality* by OMD with her, because it's got two songs about Joan of Arc in the middle, but now she rewinds the tape back to the beginning and it starts with 'The New Stone Age'. A sound like sticks rattling off the metal handrails on top of the seats. A hiss of steam from an overheated engine radiator. A frightened heartbeat.

She gets off the bus at New Heys, which is the closest stop to home, then decides to walk up the hill to the upper school, past the sports fields. Beyond the main entrance, she steps over a low wall and skids down a grass incline to the chain-link fence around the outdoor netball pitch. She puts her fingers through the wire and rattles it backwards and forwards.

The popular girls play Goal Attack or Goal Shoot. The girls picked last don't get a choice: Goal Defence or Goal Keeper. On a good day, Tracey plays Wing Attack; on a bad day, Wing Defence. Not much difference: always in the middle.

No more PE in sixth form. Only A levels. She won't be in the middle there. Does God choose her to come top, or does she choose herself? Because if He chooses her, that means He's *not* choosing everybody else. Robert, for example. He never comes top – except in art. But if he can't be the first pick, then he'd rather be the last. Maybe that's better, spiritually. THE STONE

THE BUILDERS REJECTED HAS BECOME THE CORNERSTONE. In her Physics mock, she made a deliberate mistake, so she wouldn't get a hundred per cent. She needn't have worried: she got two other questions wrong.

Tracey presses fast-forward and skips through the middle of the second side of *Architecture and Morality* until she gets to the last track: 'The Beginning and the End'. In the film, when they come to take her to the pyre, Joan asks for a cross. Tracey rubs the one round her neck between her finger and thumb. The Brethren don't really approve of external signs, but Tracey wanted it there for school, next to her treacherous skin. Like a hair shirt.

In school, she can't speak up for God. So her body speaks for her. She trains herself to endure His love. But when she pivots round a fixed foot on the netball court and the ball soars up in the air, the cross lifts off her neck too.

They took Joan's crucifix away when they chained her to the stake. They gave her another to look at, but kept it out of reach until it disappeared in the smoke. Joan called on her saints, who didn't answer. She had to endure the love of God too.

Tracey grew up surrounded by God's love; surrounded by faith. She shared it with her dad and everyone else in church. Now she wants her own faith. That's why she went to the assembly with Robert – the deliverance too. She wants to be alone with God, like Joan was alone. Maybe that's what it takes to prove your faith is real: a funeral pyre.

Robert hasn't seen the girl since the deliverance – the presence has gone too.

Four years ago, on the way to the cemetery for his mum's funeral, he said 'Goodbye' to himself over and over, because he didn't have the courage to say it in the funeral parlour. Again, at the grave, wiping soil off his hands. Goodbye, goodbye.

Too late. Wrong.

After the deliverance, Mark asked him, 'What are you doing to keep the demons away? You have to work at it, finish what we started.'

So he's been working at it. For three dead, grey months of gammon and fish fingers and broad beans and silence. He has to do his duty. Chew and swallow – and finish forgiving his dad. He can't do that until he sees him. Look him in the eye; say the words.

So one afternoon, he takes the 488 bus over to Neston again, and walks up Talbot Avenue. The pile of letters behind the door is larger. This time, when he touches the Yale lock, it clicks open.

'Dad!'

No one answers, but something's there. Its fingertips touch his cheek, smear themselves along his upper lip. He pushes the front door wider and steps into the room behind. Because the house is so higgledy-piggledy, this is a sort of gloomy dining room – or, at least, it has a table, where his dad eats – now empty, and covered in dust. There's an entrance to the kitchen on one side, and on the other, a heavy wooden door leading to the oldest part of the house.

The smell's coming from there: it's like the presence, but that can't be right.

He turns left into the kitchen. The sink's full of dirty plates and dead flies. Cracked green sludge in the bottom of a 'World's Greatest Dad' mug. Robert didn't buy this – did his dad get it for himself? He goes to the fridge. A rotten belch: flaccid, iridescent chicken and cottage-cheese milk. His dad doesn't eat much when he's drinking.

Back to the dining room. The door into the oldest part of the house is painted black, with a latch rather than a handle. He lifts the latch, and the door shifts down an inch as it swings

161

outwards, so the lowest corner scrapes against the floor at the end of its arc. Inside, there's a hall with a stone floor and a low ceiling. At its far end, there's a single, tiny window next to a crooked spiral staircase. Wooden beams on the ceiling; along the walls too – wattle-and-daub and white plaster between them: black bones; pale, flaking skin. The flagstones shine with sweat.

In the shadows at the end of the hall, to the right of the staircase, light trickles out round the edges of the door to the television room. Not natural: seared, cauterized. The smell's coming from there.

Hot. Furred, evaporated. A home within the home.

'Dad?' Robert hesitates, then steps backwards. Then out to the porch. When he gets outside, he pulls the front door closed, as hard as he can, to make sure the lock catches. Pushes it twice, to make sure it won't open again.

His stomach's still twitching from the smell, but now it contracts and growls. Another mouth inside him, opening and closing, demanding to be fed.

He can't stand that emptiness, so he prays to the presence: Come back. Show me what to do; who I am.

14

ROBERT

It's the week of Carry the Message: Garston Chapel has hired
a coach for the trip to Anfield to see Henry Prince. Robert
surveys the coach full of chattering, excited people – it feels
like the journey down to church camp last summer. A group
near the front have already started singing choruses. Robert
kneels up on his seat so he can see behind over the headrest. He
wants to pray for everyone later, so he stares at each unfamiliar
face for a few seconds and tries to memorize it. His eyes stop at
the back of the coach: Tommo Donnelly and his scally mate,
Simon, whispering to each other – a couple of empty seats be-
side them.

Robert's sitting next to Tracey, in front of Kevin and Paul. It's
the first time he's seen her properly since the deliverance, but
she's squashed herself against the window. Robert twitches his
head towards the back seat, and says out the corner of his mouth,
'How did they get here?'

'God moves in mysterious ways,' Kevin says.

'I invited them,' Paul says.

'My point exactly.'

Robert raises his palm towards the back of the bus in a frozen
wave. Tommo stares at him and silently mouths the word
'Damien'. Tommo gave him this nickname after the assembly
with Tracey. From *The Omen*. He gets the theme tune too, when
Tommo walks past him in the corridors. Tommo sometimes
sings other songs at him as well: 'While shepherds washed their

163

cocks by night, All tuned to BBC, The angel of the Lord came down, And switched to ITV.' Now he flips the hair away from his forehead and jabs at the exposed parting line with his finger. He mouths 'Six six six'.

Robert feels people's eyes on him in church, since the deliverance. But surely Tommo doesn't know anything?

The coach slows to a crawl long before they reach Anfield, as men with walkie-talkies and orange reflective jackets wave them past traffic cones and billowing lines of tape, into a closed-off street, where the driver parks next to several other coaches. When they get off, there's a line of old people in wheelchairs waiting to get on a shuttle bus.

'I thought it was Youth Night,' Paul says.

'Young at heart,' Tracey says.

Kevin slaps the back window of a Social Services Transit van. 'I'm surprised the council's helping people get to Henry Prince.'

'Keeps them off the streets,' Paul says.

There are signs tied to lamp posts pointing the way to Anfield, and Trevor Jenkins handed out the tickets on the coach, so the Garston Chapel people make their own way towards the ground, thinning out as they go. Hundreds of other people are walking in the same direction, in twos, threes, and larger groups. Some of the groups follow banners with church names and references to Bible verses: 'John 3:16'; 'Revelation 3:20'.

Paul's leading the four of them, even though Kevin's the Liverpool supporter. 'Where did Tommo and Simon go?' Robert asks, looking round.

'They know the way,' Paul says.

The four of them are in a park now, with the stadium ahead, across another closed-off road. In the park, there are more men in reflective jackets standing next to loudspeakers on poles. 'What are these for?' Tracey asks.

The steward puffs out his orange chest. 'In case everyone can't get in.'

'We've all got tickets.'

'Everyone last night had a ticket too.'

A few boys are kicking a football, dribbling around the people walking across their makeshift pitch. Their shouts rise above the talking and laughing and singing.

'It's quiet, without the cars,' Tracey says. It's not quiet, but Robert knows what she means. All the sounds are human sounds. Together, converging on the stadium. Even the boys, trying to be apart, are caught in its force field.

They cross over the final road, and enter Anfield through a large set of gates with 'You'll Never Walk Alone' written in cast-iron letters at the top. On the right, Robert can see the backs of terraced houses with chimneys and slate roofs. Imagine living there! Shouts, cries, thousands of gasps as a shot misses, but everything invisible: like a film soundtrack without the pictures. They'll be able to hear Henry Prince too.

Inside the gates, just beyond the main entrance to the stadium, there's a Radio Merseyside van with open doors at the back and thick cables running into Anfield: they're here to record the event for a later broadcast.

Robert, Tracey, Kevin and Paul walk through a tunnel and across the front of the visitors' stand, then up its central aisle to reach their fold-down plastic seats.

The pitch is much larger than it seems on *Match of the Day*. At its other end, the few people moving around on the terraces of the Kop are tiny. The grass is covered in sheets of brown matting.

'Tommo'll be disappointed,' Paul says.

'What do you mean?' Robert asks. He looks around the nearby seats; no sign of Tommo and Simon yet.

'Why do you think he's come?'

'Curiosity?' Tracey says, on Paul's other side.

'What happens at the end of the evening?'

'Henry Prince calls people to go forward,' Robert says, 'to commit their lives to Christ.'

'And where do they go?'

Everyone thinks about that.

'The pitch,' Tracey says, after a few seconds.

'Sacred ground,' Paul says.

'They see it on telly every other week.'

'But you don't get to touch it,' Paul says. 'Not even when you're here for a game. Not since they put the barriers up.'

The stage for Henry Prince to speak from is halfway down the pitch, away from the kick-off spot, close to the stand on the right. The stage has a grand piano with an open lid; a couple of microphone stands; a lectern. It's surrounded by low metal crowd barriers, which are partially hidden by rows of flower boxes and green ferns in pots. There are two short towers of scaffolding on either side, with spotlights.

The front row of the stand nearest the stage seems to be reserved for special guests. Tracey points at two small figures sitting next to one another: one in a purple shirt; the other all in black. 'That must be Sheppard and Worlock,' she says. The Anglican and Catholic archbishops.

'Bezzie mates,' Paul says.

The stadium hums. Robert can feel it coming up through his shoes, into his legs and thighs. Hundreds of feet, but one continuous vibration. People are still arriving at eight o'clock when someone walks out onstage. 'Is that Henry Prince?'

Tracey squints at the stick figure. 'I don't know.'

Grey suit, grey hair. The man sits down at the piano and lifts both hands towards the stand on the right; Sheppard and Worlock stay seated, but most of the other people get to their feet. The choir members are all dressed in red or white, and they're holding booklets, which they fold open.

166

'Isn't your cousin singing?' Robert says to Tracey.

'My aunt's one of the counsellors, too.'

'Majesty, worship His Majesty': a chorus from the *Carry the Message* songbook.

'It's not very youthful so far,' Paul says.

At the end of the song, the grey man goes to the lectern and says, 'It's a special joy tonight to welcome a guest who needs no introduction. All you need to do is mention his name where Christians gather, especially young people, and they're anxious to see him.'

Robert frowns. 'I feel like I've heard this before,' he says.

The man on the stage leans forward to get his mouth closer to the microphone, so the volume rises when he says the name: 'Cliff Richard!'

Kevin and Paul sink down in their seats; Robert and Tracey tap their fingertips politely against their palms. Everyone else in the stadium applauds as Cliff bounces up to one of the microphones. 'They can't *all* be that excited to see him,' Paul says.

Cliff's far away, but Robert can still make out all the details of his outfit, maybe because it's so familiar: a skinny tie, a red waistcoat, large tinted glasses. Cliff pushes his shirtsleeves up past his elbows and nudges the glasses up the bridge of his nose. 'The one thing that has made my life really terrific, really valuable,' he says, 'is the fact of Jesus entering into it nineteen years ago.'

'I bet he's actually the youngest person on that stage tonight,' Kevin says.

'Does this seem familiar to you?' Robert says.

'I will never understand television,' Cliff says, with a slight echo off the microphone, 'but I'll gladly switch it on and just enjoy it.' Does the distortion kick in when the volume hits a certain level, or is it triggered by specific sounds? *Pp, ss, tt*? 'And Christianity – okay, you can ask questions about it – but it needs switching on too. You need to step into it.'

'Step into the television?' Kevin says. He, Paul, Tracey and Robert form a little island of resistance in the flow of the stadium's attention. Robert doesn't feel bad about that. The crowd's big enough to contain this difference. But the moment's doubled, accompanied by its own echo, and the feedback separates him from himself.

Cliff starts singing one of his songs, and Robert prays: Help me give myself to this. Let it surprise me. He tries not to focus on anything specific; tunes himself to the background buzz from the stadium. He registers Cliff leaving the stage, and a second hymn from the choir, during which another grey, solitary man comes up to the lectern. Hunched, a V-necked jumper underneath a blazer, to protect him against the non-existent cold.

Henry Prince looks much plainer than he did on the video they played at church months ago. Almost anonymous. As the choir falls silent, he says, 'Let us bow our heads.' Robert watches everyone pray. As they all nod and murmur, Tommo and Simon slip into their seats at the end of the row. Simon's looking round, mouth open, but Tommo leans forward to catch Robert's eye. He sweeps the part in his hair aside, angling the top of his head, and jabs his finger at the part line.

Rock music is really religious music, Henry Prince explains. Elvis Presley wanted to be a preacher.

'Makes a change from backmasking and jungle rhythms,' Kevin says.

Young people are desperate for guidance – for leadership. But they look to false idols: Boy George or John Lennon.

'I don't do anything without checking with Boy George,' Paul says.

'At least he's making an effort,' Tracey says.

THERE IS NEITHER JEW NOR GREEK, THERE IS NEITHER BOND NOR FREE, THERE IS NEITHER MALE NOR FEMALE in Christ Jesus. No young or old either. No generation gap.

Henry hopes everyone has a Bible.

'No,' Paul says, 'we don't, because no one told us to bring one.'

Henry raises his own Bible in the air, then places it on the lectern without opening it. When he refers to a verse, he quotes from memory, but he wants everyone to measure his words against Scripture. And Tracey has her NIV, so the four of them all lean together.

'A father has two sons,' Henry says. 'The younger one says, "Father, I know I will inherit half of your property when you die. Can you give it to me now instead?"'

Henry's paraphrasing, not directly quoting, but Robert still knows what he's going to say next.

'I'm sick of going to church and hearing about the Bible. I want to see the bright lights, and go to the concerts and shows.'

'I'd like to go to a show,' Kevin says.

'This is the closest you're going to get,' Paul says.

'Shh.' Tracey pushes the open page towards them.

Henry beats his fist down on the lectern in time with his words; his finger follows their melody line in the air. His two hands move towards each other and rush apart; his arms sweep objections aside. His argument's easy to follow, but there are odd, American emphases in some of the words: *leeshuh* for leisure; *farther* for father.

'Life in the big city wasn't like this young fellow imagined. He tried, but he wasn't satisfied. He had bags of money; drinking companions; sex, drugs.'

'Rock 'n' roll,' Kevin says.

'Nothing could satisfy him.'

'I think there's a song about this.'

'Even Mick Jagger's younger than Cliff Richard,' Paul says.

'I want to listen,' Robert says. 'I want to be here.'

Two giant feet sink into the matting on either side of the scaffolding; two giant legs straddle the stage. The presence:

transformed, its head towering above the stadium walls. Its body's hardened and turned to gold, but its surface is beaten, stippled, covered with indentations in the shape of inverted cones, each of which has a black spot at its apex. It reminds Robert of the living creatures in Revelation, covered in chickenpox eyes. 'You left me alone,' he says under his breath. 'Why didn't you help, during the deliverance?'

The presence doesn't answer. Or maybe its changed body is the answer. *That's* the message. The Word made flesh.

The black spots inside the cones all flick themselves to white, and the presence is covered in pinpricks of light. They blink open and closed as Henry speaks.

'And he began to suffer,' Henry says, continuing the story of the Prodigal Son. 'To be in need.' His voice is part of the hum of the stadium and the hum of Robert's thoughts, and both are drawn up into a low note shining out from inside the presence. Identical with itself, continuous, but modulated underneath, rising and falling. A light, a sound: for the presence, it's all the same thing.

What is an angel? A messenger, and also a technology for recording and transmitting the message. An archive. The presence is recording Henry Prince, like the Radio Merseyside van outside the stadium. It's weighing his words, judging. But it's also playing the recording back to Robert through itself, and the speech and the playback have swapped places, like it's broadcasting directly to the microphones and the loudspeakers and Henry's just acknowledging the truth of the repetition; submitting to its judgement.

'No money left,' Henry says; 'all his friends gone. He looked for a job: he was willing to do anything. But he couldn't find any work.'

'I know the feeling,' Paul says.

'No you don't,' Kevin says. 'You're still at school.'

If this is God speaking through Henry Prince, then why are the words so ordinary, so banal? It's like when someone translates tongues. The revealed message is always disappointing. Why would God go to the trouble of using an angelic language to say something so uninspiring? Maybe that's the point. MY STRENGTH IS MADE PERFECT IN WEAKNESS.

Henry continues the story. 'Lying in the gutter, a thought came to him: "I used to look down on my father's servants, but they get more than I have now. At least they don't go hungry. I'll go home and ask if I can be a servant."'

On the son's painful journey home, he rehearses the speech he knows he has to make, admitting his faults and asking for mercy. But when he finally reaches home, the father embraces him: 'Kill the fatted calf! My son was lost; now he is found.'

Robert looks up at the chest and arms of the presence, and his gaze finally ascends to its summit, far above the walls of Anfield and the echoing souls in the stadium. Its head is enveloped in a Pentecostal flame. It's too bright to see anything up there but the flame itself: the whole presence is now a vibrating organ.

He doesn't have to make it speak; he doesn't have to make it do anything. It's here to bear witness. To enter history; to become history. On this day in Liverpool, in July 1984.

'The Father says: "Come back! Find your way home." It's the same message for everyone here tonight.'

The words enter Robert's ears and leave his mouth at the exact same moment. But he doesn't say them aloud: he exhales them. They pass through him. Breath, spirit – current.

'The Father is waiting for you with open arms. Let Him welcome you into his mansion.'

The counsellors are already streaming out from the front rows of each stand, ready for the call to come forward that Henry's about to make. They make their way past the wheelchairs and the St John Ambulance. They spread out on the pitch, standing apart from each other. When they've chosen their individual spot, they bow their heads and fold their hands together.

Robert can feel the charge coming off the presence: like standing underneath a pylon. No one else even acknowledges it's there, but the counsellors on the pitch avoid its feet. Robert's already been saved. If he went forward, wouldn't that be a lack of faith? As if he got it wrong the first time, as if God hadn't answered his prayer.

A doubt. A flicker, a ripple. A shape on the edge of his eye, running from the top of the stand down the steps in the middle. Naked, small.

Robert stands up.

'You're keen!' a man in a dog collar on the row behind says.

Robert pushes past knees and feet; past Tommo, who shrinks back as if he's contagious; past Simon, whose eyes are closed. He looks down the centre aisle towards the pitch. A figure disappears round the edge of the front row of seats, towards the exit tunnel. He follows.

Henry says, 'When Christ was crucified, He died for you. He took your place. God took your sins – my sins too – and put them on Christ. He carried them for us. He became sin for you and me.'

As Robert comes up to the corner of the stand, he can hear the skittering feet inside the tunnel. He follows. He can still hear Henry Prince, but the signal's weaker, swallowed by the concrete walls and ceiling. 'And God doesn't see our sins any more; He sees the Cross. And so He says, "Because of the sacrifice of my son upon the Cross, you're forgiven."'

A walkie-talkie squawks and feeds back. A steward tries to step in front of Robert, but he dodges past. 'It's not that bad!' the man shouts after him.

'Not just forgiven,' Henry says, receding into the background, 'wiped clean; made spotless. God records over our sins on the tapes.'

Outside in the car park, the girl's swinging off the cast-iron gates under the motto. Robert knew she'd come, as soon as he saw the presence. That's how it is: he can't have one without the other.

She says, 'The Prodigal Son. We all know that story. But what about the elder brother?' She moves her feet along from one slot to another between the railings, clenching and un-clenching her fists. 'Can you remember that part? He stayed at home. Day in, day out. Never got a party. Who do you think Tracey identifies with?'

'Shut up about her!' Robert shouts. The stewards stare, but they're used to people praying out loud, talking to God.

'You don't deserve the fatted calf,' the girl says. 'You wouldn't eat it anyway.'

He imagines the marbled flesh on his plate, the stiff rind. Strip every sliver of white; snip every greasy edge. It's not enough.

'What if the father didn't kill the fatted calf? What if he killed the elder son instead, the elder daughter? What if he asked the Prodigal Son to do it for him?'

'No! I won't do it.'

'You're already weak,' the girl says. 'But it's not too late. You can save your mum – you can save yourself. Come home.'

Robert turns around and walks back towards the tunnel.

'Why did you come out here then?' the girl calls after him.

People are leaving the ground, and Robert has to duck and squeeze and push against the flow. 'I'm trying to find my friends,' he says to the steward with the faulty walkie-talkie when he gets to the corner of the pitch.

The presence is gone. Where its feet rested on the matting, the surface of the pitch is smooth, unmarked. People are huddled in groups of two and three: those who went forward talking to counsellors. Robert looks round; dizzy, tingling with panic.

The presence is a witness. So Robert has to imitate it; he has to be a witness too. He scans the pitch. Down here, there's no broader perspective. He can only see what's right in front of him.

Simon. Juddering and gulping. His face is almost unrecognizable: swollen, smeared. He's standing next to another grey man. No sign of Tommo.

Robert strides over to Simon and puts his arm round his shoulder. 'I know him,' he says to the counsellor, who takes a step backwards. He says to Simon, 'It's okay. It's going to be alright.'

Come home. But Robert's already been home. There's no fatted calf in Neston. No father waiting with open arms. Only a door he doesn't want to open. What's behind it? Something important. He's not pure enough to look; not yet. He has to offer a sacrifice first. Like on the Day of Atonement.

A sacrifice: the girl got that much right. But it's not Tracey who's going to die – it's the girl. It wasn't enough to cast her out, because she'll keep coming back. Mark doesn't understand that if you want to keep the channel open for God, other things can broadcast on it as well. There's only one way to shut the girl up: kill her. It's not the presence he has to wrestle – it's her. He has to put his body against hers, like Jacob with the angel.

15
ROBERT / TRACEY

Robert's in his room. The angry child from the cover of U2's *War* album scowls out from a poster above the table with model aeroplanes. It's the same face as the one on the *Boy* cover, but older and wilder. Robert's sitting on the floor, legs crossed, leaning back against the bed. The girl's in the same position on the other side of the bed; at least, he assumes she is. He's deliberately not looking: waiting for her to come to him.

She says, 'MY KNEES ARE WEAK THROUGH FASTING; AND MY FLESH FAILETH OF FATNESS.'

Robert doesn't reply.

'Come on, that's easy. MAN SHALL NOT LIVE BY BREAD ALONE, BUT BY EVERY WORD THAT PROCEEDETH OUT OF THE MOUTH OF GOD.' She pauses. 'Like a bird regurgitating food for its chicks.'

Robert wraps his arms around the cage of his ribs; his heart flutters.

The girl continues. 'In the gospel of John, Jesus says, I AM THE BREAD OF LIFE. Does that mean He's eating Himself? Carving the flesh off His own bones?'

She knows the Bible better than Robert does. He can't win with words, but he doesn't need to. He just needs her to get close.

The floor shivers; outside on the landing, the banister creaks. Uncle Edward is coming up the stairs.

'Why didn't you ask him to Henry Prince?' the girl says.

'He'd never come.'

'How do you know? You don't know anything about him.'

'I know every time he goes the bog,' Robert says.

'You never talk to him.'

'What would I say?' Robert's world reaches up to the heavens and down into hell. Uncle Edward's goes from the television room to the bedroom.

'Well, anyway,' the girl says, 'maybe Auntie Rose wouldn't *let* him go to Henry Prince. She doesn't like it when he goes out by himself.'

'Because he comes back drunk.'

Uncle Edward does have one regular weekly excursion: to William Hill on Friday afternoons. One day in the holidays, with nothing better to do, Robert followed him. Uncle Edward's metal heel taps clicked on the paving stones, and every few steps he made a juddering half-skip as he pulled up the elastic waist-band on his trousers.

He's probably doing that now, on the stairs. Thud, thud; pause.

'What if I let him see me?' the girl says.

'You can't.'

'Yes I can.'

'You've never appeared to anyone else before.'

'Yes I have.' She grabs hold of the bedpost and swings herself onto her feet. Robert stands too; turns around. Now they're looking at one another over the bed. She puts her tiny fists up, like a boxer.

She's *his* cross to bear. Only he can see her, touch her. Kill her. 'Uncle Edward doesn't know anything about God,' he says.

'You should be grateful then.' She takes a step backwards. 'I'm giving him a push in the right direction – doing your dirty work for you. I do all God's dirty little jobs.'

'Stop.'

'Maybe God will stop me.' She jumps for the door.

Robert follows, but she's already grabbing at the handle. She opens a gap – a few inches. She flattens herself against the wall and slides her cheek and shoulders along; wriggles through.

Robert can't stop himself in time and his shoulder slams the door shut behind her. The handle snatches itself away from his fingers; it takes him several seconds to get out onto the landing, where he just manages to stop himself colliding with Uncle Edward, who's leaning on the banister at the top of the stairs.

Edward flinches. He grips the newel post to stop himself toppling backwards.

'I …,' Robert says.

Edward's left hand flexes on the post. He presses the other against his chest. He purses his lips; nods his chin. He wheezes, coughs – like he's got something stuck in his throat.

The girl leaps out from Edward's bedroom. 'Boo!'

His neck jerks; his eyes pop. His left foot steps back off the top stair and his legs collapse. As he goes down, his shoulder and the side of his head hit the banister. His hip bumps down, stair by stair; his shoulder drags across the banister posts. He slides down until he's sitting awkwardly, legs splayed, on the small landing at the turn of the stairs.

Robert steps forward.

Edward gets up on his knees, mutters something to himself. The girl stays over by the main bedroom door, out of Robert's reach.

Ignore her – for now. He puts one foot onto the top stair.

Edward reaches across the landing carpet for his glasses. One of the arms is twisted at an angle.

Silence, except for the television blaring downstairs. 'I'll fix your glasses,' Robert says, and takes another step down.

Edward blinks. He leans in against the landing post, and staggers upright. He slides the left arm of the glasses in behind his ear and tries to press the pads in against his nose.

Robert keeps his eyes on Edward. His foot gropes blindly down onto the next step, where it finds something loose. He wobbles and lurches towards Edward, who steps back – off the landing.

Edward windmills over and lands on his back, head facing downwards. His body ripples down the main flight of stairs, all the way to the bottom, where it collects in a broken heap. The house shudders and groans.

The girl's still on the upstairs landing. 'Penny for the guy,' she says.

Robert looks down, to see what he trod on. Edward's abandoned slipper. He kicks it aside, then sits down at the top of the main flight of stairs. He leans forward, hands on his thighs, head between his knees; paper skin sticking to his ribs. He can't breathe.

'You're not very fit,' the girl says. 'You only ran across the room.'

Robert looks back at the stained-glass window and the statue of Joan of Arc, but Joan keeps her eyes averted and her hands clasped together in prayer under the cross guard of her sword.

'Why don't you go and help him?' the girl says.

Auntie Rose opens the door to the television room, but hides behind it. She calls, 'Edward, Edward? What's happening?' She peeks out.

'He fell,' Robert says, standing up so she can see him over the banister.

'Edward! Are you hurt?'

Robert can see his uncle's chest rising and falling, but his mouth looks wrong: disjointed. His teeth have probably come loose. 'You should call an ambulance,' he says to Auntie Rose, who's now at the foot of the stairs.

'Oh oh. What's happened?' Auntie Rose leans down and places her palm against her husband's forehead, as if she's checking his temperature.

'Is she going to close his eyes?' the girl says from above. 'Bit premature.'

Robert waits outside for the ambulance, by the front gate. The girl's with him, but she's over by Tracey's driveway, still out of reach.

The ambulance approaches slowly along South Mossley Hill Road. A man in the passenger seat leans his head and arm out of the window, scanning his eyes along the house fronts, jumping from one porch to the next. No siren or blue light, but there's a horizontal orange stripe round the middle: the same jam-butty pattern as a police car.

Robert waves. When the ambulance reaches him, the man says, 'Is this 113?' He has a moustache and sideburns.

'It's my uncle. Inside, at the bottom of the stairs. He fell.'

The man with the moustache slides back the passenger door and hops down; the driver does the same on the other side. They go to the back of the ambulance and get a stretcher out. Close up, they look like policemen: dark jackets, white shirts, clip-on ties. Robert almost expects them to arrest him. 'I couldn't do anything,' he says. 'To stop it.'

Are these the same men who took his dad? He can't remember faces: only uniforms. The blue serge is a disguise. Both of them disappear inside the house.

The girl leans back against the garden wall. 'Poor Uncle Edward,' she says. 'Your dad joined the merchant navy at sixteen – made everyone look bad. Edward had to wait till he was eighteen for the army. He made up for lost time though: won the DSM in Italy. He doesn't like to talk about it, so he never gets the credit.'

The two ambulancemen manoeuvre the laden stretcher back out through the porch doors. Red faces, arms straining. Uncle Edward's piled in a heap under a scarlet blanket, but they've left his face uncovered. Robert stays by the gate. He's been holding it open all the time they've been inside.

'Broken foot, concussion,' the man with the moustache says when he reaches Robert. He stops speaking for a second to get his breath back. 'He might have had a stroke.'

Robert imitates the man's serious expression, but with a stronger frown, as if he's the one delivering the bad news.

They put Uncle Edward in the back of the ambulance, and wait outside with Robert. The light goes on behind the curtains in the little bedroom upstairs; Auntie Rose is getting dressed.

'Are you coming too?' the second man says to Robert. He has a Coal Not Dole badge on his lapel.

'There isn't room.'

'It'll be fine.'

'The least you can do,' the girl says.

'You're doing well,' the moustached man says. 'Being brave. Supporting your …'

'Auntie. … Uncle.'

'We're going to Alfred Jones Memorial. Not far.' He moves to one side of the ambulance door.

Robert puts a foot onto the fold-out step. He feels like he's been here before.

'Good lad,' the man with the lapel badge says.

'It's going to be crowded,' the girl says. 'I'll see you down there.'

The church youth group does visits to the geriatric ward at Alfred Jones, so Robert knows the building. It's in Garston village, on Church Road. It stands by itself on top of a hill. A Victorian brick facade split into sections by pillars. Each section has four rectangular sash windows, two on each floor, and four chimneys on the slate roof above.

Ordered, logical. Safe. But not tonight. Not now the girl's here.

There's a driveway up to the side entrance, where a nurse is already waiting for them. 'Hello,' she says. 'We'll soon get you right as rain.' She's speaking to Edward, but she looks at Robert and Auntie Rose.

The ambulancemen carry Edward inside, and lift him onto a sturdier stretcher-bed with rails on each side. As they leave, the one with the lapel badge squeezes Robert's shoulder and pats the side of his face. 'Chin up.'

The stretcher-bed's on wheels, and it has an angled upper half, to raise Edward's head and shoulders. The sister pushes it along a corridor and into a large alcove, where there are several bays, separated by curtains. The curtains are the same colour as mushy peas; the walls are chip-fat yellow.

'What's going to happen?' Auntie Rose says. She keeps tight hold of her handbag.

'He fell down the stairs,' Robert says again.

Uncle Edwards groans. He rearranges himself under the blanket. His hand peeps out and plucks at his lips.

'We're going to X-ray his foot, and check for signs of stroke.' The sister leans over Edward and raises her voice. 'Can you understand me?'

Edward puts his hand over his mouth. 'Where are my teef?'

'I'm sure they're safe. Can you tell me your name?'

'Ewward.'

'Do you know where you are?'

'Hoshpital.'

Robert doesn't want to look at Edward, so he concentrates on the nurse. A blue one-piece dress buttoned all the way up; a watch on a ribbon, hanging like a medal, pinned to her left breast; a plastic name tag on her right. 'Riordan'. Robert wishes he had a uniform: a job; a script. He wishes he knew exactly what to do – like the ambulancemen. Or Mark. Except Mark got the deliverance wrong. Didn't he?

Sister Riordan folds the red blanket down and takes hold of Edward's right hand. 'Can you squeeze? Good. Now the other.' She folds the other end of the blanket back to reveal Edward's socks. 'Which is the one that's broken? Can you wiggle your toes?'

'Is Jane Gibbon on tonight?' Robert asks. She goes to church, and she's a nurse here too. She arranged the youth-group visits.

'I don't think so, but the doctor will be here shortly.'

Auntie Rose's eyes are watering. 'Don't leave us,' she says.

'It's okay. I'll be back soon.' Sister Riordan's rubber soles squeak off down the corridor.

In the alcove, all the curtains are pushed back against the walls. Robert looks across at a shirtless man, who's in one of the other bays. There are sticky pads on his chest, but no monitor nearby. He's alone, with a single plastic chair next to his stretcher-bed.

Robert walks over. He clears his throat. 'Is anyone using this?' The man says nothing – just stares at the ceiling. Robert scrapes the chair over to their side of the room. Auntie Rose sits down hard, as if her body's suddenly got heavier.

'I'll see if I can find a cup of tea,' he says.

She grabs his wrist, and looks at the ragged man on the other side of the room. He peels her fingers off. He doesn't want to be here when Edward starts talking.

There's a nurses' station opposite the alcove, but no one's there, so Robert continues down the corridor in the same direction Sister Riordan took. He goes through a set of double doors, which swing backwards and forwards behind him.

A T-junction. That can't be right. He tries to picture the outside of the building. As far as he can remember, it's just a box. Like trying to guess how the intestines are packed inside the stomach. He's in the gleaming white guts of the hospital.

No signs on the wall, no clues about where to go. Only a vending machine. Not for hot drinks though: it's full of chocolate bars. When did he last eat chocolate? He doesn't even get

182

hungry any more. He had to punch a new hole in his belt last week.

He stares at the machine. Fishes around in his pocket; sticks two ten-pence pieces in the slot; turns the knob. He pulls the tray for Dairy Crunch and takes a bar out. He's suddenly dizzy. His hands shake; his stomach clenches. The walls shift and spasm.

He rips the outer wrapper off and snaps the bar in half. Gets his nails underneath the edge of the silver paper and scrapes it back off the exposed chocolate. He jams the broken edge of the bar into his mouth, and bites down hard.

'Ow!' He's bitten his tongue. Blood mixes with spit as he churns the chocolate into brown slime. He retches, swallows. Chews, swallows again. He sticks a finger into his mouth to pick the paste of ground Rice Krispies off the surface of a molar. Thinks about sticking the finger farther in, but he doesn't want to leave a mess.

He wolfs another bite. Suddenly, he hears the girl laugh: she's halfway down the right-hand corridor. She doesn't have a uniform either, unless being naked is a kind of uniform. But she has a script – a role. Robert's the only one who's got to make it up as he goes along.

He drops the remains of the Dairy Crunch, and stumbles after her. Crashes through another set of doors and finds himself in a darkened ward with shapes in the beds. He freezes, but no one reacts to his arrival. It takes him a moment to orient himself, because he's on the opposite side to the one he normally comes in by: it's the women's geriatric ward.

There's a small glass-sided cubicle in the corner to his right, with a desk, a chair and a nightlight. A steaming cup of tea on the desk.

He shouldn't be here. It's even more horrifying in the dark – even more intimate. Sighs, snores, muttering. On the few times he's been here with the church, he can't bear to look at the women's faces. It feels like an imposition, singing hymns at them – or it would be, if they understood what was happening. One of them usually moans and claps along, but he can't remember which bed she's in.

The doors at the other end of the ward creak open; the girl pokes her head and shoulder through. Beckons Robert with a curling finger. Bodies toss and turn; mouths slacken. Blankets bunch at the foot of beds; fall on the floor. 'No, no,' a voice says, the head turning from side to side on the pillow.

By the time he gets through the doors, the girl's already running away again. He's completely lost as he follows her round a corner. She's gone, but there's a single, open door at the end of the corridor: nothing visible beyond.

He walks up to it; steps through.

Back into his bedroom.

The girl's standing on the bed, looking down at him. He's alone with her, in an empty house. 'You should have used a ball of thread,' she says. She puts an index finger on either side of her forehead to make horns, and paws the duvet. The mattress shifts under her foot; she hops to regain her balance. 'Time to put right what you did wrong, and save your mum. Time to give me what I want.'

'No,' Robert says, 'you're the sacrifice. Not Tracey. You. I'm going to kill you.'

'Well, if you won't sacrifice her, then I'll do it for you.'

The girl jumps off the other side of the bed and bends down in front of the derelict fireplace. It gapes around her, opens its black throat. She wriggles like a tongue, and worms her way inside.

Into the wall. Through the wall.

Robert reaches into the fireplace after her. Closes his fist around emptiness. He rushes to the stairs, where Joan of Arc's still praying. He runs his thumb along the edge of her sword. Rattles the pommel and the blade against her ceramic armour. He'll need something sharper tonight.

He hurries down the stairs; turns locks, opens doors. In the kitchen, he wrenches a drawer open and rummages past a can opener, a turkey baster, wooden spoons – until he finds a chopping knife with a long, triangular blade.

Back upstairs, into his bedroom. The sugar rush from the chocolate's wearing off, and he's weak again. His bones are chalk. God, make me strong. Just this one time.

He sticks the knife between his teeth. Gets down on his knees in front of the fireplace; drops to all fours. His body against the girl's. And he's alone: there's no sign of the presence.

He closes his eyes, and starts to crawl.

Tracey went back to see Henry Prince again tonight. When she gets home, her dad's reading *The Times*. She stands in the lounge doorway without saying anything. The headline blocking her view of him says: 'Danegeld in Liverpool'. 'What's Danegeld?' she asks.

'Hmm?' Her dad turns the page over to scan the editorial. 'The Vikings. If they turned up to sack the town, you could pay them to go away instead. But it never worked. They always came back.'

'So Hatton's a Viking?' A delegation from the council's just been down to London to try and get more money from the government for the budget.

Her dad moves his mouth from side to side as he thinks about this. 'Were they pillaging the government in London? More like threatening to commit suicide. "If you don't give us more money, we're going to spend it anyway."'

'It worked though. They got more.'

'Until next year.'

'So that part fits.'

Her dad squints down through the bottom part of his bifocals and reads, 'A third-rate provincial politician, a self-publicizing revolutionary whose organization of "the greatest demonstration by the working class in the history of Merseyside" produced a turnout less than half a Saturday gate at Anfield.' He chuckles. 'Was it full tonight?'

'Ish,' she says. She doesn't want to be too enthusiastic. 'Why didn't you come?'

'I'm going on Friday. But my job's done, now that it's actually happening. Other people can take over now.'

'Henry Prince is less shouty than I expected.'

'He doesn't need to be; it's not up to him if people go forward.'

'Robert went down, yesterday,' she says.

Her dad's got one leg crossed on top of the other, and the foot up in the air twitches. 'I'm not surprised,' he says. 'It's public. Appeals to his sense of drama.' He puts the newspaper down. 'Is he better now?'

Tracey doesn't answer. She hasn't talked to her dad about Robert since the deliverance.

'I don't agree with everything Mark does,' he adds. 'Some of it might even be dangerous. Especially for people like Robert.'

'People like Robert?'

'Vulnerable people.'

She crosses her arms. 'Do you think people can be oppressed by demons?'

'There's no need to go looking for demons. FOR FROM WITHIN, OUT OF THE HEART OF MAN, COME EVIL THOUGHTS, THEFT, MURDER, ADULTERY. ALL THESE EVIL THINGS COME FROM WITHIN, AND THEY DEFILE A MAN.'

'He's happy when we do sin though,' Tracey says. 'The Devil.' That's what she's been told at church for the past sixteen years.

Though the precise mechanism of influence is never explained.

Her dad says, 'The best way to resist the Devil is by drawing closer to God.'

She looks out the patio windows, into the back garden. 'Paul brought two friends from school yesterday, to Henry Prince.' Which is two more than Tracey managed.

'I like Paul. He's very sincere.'

'He's a Hatton fan,' she says, although she's not sure that's true.

'Is he going to camp with you on Saturday?'

'Derek Hatton?'

'Paul.'

'Yes.'

'First year at Seniors,' her dad says. 'All grown up.'

She sticks her tongue out at him, but he's already hidden behind the paper again. She turns her head back to the garden. And jumps. In the middle of the grass, there's a naked figure, standing still. Like a statue: legs together, arms flat against its sides.

Robert. Not Robert.

Smaller: like he used to be, when he first moved here. Like he was in her horrible dream. Hairless, dead white against the deep twilight. A dark stain between his legs. He's looking at her. He moves a finger up to his neck, and draws it across his throat.

'Dad,' she says.

He rustles the paper.

'Dad.' Her eyes flick to him. 'Look in the garden.'

He puts the paper down again, and they both peer into the gloom.

Nothing.

16
ROBERT / TRACEY / ROBERT

How big is he? He's lost his sense of scale. He could be a booming giant. He could be a tiny homunculus. He stays down on all
fours. He's crawling through a tunnel to be born. Born again.
Because he didn't get it right the first time. He couldn't save his
mum – but he can save Tracey.

He opens his eyes, not that it makes any difference. Nothing to
hold onto in this no-space: nothing except the past. And the girl's
invaded his memory. Changed it; remade it in her own image.
He's forgotten how to remember by himself, how to find strength
in who he used to be. He's moving towards Tracey's room. What
happened there, in the past? What gave him strength?

He slept there when Auntie Rose was in hospital two years
ago. They set up the airbed and gave him a sleeping bag. It
had a fancy hood, with drawstrings, which you could pull tight
around your face. He imagined himself at the South Pole, toasty
toes and fingers but frostbite in his nose and lips and eyelids.

Keep moving, or freeze to death.

He's holding the knife between his teeth, like a pirate. The
blade touches the metal in his fillings. He tries to suck the spit
in around it; he can't stop drooling. He moves the knife to his
left trouser pocket, which isn't deep enough to take the entire
blade, so he'll have to keep remembering to push it back down
as it works itself out. Forward again. The floor's smooth, but it's
coated in fine grit. He must be leaving a trail behind, forming
and erasing patterns he can't see.

He gets up onto his knees. The grit trickles off when he wipes his hands against one another, or puffs into the air when he claps them together. Dust is made of skin and hair. Whose body is Robert clouding up around him? Who is he breathing in?

Cough; swallow.

One night three years ago, Robert woke up crying. He struggled out of the sleeping bag; kicked his feet and legs across the wobbling airbed. Tracey lay on the other side of the room, turned towards the wall, the line of her spine curved like a bow. Obviously awake, but not going to admit it. In the grey, he could still make out a poster on the wall: the cover of *Unknown Pleasures* by Joy Division. A pattern of lines shaped like a receding mountain range, one peak in front of another. Tracey explained it to him – a graph plotting a series of radio transmissions from a pulsar: a distant star.

A hard line of light appeared under the bedroom door, broken in two places. Flickering interruptions in the signal: except in this case, the interruptions were the signal. No shadow without presence.

The door opened a few inches, and Tracey's mum whispered, 'Robert? Are you alright?' A silhouette with a halo, like the empty bodies of angels in the Old Testament. She came over to Robert's bed. Took him in her arms and pressed his cheek against her thighs.

As he crawls forward now, he tries to remember his own mum, but he can only see the silhouette in Tracey's doorway. Only feel the enveloping body around him. A screen of flesh, a veil over his own childhood.

He imagines the signal from the pulsar, sweeping through space like a lighthouse beam, crackling with tiny specks of interstellar matter like the prickle of dead light on the inside of his eyelids. Tiny specks. Moons, planets.

The knife's worked itself up, so he shoves it back down, and it rips the lining of his pocket; pricks his thigh. 'Ow!' He twitches away from himself.

Somewhere ahead of him, a thin vertical crack of light, as if the knife has slashed the darkness open. It's not a doorway. Tracey's room has a set of walk-in wardrobes, and he's looking at the thin gap between two of the sliding panels. From behind.

Only a few strides away. He stands, and steps forward into the back of the closet, where he's surrounded by dresses and blouses. He slides the wardrobe door open and blinks into the light of her room.

The girl's not here; nor is Tracey. He turns around to look back at where he came in, and sweeps the dresses on the rail aside. The wall's closed behind him. He looks for the X where Tracey bangs her fist. There. He runs his finger over the two lines; taps the point where they join.

Back to the room, and *Unknown Pleasures* is still on the wall by the door, but there's a new poster next to it, with camouflage patterns from the cover of *Dazzle Ships* by OMD. A bible and a *Daily Bread* pamphlet on the bedside table; a nightie folded on the pillow.

This house is a sacred place. He comes here to worship, to offer his life back to God. Home. Not home.

The writing on the posters is correct, but the rest of the room's the wrong way round, as he knew it would be. There's no avoiding the floor-length mirrors on the wardrobe doors, so he steps forward to the centre of the room and spins towards them. His reflection looks how it always does. Which means he's reversed in the mirror but not in the room – and the room's reversed behind him but it's the right way round in the mirror.

There's a kind of shimmer around his image in the mirror, like a heat haze, and he can't quite focus on his eyes, or on the outline where his body separates itself from the room. He steps up to the wardrobe doors and places his dusty palms on the

191

glass. The surface is quivering like the skin over his heart, and the blood in his ears beats to the same rhythm.

The girl's an unclean spirit – an unclean body too. Is this still a sacred place, if she's here? He can purify it – by sacrificing her. But he has to find her first.

He takes the knife out of his pocket. There's a spot of blood on his jeans where the point dug in. He tugs the denim off the clot and feels it break underneath. Presses the cloth back against his leg: a second stain, lighter than the first.

He steps out onto the landing. Joan of Arc's travelled with him, but she's headless. Someone's knocked the top off the statue.

He pads down the stairs. Leaning out over the banister, he can see a light shining through the gap under the closed door in the back room. He moves the knife from his left hand to his right; wipes his palm against the front of his shirt; moves the knife back. He's suddenly ashamed. He wants to hide, go back.

Something at the bottom of the stairs, blocking the way. Another Robert. A version of himself, but not his reflection, because it's naked, smaller. How it used to be, three years ago –when his mum died. Fat calves, fat thighs, fat belly. Nothing between the legs. Only red jelly. Livid, raw.

He presses the blade against his thigh, touches its tip against the red spot on his jeans.

'You're Azazel, aren't you? In disguise.'

'I'm always in disguise,' the double says. Is that her voice? Or his own, before it broke? It's difficult to be sure. The double reaches between its legs; rubs its hand across itself. Holds the palm up towards Robert, then wipes the blood across its face. 'If you kill me, doesn't the presence go too? Is that what you want?'

'No, but I have to do it. To save Tracey.' Robert steps down, knife held out. The double moves backwards, away from him, off the stairs and around the banister, towards the closed door at the back of the house.

A line of light underneath, broken in two places.

The door opens, and the double's gone. In its place, a backlit silhouette – it has the same shimmer around it as Robert's reflection in the mirror upstairs. Is this the presence? Something's wrong. 'Hello?' it says. 'Is someone there?' But it sounds muffled, as if it's speaking from the next room.

The darkness at its centre dissolves; fills itself in. No stippled gold – more like it used to be when it first appeared: waxy, translucent, unstable. 'Robert? What are you doing here?' The words seem to leak out of the bubbled slit in its head.

Not his mum's voice, but the sounds are as smeared as the figure's outline. He can't think; can't focus his mind. The throb in his blood fills his head. Is this what being drunk feels like? In drink; in a demon.

He says, 'Are you the presence? Whose words are you saying? Who's sending them?'

The girl's standing behind it, back in her familiar form. She leers, knowing he can't reach her.

'How did you get in?' she says. Is that Tracey's voice?

'I followed you. Why are you talking like her?' But didn't the girl use Tracey's voice before, when she took him back to Harmon House? Or was it the other way round: the girl's voice coming out of Tracey's mouth? He can't remember.

He looks at her again. That is the girl, isn't it?

'Go home,' the presence says. It's still muffled, but he can make out the words. 'You can't be here. You have to go home.'

'Get out of the way.'

'I can't do that.'

'I have to sacrifice her,' Robert says. 'The girl. Azazel.'

'You're not going to do anything,' the presence says, through the shimmer around it. 'Give me the knife.'

The girl's outline ripples too. 'I don't understand what you're saying.'

'Stop using her voice!' he says.

The presence has an arm now: a hand. It pulls its wet fingers apart. Reaches towards Robert's trembling hand.

'What are you doing?' Robert says. 'You're supposed to bear witness. Not get in the way.'

'Give me the knife.'

This is the last part of the test. The girl's using the presence, somehow. She's turned it against him. It doesn't make sense – but he knows one thing. He has to get through it to reach her: kill her. Does the girl feel pain? Robert doesn't want to imagine her pain.

'It's your fault,' he says to the presence. 'You won't get out of the way.'

Step inside the vision; take the blessing.

As the knife goes in, the waxy flesh slides against itself, then sucks itself closed as he pulls the blade out. The suction nearly takes the knife out of his hand. The presence gasps. It tries to grab the blade. Robert slashes its hand away, and pushes the knife in again.

'No!' the girl screams.

The edge of the metal catches on something hard inside the presence. Robert jiggles the knife about, like a key in a lock, and it comes loose. Its body sighs as he pulls the knife out. The presence falls to its knees, and he slices its face. Maybe he can cut out the red disc hidden inside its head.

The girl runs forward and flings her arms around the presence; it topples back against her. Why is she trying to protect it? But now she's within his reach. The knife's slippery, so he puts both hands over the handle. He lifts it up over his shoulder.

'Stop it! Stop!' the girl shouts.

The head of the presence opens below him, and blood bubbles up out of the gap. A voice forms itself out of the blood: speaks through it. It says, 'O my boy, my darling boy.' A woman's voice: he knows who it is. There's no distortion at all.

'Turn it off!' Robert shouts, but he knows. This isn't a recording. Nobody's ever said these words before. They're coming into being now.

'What have you done to yourself?' his mum says. 'What have you done?'

He drops the knife; puts his hands over his ears. The room reverses itself. Robert swaps places with himself. And finds himself staring down at Tracey, holding Bill Forester's body, both of them collapsed on the floor in front of him.

'Dad, Dad!' Tracey tries to grab fistfuls of shirt cloth to lift him, but he's too heavy. White palms and face around the ribbon slashes on his hands and the sides of his mouth. Blood gouting from his side. She's on the floor with him; he's lying across her lap. The carpet's slick. She can feel it squish against her legs.

Time cleaves in two: before separates from after. But it's not a lightning flash of illumination. It's a chasm. Her past and future are rewriting themselves. The crack's spreading out from this moment, and she can't stop it.

In the hallway behind Robert, another figure steps out of the darkness. Another Robert, naked, with a dark stain between his legs. A gap: an absence. The double looks at Tracey, and laughs. 'Yes,' it says. 'This is a vision; *and* it's really happening.'

Robert's on his knees in front of her, his trousers soaked in red. Bent forward; she can't see his face. He looks like he's trying to get more of the blood on him. Like he's lapping it up.

The double picks up the knife with one hand, and grabs Robert's hair with the other. It pulls his head up and presses the knife against his throat. But he's already a death's head, his skin vacuum-sealed around his bones. The double looks almost bloated by comparison. An obscene cherub. 'Shall I kill him as well?' it says.

'Yes,' Robert says.

'No,' Tracey says.

The double looks at Tracey; pulls back its lips. She can't tell if it's a grin or a snarl.

'In Jesus' name,' she says, 'I cast you out. Both of you.'

She's finally alone with God.

Robert knows: this hasn't happened yet. It's always happened. And it's never over, so he can't press 'Stop' – or even 'Record'. He won't hear this replayed on the Day of Judgement. *This* is the Day of Judgement.

The double leans down to whisper in his ear. 'Did you really think you could kill me? You're so easy to fool.'

'No! I saved Tracey.'

The double laughs. 'Do you think she's grateful? Don't you get it? You're not the hero. You're the monster.'

Robert stands up, hands gloved in blood. Turns away from Tracey, towards the double. 'No,' he says. 'It's you. You did this.'

'They opened their house to you. And this is how you repay them.'

He knows it's true. He can't ever be the person who didn't do this.

The double points at Bill's body. 'This fool, sacrificing himself. God can have him. But if I can't have Tracey, I'll take you. You're the scapegoat.'

Robert can feel the two houses ripping apart along the seam that joins them; he can feel himself, ripping away from Tracey. He can't stay here any longer; he can't go back next door either.

He falls into the space between the houses. Into Azazel.

17

ROBERT

Empty, flapping; full of teeth. Holes where its eyes used to be. Ragged limbs. Robert averts his gaze.

He seems to be in his dad's house, standing in the open doorway to the television room. But he knows where he really is – in the wilderness, outside the camp. He steps into the television room: the carpet pile is stiff and brittle. And it's covered in little pellets. He bends down to look closer – like liquorice torpedoes, but hollow.

The electric fire throbs. The room feels swollen, feverish; panting; it can't get cool. He goes over to turn the fire off at the wall, and it pings and creaks with relief. The television's on too, but the sound's down.

The presence is sitting in his dad's armchair. Robert turns to watch as it uncollapses and reconstitutes as his dad, sitting in striped pyjama bottoms, with a thick glass gripped between his knees and a bottle squeezed between his thighs.

'Dad,' Robert says. But he's also in the chair, listening to himself speak. His head lolls back; his knees open. The glass falls on the carpet. The bottle tips forward on the chair and leaves a brown dribble on the cushion. Its wet lip points outwards, towards his other self, standing in the room.

Damp, cold air coming through the open window, fighting with the dry shimmer off the fire. The two currents touch each other, the boundary between them shifting: advancing, receding.

Robert can't feel his own body any more. He's coming loose from the flaking red mask on his face, the crusted lines on his palms and under his nails; the tortured belt knotted into his stomach; the blood-soaked jeans sucked in against his calves and ankles. All the miserable, inescapable weight of his guilty self.

He's inside the body on the chair. Its eyes stare. The face gets paler; hands and feet swell pink, then red. A locked spasm spreads downwards from its jaw and neck, following the pooling blood. An unbecoming. A becoming, unfolding from inside the unbecoming. Robert, unfolding inside the presence.

The skin on his new body sweats and blisters, but it's not sweat. It's the inside and outside beginning to change places. He's not alive, but something is, and it's multiplying, spreading. Gut, lungs; climbing up his throat into his mouth.

The suffocated blood settles: turns deeper red, purple, blue. The network of threads stitching his flesh together reveals itself. Turns black.

Outside, the sun comes up. Birds sing.

A fly lands on the frame of the open window. Pauses there for a second before moving to Robert's slack mouth, where he can feel its feet dancing over his lip. Its abdomen swells and pulses. It expels sticky white cylinders, like grains of rice. They form a crust over Robert's lips.

Another fly arrives, and lands just outside the gaping flap at the front of his pyjama bottoms. It crawls inside and disappears. A third lands on his eye. He's being colonized, possessed. From the outside in; from the inside out. The inside's part of the outside now. And Robert's part of his dad.

His abdomen glistens: metallic green, like the bodies of the flies. His muscles begin to lose their grip on themselves. The electric fire beats on, and his belly begins to rise in the oven of the room. The things between his legs swell. His lips and tongue bloom and flower.

Something says, 'For i delight in the law of God after the inward man: but i see another law in my members, warring

198

AGAINST THE LAW OF MY MIND, AND BRINGING ME INTO CAPTIVITY TO THE LAW OF SIN WHICH IS IN MY MEMBERS.' Are the words coming from the mouth in the chair? But it doesn't move – and Robert doesn't hear them with his ears.

The sun sets and rises; sets and rises.

Little mouths, hungry; plenty for everyone. At first, they lick and suck. Later, they burrow across his face and groin. Work their way under separating layers of skin, which puff and slip.

He splits; his stomach bursts. He exhales himself into the air around; pours himself into the chair underneath. It sops him up. Wasps sip the fermenting juice. Clouds of flies. More eggs, in the gaps his body has created for itself.

The sun sets and rises; sets and rises.

At his edges, individual maggots separate themselves and drop down the sides of the chair. They fall onto the floor, and crawl underneath. Curl up; wait for their skins to harden.

The pupae vibrate and split. Wingless flies suck themselves out. They totter between the fibres of the carpet, until they dry out and stagger into the air. The light bulb overhead pops dead with a rattling pupa inside, but the orange glow of the fire shines on like a beacon as spring turns into summer.

His organs spill into one another. His brain leaks out through his ears. Beetles and ants pick and nibble. Mould and fungus fur his surface, but now he's nothing but surface.

No more secrets. Something says, 'O WRETCHED MAN THAT I AM! WHO SHALL DELIVER ME FROM THE BODY OF THIS DEATH?'

The presence re-enters itself – re-enters Robert. The ragged throne on which he sits rests on four sunken castors. He regards his greasy skull through the compound gaze of buzzing flies. He can't see a cone in the head of the presence, but that's because he's looking through it – *with* it. And the disc at its truncated apex is a mirror, reflecting his vision back into his superimposed self.

A wax figurine; a bloody fountain; a ceramic saint; a giant

punctured with light. That's what angels are made of. All stripped away now. Stripped down to bone.

Robert's carrying the presence inside him. He's carrying it, but it's carrying him too. They're inside each other. They've swapped places.

The presence isn't his dad any more. It's the Angel of the Lord. And as it appears, it also disappears.

It's cast Robert back now, into his own body. 'I'm sorry,' he says. 'I didn't know; I didn't understand.'

When the Angel of the Lord speaks, the words aren't sounds; they're fashioned out of itself. And the Word made flesh says, 'TAKE, EAT: THIS IS MY BODY, WHICH IS BROKEN FOR YOU.'

Robert kneels down on the floor in front of the chair. Insect shells splay and crack. He closes his eyes, and opens his mouth to receive Communion.

18

TRACEY

When Tracey gets into the front seat of the Beetle, Aunt Rachel turns the ignition off. Tracey can hear her leather jacket shift against the seat covering when she turns. 'Did you get what you wanted?'

Tracey doesn't reply. She was looking for papers in her dad's room. She's not sure she got the right ones, or even what the right ones are. Mainly she wanted to change into the dress suit she wore to her mum's funeral. It's uncomfortably tight now, but that's good. The more uncomfortable, the better.

Rachel picks a few pieces of fluff off Tracey's lapels and shoulders. 'We have to help you. You have to let us help you.'

'Everyone wants to help,' Tracey says. 'But really they need you to play the part. "If there's anything I can do." Special voice: like a BBC announcer. And then I've got to say, "No, there's nothing." Forgive them for not being able to help. Just shut up; leave me alone.'

Rachel says, 'I'm not going to leave you alone. Nor are Maggie and Josh. We can help you, and we're going to.'

'I want to do it myself.'

Rachel sighs. 'There's legal stuff. One of us might need to be a guardian.'

'It's my house,' Tracey says. Her voice sounds angry.

'Yes, it is. Maggie thinks your dad paid the mortgage off with the insurance after your mum died. Even if he didn't, he was insured too.'

'I don't care about that.'

'You can't live there by yourself. Stay with Maggie for a while. She's got a spare room.'

'Do you want me to leave?' For the last week, Tracey and Rachel have been sleeping in the same bed at Rachel's flat. Last night, they fell asleep in each other's arms.

'Of course not. I'm talking about the future.'

'I want to stay at New Heys. Do my A levels.'

'You can.'

Tracey tugs at her too-tight jacket and skirt. 'I should have planned the service today.'

'Everything you asked for is in there. We can go over it now.'

'Who's leading?'

Rachel pauses. 'John Cooper.'

Tracey squeezes her eyes shut and presses her palm against her forehead. 'It should be Trevor Jenkins. Or Uncle Josh.'

'There was a meeting. Trevor was the one who asked John to do it … John and your dad knew each other a long time. They built the church together.' Rachel lets go of the steering wheel and flexes her fingers, as if they're stiff.

'I know,' Tracey says. 'I was there.'

Rachel takes Tracey's chin in her hand and tilts her face towards the light. 'Are you wearing mascara?'

'What does that matter?'

'It'll run.'

Tracey twists around and reaches behind her shoulder for the seat belt. It's the old type, so it hangs loose in her hand instead of pulling back against her. She looks across at Robert's house. 'Auntie Rose,' she says.

'What about her?'

'Did anyone let her know? She might want to come.'

'Do you think that's a good idea?'

Tracey juts her chin out. 'Yes.'

'We're going to be late.'

'They're not going to start without *me*.' She hangs the seat belt back up, and opens the car door.

Rachel has to park halfway up Long Lane, near Paul's house. Tracey walks with Auntie Rose, who leans on her arm. She's wearing a tweed coat and a hat Tracey's never seen before. A smell of mothballs. Her outfit's too heavy for this humid July day.

'How's Uncle Edward?' Tracey asks, taking smaller steps. But she still has to stop for Auntie Rose to catch her breath.

'He's not well. So he couldn't come.' Auntie Rose's arm is trembling inside the heavy coat.

'It's okay. We're glad you're here. *I'm* glad.'

Rachel's several feet ahead, swinging her keys round her index finger. She doesn't look back, but she must know they've stopped, because she stops too. Cars all along the pavement; across the road, up onto the central reservation in the middle of the dual carriageway. A limousine and a hearse directly outside the church entrance, with two uniformed drivers smoking by the back. They drop their cigarettes and stub them out when they see Tracey coming.

Rachel waits at the bottom of the church steps with Trevor Jenkins, who's on greetings. 'Welcome,' he says to Auntie Rose, but he's looking at Tracey.

'Can I leave my friend with you?' she says, patting Auntie Rose's arm as if Trevor doesn't know who she's talking about. 'I have to go down the front with my family.'

'Absolutely,' Trevor says, head bobbing up and down like it's on a spring. 'We'll get her a seat at the back, and save the one next to her for me.' Like Auntie Rose is a child who can't understand.

Tracey thought everyone would fall silent when she walked in, but the hall's full of life: whispering, nudging, primping ties and hats. She stands at the back and allows herself to hate them all, for a few seconds. It has to come out somewhere. Someone should play the organ when she starts walking up the aisle. 'The Funeral March' instead of 'Here Comes the Bride'.

As Tracey steps forward into a future without her dad, Rachel stays close behind, with her hand on Tracey's shoulder. People do stop talking when they pass, but the chatter starts again after a few seconds, as if Tracey's carrying a bubble of silence around her.

Aunt Maggie and Uncle Josh, her dad's younger brother, are on the front row on the right. Tracey's cousins Sally and Richard are on the row behind. Her mum's sisters, and her older cousin Judith, are at the front on the left.

The coffin's on a collapsible stand near the front. It shines with varnish, and its handles gleam with polish. Tracey wanted something simpler, but she was overruled. There's an easel on either side of it: one holds a wreath of lilies and roses from her mum's family, the other a cross made of roses and chrysanthemums from her dad's. There are other flowers from church members in baskets against the walls. The air's humid with them, and the smell's a little overpowering: like being in a greenhouse.

On the right side of the aisle, there are spaces for Rachel and Tracey to sit, each with a photocopied order of service to mark it off. Rachel takes the outside seat, so Tracey's between her and Aunt Maggie, who has a box of tissues ready on her lap.

Tracey looks behind her. Mark and Jenny are on the third row, surprisingly sitting next to one another, but not talking. Kevin and Paul, just back from Seniors camp, are on the opposite side of the hall, arguing about something. She envies their distraction: they can *choose* if they want to be here. When Paul sees her looking, he raises a hand and smiles, then remembers he's not supposed to. Kevin won't meet her eye, and Paul looks away when Kevin jabs him in the shoulder.

John Cooper stands silently at the front, behind the lectern. There's an overhead projector next to him. 'What's that for?' Tracey says to Rachel.

'I don't know.'

She looks down at the photocopy in her hand, which offers no clues. There's a degraded copy of a black-and-white picture of her mum and dad on the front, taken on their wedding day.

The congregation rises for the first two hymns. Her dad's favourites: number 168, 'O for a thousand tongues to sing', and number 265, 'When I survey the wondrous cross'. No guitar or piano. The first song includes a round on the last line of each verse, which is repeated several times and split into alternating male and female parts; the second hymn is quieter and sadder.

After everyone sits, John Cooper grips the sides of the lectern and leans forward. 'I've never seen our church this full,' he says. 'I know why. We had to come. To pay our respects to our friend. My friend. Tracey's father. We all knew him. We know what he stood for. A man of faith, a true Christian.

'And yet, in another sense, none of us want to be here. How cruel it seems, only a year after Sara was taken from us, to lose her husband Bill as well.'

Tracey blinks and blinks again. She gulps and wipes snot off her upper lip. Her throat feels raw from swallowing. Aunt Maggie pulls a tissue out for her, and passes the box along. She's crying too.

'Sara died in an accident. But *this* was no accident.

'Until we meet with God in the Kingdom of Heaven, where I know Bill is joined with Sara today, we cannot escape suffering. Why did God permit this? I cannot say. But He will use it for His glory. When Jesus died, Satan thought he'd won. He could not imagine God's wonderful purpose. And so he lost.

'I do not speak of the person who held the knife.'

Rachel and Maggie turn inwards towards Tracey, press their

thighs in tighter against hers, squashing her between them. Farther along the pew, Josh leans forward and stares at John: thin mouth. Tracey feels sorry for Auntie Rose, at the back, having to hear this.

'One of us,' John says. 'It would be easy to pretend otherwise. Cast him out, call God's judgement down. And let us be clear – God will judge him.' John pauses. 'As He will judge all of us.'

'Perhaps this boy knew not what he did. And perhaps we failed him. Perhaps some of us even encouraged him.' John looks towards Mark, and a few people turn around. 'In his fantasies.'

Robert acted alone: that's the fiction. But Tracey saw something standing behind him. It spoke to her; she spoke to it. Then it was gone, and Robert went upstairs. He locked himself in the bathroom and smashed the glass on the cabinet mirror.

'There'll be time to think about this,' John says, 'and each man must come to his own conclusion.'

In the police interview, Tracey just recited the physical facts in a monotone, and finished with her dad dying. Because nothing after that mattered. Not to them. They didn't need her as a witness anyway – Robert couldn't stop confessing. But he didn't tell the whole story either.

She knows the police spoke to Mark. She doesn't know what he said; no one in her family's talking to him now. It's not fair. He was the only one who tried to help.

'I can't presume to forgive on someone else's behalf,' John says.

'Don't then,' Rachel mutters.

'But I can speak for all of us when I say I loved Bill Forester.'

If Robert went on trial, Tracey would have to stand in the witness box, pale and luminous, and say what she saw. But there won't be a trial. Robert's in a psychiatric hospital, and there'll be some kind of a hearing to make sure he stays there. She gets to keep her secret with God – and Robert.

Don't remember him. Remember Dad.

'We'll hear from Bill's family shortly,' John says. 'But let me share one thing.'

He wipes his forehead and smooths his hair down. Tracey can smell his sweat from here. He moves his Bible to his left hand and hitches up his belt with his right. He throws the Bible onto the lectern and leans against the wood, as if he's scared of falling over. Maybe this is difficult for him too.

'Henry Prince,' John says.

'Some of you are new here. You only came here because you went to Anfield last week. You might not even know Bill, and you're wondering what you've got yourself into. I was never against Henry Prince's visit, but at first, I wasn't really *for* it either.

'If you're new here, you are welcome. God brought you to us, but Bill made it happen. He was the one who convinced us to take part.

'We just sang two of his favourite hymns. They're both in the *Carry the Message* songbook, but they were written in the eighteenth century. By a Puritan and a Methodist: Isaac Watts and Charles Wesley. That was before the Brethren existed. These men are part of our history too. Because it begins with Christ, and any man who acknowledges Him is my brother. Bill taught me that.

'I don't follow the football. I understand Liverpool had a respectable year.' Laughter from the audience. More than the comment deserves – out of relief. 'Let me see,' John continues. 'Top of the League, Milk Cup – and the European Cup.' He ticks each victory off on his fat fingers. 'Not too bad.'

He takes a few steps away from the lectern, down the aisle, to where Paul's sitting. He reaches down to squeeze Paul's shoulder. 'And yes, my friend, I haven't forgotten: there are two clubs in this city. The other one won the FA Cup.' He speaks over Paul's head, and Paul doesn't look up, only twitches his shoulder under the grip of John's paw.

John says, 'Bill told us to take the gospel into the heart of our city.

'I never much liked the word martyr; nor the word saint. We're all saints. But martyr just means "witness". The Greek word for witness. So Bill Forester is a martyr. He died for his faith.'

Her ears burn; her eyes spill over again. What was it Tracey said at Mark's home group, months ago, before the assembly with Robert? 'If God told my dad, "Kill your daughter," he'd reply, "Take me instead. Kill me instead."'

John continues, 'Bill didn't put himself forward during the week at Anfield: you might not even have noticed him. He knew his work was done by bringing us there. But we took over the stadium for a week. Now I want to borrow something else from Liverpool Football Club. A song. Not a hymn, not in *Carry the Message*. This song doesn't even mention God. But the promise it makes can only be fulfilled through Him.'

John turns on the overhead projector, which beams a transparency onto the bare wall of the church hall. The words of 'You'll Never Walk Alone'.

'Again: how cruel for our young sister to be left alone in this world. And yet I say to you, Tracey, you are not alone.' He waits for her to look at him, but she can't see anything through the tears. 'God stands with you, and we stand with God.'

The last time she heard this song, Paul was singing it. Different words: 'Sign on, sign on, with no hope in your heart, And you'll never work again! You'll never work again.' She whispers Paul's version to herself, to help her get control of her face. It doesn't work.

When the singing stops, Uncle Josh gets up to speak, but Tracey can't concentrate, waiting for her turn. She's prepared a little speech. Sober and dignified; quiet, so people have to lean forward to hear. Only that's not what happens when she gets up to the lectern. She sobs and shakes – like she's possessed by the Holy Spirit, like she's speaking in tongues.

When she was alone with God, all she could hear was His silence. If she wants to hear God speak, she has to come here. That's always been true: she just forgot.

Faith isn't a secret. You have to share it with others.

Six men carry the coffin out: John and Trevor, Uncle Josh and Miriam's husband, Graham – plus the two limousine drivers, because they know what they're doing. But the church men manage to walk in lockstep too. Did they practise? Somehow that thought appals Tracey.

When the coffin's gone, Rachel takes her out to the loos to clean up, and by the time they come back, the church is almost empty. 'Are we going in the limousine?' Tracey asks. The burial's in Allerton Cemetery, which is just around the corner.

'Yes,' Rachel says.

'It's hardly worth it. Isn't everybody walking?'

'It's so we arrive together. As a family.'

The hall's silent, but there's chatter and clinking plates in the kitchen from the women who are staying behind to prepare for the reception. It obviously couldn't be at the house.

'What happened to Auntie Rose?' Tracey asks.

'Trevor drove her home.'

Tracey picks up her jacket and checks the pockets for snotty tissues. 'Where's the order of service?'

'Josh kept it for you.'

There's something else on her seat. A folded piece of paper. She picks it up. THESE ARE SPOTS IN YOUR FEASTS OF CHARITY: TREES WHOSE FRUIT WITHERETH, WITHOUT FRUIT, TWICE DEAD, PLUCKED UP BY THE ROOTS; WANDERING STARS, TO WHOM IS RESERVED THE BLACKNESS OF DARKNESS FOR EVER.

It's the King James Version, which narrows the list of suspects

– but it can't be John Cooper. Not after that speech. Is it supposed to make her feel better? She screws it up; throws it away.

A week later, the police find Robert's dad at the house in Neston. Tracey goes to that funeral as well. A non-denominational chapel in Chester Crematorium, with the next lot of people waiting outside for their slot in the schedule.

The Brethren don't believe in the resurrection of the body – at least, Tracey doesn't think they do: not the *same* body – but cremation's still a bit disreputable. Like getting married in a registry office. Well, it's not like there's anything much to bury, in this case.

Apart from the minister and the coffin, Tracey and Auntie Rose are the only ones there. They sing 'For those in peril on the sea'. When they stand up and sit down, the creak of the pews echoes.

19
ROBERT

To Robert Fisher from Sarah Crick. You'll have to pay me if you want me to be your mate. I'm quite cheap. A sausage roll usually bowls me over.

After the years in the hospital, the first place Robert can remember is a B & B, somewhere near Toxteth. Other people's toenail clippings in the carpet; other people's shit stains in the toilet. A hollowed-out space in the middle of the yellow sheets. Maybe that's from someone else too.

He never sees the girl, but wherever he goes, he knows she's there. She's in charge.

Darling Honk, do I still remind you of a SPOTTED PUDDING!

Once, an American tourist accidentally books a room in the B & B. She has a Beatles T-shirt, and she smiles and says hello in the corridor. Until someone mugs her and takes her purse outside the front door.

Robert, 100% for Jesus. Always. Never give him up. All love and prayers, your new friend, Louise

He carries his clothes in a bin bag; tips them out in the corner of the room. He's kept his Walkman with a dozen cassettes, even though the batteries are usually dead. His only other possession is a booklet from Merseyside Christian Youth Camps. Where he found God, in the summer of 1983: where he was born again.

The booklet has the schedule for the week at camp, and daily questions for group discussion, but he never looks inside: only at the scribbled messages from other campers on the cover. They're all over the front and back, at different angles. When he reads them, he has to turn the booklet round and round in his dirty hands.

Hello Honkie Tonk, The week wouldn't have been so cool without you (corny!). Henry's cat loves you! Keep it mellow dood, love Helen

On the coach down to the campsite, he answered every question with the word 'honk'. He wouldn't say anything else. He can't remember why. Maybe a chicken cluck was too complicated, too expressive. It couldn't be reduced to a single syllable.

Robert, carry on eating spam. It's good for you. See yer soon, Kathy

The booklet's bound with staples and tape, but the staples are rusty and the tape's not sticky any more, so the pages are falling out. He keeps it all held together with an elastic band, and when he takes the booklet out to read the messages, he tries to only touch the cover with his fingertips. But it gets more smudged and dog-eared every year.

Hi Robert, yes it's Nick who never knows what to write because he is insecure.

One evening, he comes back to the B & B, and he can hear voices in his room: a man and a woman with a baby have

212

moved in. No one pays any attention when he tries to object, so he just takes his bin bag and leaves.

He knows that's because of the girl too.

He sleeps outside for a few nights, until he realizes he can go wherever he likes, now that he's invisible. The only hotel he can think of is a posh one in the town centre, where one of Tracey's aunts had her wedding do. He wanders around the reception area, where there's a porter slumped asleep at the check-in desk. What time is it? He looks at the clock above the porter. Three o'clock. It's always three o'clock in the morning now. Or maybe it just feels that way.

He walks up a wide flight of stairs into the ballroom – where they had the dance after the wedding. Fake marble pillars; arched alcoves with glass partitions; an enormous chandelier. A place with a history, but he doesn't want to be in a place, and he doesn't want to have a history. He wants to be nobody, nowhere.

So he stays at the hotel and moves from floor to floor, from identical room to identical room: whichever one's left open for the cleaners after the guests leave. He puts the Do Not Disturb sign on the door, makes sure the curtains are pulled tight, and crawls into the unmade bed. Once he's inside a room, no one ever disturbs him, but if he leaves and comes back, the door's always locked, and he has to find a new one.

Robert, you are the most stupid guy I've ever met. But there you are, Kevin

Eventually, other people disappear altogether. He can still see the traces of their presence; he never sees their bodies. He checks the abandoned meal trolleys for bites of pasta and scraped fish skins in the evenings, but there are more leftovers after breakfast. Toast crusts, soggy cereal, congealed egg: like the buckets for feeding the chickens at Harmon House. His body still wants to be fed, and he doesn't care enough to fight it any more, but he doesn't want to indulge it either.

To Robert, thanks for your very peculiar message. I'm still trying to work it out. Take care, Rebecca Miller

No one answers if he calls room service, but if he closes the room door behind him and then opens it again, there's a bottle of whisky placed on the carpet, just outside. A present, from the girl.

The brands vary – J&B, Johnnie Walker – but more often than not it's Teacher's: the one his dad used to drink.

It's several weeks before he gives in. He breaks the polythene wrapper on one of the clear plastic cups in the bathroom and twists the metal cap off the whisky. As he pours, the cup trembles with the weight of the liquid.

Has he ever had whisky before? He can feel it sting his lips and bite into his dry tongue before it burns the back of his throat. Antiseptic: purifying. He fills the top of the cup with water from the bathroom sink, and opens one of the packets of shortbread biscuits by the kettle.

It takes him a week to finish the bottle. When it's empty, he decides to change rooms. When he opens the door on the way out, there's a new bottle waiting for him. He takes it with him.

Honky, I think you have wonky, Long sideburns. But don't fret, The Lord can use you yet, In ministry to old ladies. Fondest regards, Lindsey

So long as there's whisky left in the bottle, the corridor outside stays empty, but seconds after he shakes the last pregnant drops from the lip of the bottle neck, there'll be a replacement waiting. He tries emptying the bottle directly into his mouth while holding the door open with his foot. That keeps the replacement away for a while – until he closes the door again. He also tries snatching at the handle seconds after finishing, fast as he can, but he never catches anyone outside. The only sound is the humming of the strip lights above; the only movement is the blip of the battery light on the smoke alarm.

At first, it takes him several nights to finish each bottle, and whenever he collects a new one, he changes rooms as well. But now that he's going through the bottles faster, he stays in the rooms longer, until the sheets start to smell.

Robert, I enjoyed our talk the other day when we gave the slate mines a miss, Ian

There's always a desk at the foot of the bed, with a mirror. He looks into it. The main light's off, and he adjusts the anglepoise lamp so it shines directly on his face. Blotched skin, cracked lips. He looks like he's been stretched on a rack, all his limbs and features out of proportion. He scowls; the image scowls back. His mouth falls open, and that looks wrong too. He peers into its black cave: chipped yellow teeth.

To my little Honky Ponky, cauliflower tastes nice with custard. Never change. I love you as you are! God bless, from Mandy Pandy

It takes him a while to realize he's up to a bottle a day, because with the curtains closed, 'a day' is no longer a meaningful unit of time. He sleeps as much as he can, but his back hurts if he stays in bed too long. In the bathroom mirror, he seems swollen as well as stretched, like his skin's about to burst. There doesn't seem to be enough room inside for his organs. They're pressed up against each other, and everywhere he touches feels bruised.

*Honk and eggs, have a busk on me, love Paul the Chicken Dancer
(don't tell!)*

Empty bottle. He opens the door to the corridor. No whisky. That's not good. But there's something else: a small brown bottle with a childproof plastic cap. No label. He shakes it, and pills rattle inside. Not Largactil then, since that comes as a liquid. Worth a try.

When he takes the pills, he can't remember who he is or why any of this matters. Not exactly pleasure, because pleasure's a feeling and this is just an absence where a feeling used to be. He likes it. He likes feeling nothing. He falls over; his arms and legs don't seem to want to obey his brain. But mainly he just stays in the chair – even the bed's too far away now.

*Whether it's logical or illogical doesn't really matter. What matters is we're brothers and I love you in Christ,
Trevor Jenkins*

He starts to feel anxious again: he's worried that the pills will stop working. And once that thought's entered his head, they do seem to become weaker. They still keep him paralysed, but now some version of himself stands outside himself with unblinking eyes and a dark stain between its legs.

The next time he opens the door, there's a bottle of whisky – *and* a bottle of pills. That works for a while, but it's like the princess and the pea. He's unconscious, even while he's awake, but even while he's unconscious, some tiny kernel of self is trying to get out, screaming and banging on the walls. Like being awake on the operating table and unable to tell anyone.

He knows who he is now. He's the rotting thing in his dad's

house. He's a maggot, feeding off the dead body of Christ, add-ing to His suffering by refusing to suffer himself.

To my dear Honky Doodle Dandy, please don't inspect my bra very very closely, love Dave the Kettle ☹

No whisky outside; no pills. Only a thin cellophane packet of powder. He sits down on the floor, with his foot wedged against the door to keep it open, and holds the powder up against the blurred light in the corridor ceiling. He squints – even the corridors are too bright for him now – and flicks the bag with his index finger.

He drags himself back inside the room and lets the door close with a pneumatic sigh. He leans back against the wall and pops the ziplock seal on the bag. He licks his fingertip and dips it inside; wiggles it about in the powder. He presses the finger against his tongue. The powder fizzes and crackles, like bitter Space Dust.

The phone in the room behind him blurts out half a tone, as if it's clearing its throat and isn't sure whether to continue, then settles into a steady pulse. That's never happened before – but he doesn't care. He gets his Walkman and puts the headphones on. Presses play and turns the volume up.

Reckoning by R.E.M. Did Jenny bring him that – back in the hospital?

He waits five minutes and lifts one foam headphone away from his ear. The phone's still ringing, but nothing else has changed, so he takes another fingertip of powder from the bag. Again, he can't feel anything, so he tilts his head back and empties the packet into his mouth.

He can feel something now. He can feel it eating into his teeth. For the first time in years, he prays: Let me die. Let it kill me.

The music on the cassette finishes, and behind the tape hiss, the phone won't shut up. Robert stands up and lurches towards the bedside table. He picks the receiver up.

'Is that Franny?' a Scouse voice says in his ear. 'I *knew* you were there.' Robert doesn't reply, and the voice says again, 'Franny?'

'I think you've got the wrong number.' His own voice sounds strange to him, and the words echo on the phone line.

'Is that Stu?'

'No.'

'Tell Franny from me, she's a fuckin' slag.' The woman's mouth comes closer to the speaker for the last two words, which pop in Robert's ear.

'You can hear me,' Robert says.

'Yeah Stu, I can hear you. You meff.'

He's about to put the phone down, but he hesitates. He can't remember the last time he spoke to anyone. For some reason, he remembers the assembly, when Tracey spoke with him to the school. And the camp booklet. Where is that? When did he last look at it?

Honk, I regret sitting on the front row, Mikey

'What did Franny do?' he says to the stranger on the other end of the line.

'She snogged Jimmy.' The voice wavers. 'I love him. I can't stand it.'

Has Robert ever loved anyone? Did he love Tracey? Not like the woman on the phone means. He wishes he could speak to his mum. Tell her how sorry he is, for what happened to her. Put his arms round her and try to comfort her, like she used to do for him. Say thank you – for loving him. Because she did love him: he doesn't have any doubts about that.

His dad loved her too, and Robert wishes they'd been able to talk about that.

His mouth is made of rubber, but he manages to speak. 'I'm sorry,' he says to the girl at the other end of the line.

'Fuck you, Stu.'

A dead, continuous tone – like the sound of a heart monitor after someone goes into cardiac arrest. Robert's still got the phone stuck to the side of his head, but even when he drops the receiver, the sound remains, and now it's all around him. The whole room's an ear.

To Robert, I've learnt so much from listening to you! Everybody should think so deeply and carefully, Jenny. Philippians 4:19

20

ROBERT / TRACEY

'Can you tell me your name?' The nurse is shining a pencil light in Robert's eyes.

'Wha?' His mouth won't move. He tries to wipe the drool off with the back of his hand, but he can't lift his arm either. He blinks: he can manage that. He can also move his head: a few inches to the left; a few to the right. He's lying on a paper sheet, propped up on a stretcher-bed, in a curtained alcove. Sticky pads on his bare chest, but no wires or monitor.

'I'll come back to you later,' the nurse says.

He's shirtless; shoeless too. His feet are rigid, curled. He tries to relax the toes, straighten them out. He has to focus his attention, move each toe in turn, one by one.

The nurse pokes her head round the curtain. 'What's the matter?'

He realizes he's been groaning. He tries to speak again, but just makes a gargling sound. He lifts his thumb and index finger and pinches them together. Moves them backwards and forwards in the air.

'Pen? Paper?'

He nods, and the nurse disappears again. He remembers this place from when Uncle Edward fell down the stairs: Alfred Jones Hospital, in Garston. How did he end up here? It's miles from the hotel.

The nurse swishes the curtain open and hands him a pad and a biro. He presses the pad against his thigh with the base of his palm, and holds on to the pen as tight as he can. He doesn't have much sensation in his fingers, so it takes him a while to write 'Sister Riordan?' in toddler letters. It's not like she'll remember him. But if she's here, it'll prove this is really happening.

The nurse looks at the pad. 'Repeat customer, are we? She hasn't worked here for a while.'

He writes again. 'Bag?' He's surprised the nurse can read any of it.

She points under the stretcher-bed, then returns to the reception area. He eases his scabby ankles off the paper sheet and inches his bum forward until his feet touch the floor. The creased sheet falls off behind him, and his arms and legs sway, but he doesn't fall over. The nurse picks at an open packet of sweets without looking up from her magazine.

Robert focuses on his jaw, his teeth, his tongue. He smacks his lips, like he wants to get rid of a bad taste. He tries to say, 'I can't speak.' An exercise in futility.

He bends down slowly and twitches the fluttering edge of the crinkled bin bag towards him. He can see the MCYC booklet and the earphones from his Walkman inside, on top of his scrunched clothes. Everything smells of mould.

He straightens up; shuffles forward. The hospital entrance is on his left. Someone's having a smoke outside, and the automatic doors open and close whenever the edge of their foot strays into the sensor zone.

He turns back to where he came from. There are other stretcher-beds, other alcoves, but his is the only space with the curtain pulled out to separate it from its surroundings. Someone's lying on their side on one of the beds, asleep. A woman; a doctor. Cheek pressed into the cracked vinyl padding, eyelids flickering.

She's different from how he remembers her – clothes, hair, body; glasses clutched in her clenched hand – but it's her. Tracey.

Robert stays outside the invisible boundary where the curtain would close her off, if it was pulled out; he's scared he might touch her. He's scared all this is real; he's scared it isn't.

He turns to the nurses' station, and finds he can speak now, if he goes slowly. He tries to whisper, but it comes out loud. 'Ish she shick?' He sounds like Uncle Edward without his teeth.

The nurse looks up from her magazine; narrows her eyes. 'Leave her alone. She's been on duty all night.'

Robert goes back to where he came from; sits down; pulls the curtain closed around him.

For Tracey's final year as a registrar in emergency medicine, they gave her a cushy placement: Alfred Jones Memorial. Not just because it's near home, but because they've shut down most of their inpatient treatment. It's mainly outpatient clinics now – they just keep a small A & E open for walk-in patients. Tracey's in charge of the whole place whenever she's on a night shift, with only a senior house officer and a couple of nurses in support. And tonight the SHO's called in sick.

It's quiet now, after an early car accident – the driver's been transferred to the Royal after Tracey stabilized him. There's no on-call office here, but she can take a nap in a corner of the pa-tient area, if she turns the sound down on the television. When she wakes up, she checks in with Linda at the nurses' station.

'Overdose in there,' Linda says, pointing to the closed cur-tain. 'No one else has come in since.'

'You didn't wake me.'

'No need. Everything stable.'

'Where's Barry?'

Linda nods towards the entrance. 'Keeping watch.'

Tracey snorts. 'What for?'

'Anything that might actually require him to do any work.' He's probably avoiding Linda: a divorcee with a tendency to overshare about her love life.

Tracey looks down at the notes left by the paramedics on the patient behind the curtain. She asks Linda, 'Is he conscious?'

'He was ten minutes ago. Not very lively.'

Tracey pulls up the elasticated waist on her blue scrubs, which are a size too large. They never have any that fit her. 'We don't know what he took?'

'I don't think *he* knows. Some kind of dissociative.'

'They didn't take a blood sample?'

'He refused.'

'Lively enough for that then.'

Tracey walks over and pulls the curtain open, keeping her eye on the chart. She sees his filthy feet before she sees his face. She's imagined this, without ever thinking it would happen. She thought she might be scared of him – but he looks like an old man. Not just dirty: stained, worn-out.

He's a patient; she's a doctor. That thought keeps her safe. And she doesn't need to ask 'Why are you doing this to yourself?' She knows why.

She doesn't want to touch him. She looks up at the television. It's on a wall bracket; they only put it in last month. On the screen, Tony Blair's leaning forward in his chair, trying to get as close as he can to the interviewer. 'Do you know who I am?' she asks Robert, still looking away from him.

'Yes.'

'When did they release you?' she says, although she knows. They sent her an official letter before it happened. Robert doesn't reply, so she says, 'Mark used to visit you.'

Robert squints at Tony Blair. 'Jenny? Did she come too?'

'Yes.'

He swallows – painfully, as if he's chewing paracetamol. 'But not you.'

'No. Not me.'

He puts his hands on his knees. 'When is it, now? What year is it?'

'Year?'

'I'm serious. I don't know.'

'1997.'

He opens his mouth.

'Don't.' She says this too loudly, and Linda looks over to check everything's alright. Tracey waves her away. 'Whatever it is,' she says to Robert, 'I don't care.'

'I ruined your life.' His jaw quivers.

She's disgusted by this self-pity. 'You're not that important,' she says. 'I don't even think about you. Why would I think about you?'

'Did you stay there? In the house.'

'Why not? It's mine.' When she moved back in, she wanted Mark to perform an exorcism, but he wouldn't – he said demons don't dwell in buildings – so she got a priest to do it.

'Auntie Rose.'

Tracey holds the clipboard against her chest. 'She's still next door.' Where else would she be? 'Edward too.' Not that Tracey would know if he wasn't. She adds, 'Paul mows the grass.'

'Paul?'

'He comes round, sometimes.' Why did she mention that? It's none of Robert's business. Or anyone else's.

'Where are you staying now?' She looks at the chart again and taps it with the end of her pen, as if this question's written there and she's ticking it off.

He squints. 'A hotel?' He looks down at his shaking hands. 'I don't know.'

'I'll get Social Services in. It won't be until the morning.'

'It's morning now. Isn't it?' He looks towards the entrance doors.

She can hear the birds, but her brain's still scrambled, and it's just white noise to her. She says, 'Are you going to hurt anyone else?'

225

Robert cringes. 'No.'

She pulls the curtain closed behind them. He's harmless now, and she doesn't want Linda to see her lean in close. 'Do you still read the Bible?' she asks.

'No.'

'But you remember.'

He closes his eyes. 'Some.'

'Do you remember David, following the Ark into Jerusalem, DANCING BEFORE THE LORD WITH ALL HIS MIGHT?'

Robert doesn't reply.

'I used to think that was you. And I was Michal, the daughter of King Saul, high up in the palace window, watching. Michal hated David, for making a fool of himself in front of the servants. He told her off. "I don't care how I look. I'll humiliate myself for God."

'I thought God was going to speak to me through you.

'But there's another part to that story. When they brought the Ark into Jerusalem, it nearly fell over. A man called Uzzah put his hand out to stop it. God struck him dead. Because Uzzah thought God needed his help. He thought he was God's equal.

'Why didn't God strike *you* dead?'

Robert says, 'I think He did.'

Tracey takes a step back away from him, through the curtain. It falls back into place in front of her, blocking him off. She goes back to where she was sleeping before and lies down.

Robert, remember that you have to fight the enemy to claim your blessing. I'll pray for you, Mark

21

TRACEY

Summer 1983: the revue concert on the last night of church camp in Wales.

Tracey's watching someone standing on the makeshift stage at the front of the rec room. They're wearing a chicken costume: a fake-fur bodysuit with a zip up the front and flapping decorations around the collar and zip, like rows of bunting. A rubber mask with round, dead eyes and a gaping beak. The costume's for outreach to kids in the local village. She'd never seen anyone use it in the concert before.

The stage is made up of several tables from the dining hall, pushed together. The chicken stamps up and down to test its stability, then it lifts a smaller table up onto the platform.

Tracey's at the back of the rec room, watching the stage. She's in her hospital scrubs. Robert's here too, still dirty and shirtless – there's an empty chair between them. 'What am I doing here?' she says. The last time she went to camp was over ten years ago. 'Is this because of you?'

'You went back to sleep.' Robert says, shivering. Slurring his words.

'If this is my dream, then why are *you* here?' She nods towards the stage. 'Why are we watching you?'

Robert makes an effort to shape his words. 'You can't share a dream.'

'The same old crap then: you dragging me into your messed-up reality.'

227

Onstage, the teenage version of Robert from 1983 reaches into a plastic bag and pulls his props out, one by one. First, a large bottle of tomato ketchup from the dining hall. Squeezy: red with a white nozzle. He places it on the small table he's dragged up onto the stage. Next, a large carton of eggs. He opens the lid, pressing the top down twice until it stops trying to close by itself. Finally, he brings out a metal tablespoon, which he holds up for everyone to see before placing it next to the eggs on the table.

'You kept the secret,' Tracey says to Robert, who's impassively watching his younger self. 'You never said anything – to the police.'

'The secret? You mean Azazel. What good would it have done? She won. I belonged to her. I was *inside* her.' He looks around at the rec room. 'But this isn't part of her. It can't be.'

'I don't need to see this,' Tracey says. 'I know who I am. I know where I came from.' She turns to Robert. 'And *you've* got nothing to do with it.'

He doesn't reply.

'That thing – Azazel – it said to me, "My existence. That's my gift to you." I don't accept that. *I* decide what I believe.'

'So what do you believe?'

'That I'm not alone,' Tracey says. 'I've never been alone.'

At the front of the rec room, a second performer steps through the door near the stage, dressed in a bulky collection of clothes. A German-army parka over a leather motorcycle jacket; two open shirts on top of each other: one checked, one stripy; two T-shirts under that; baggy swimming shorts pulled over tracksuit bottoms; an unlaced boot on his left foot, a flip-flop on his right.

He also has a bin over his head. Blue plastic, from the craft room, with vertical slots cut in it all the way round. A wide strip of paper taped round the inside – Tracey can see the white flash through the slots – but with a letterbox gap at the front, so the bin wearer can see out.

He climbs up on the stage. He moves slowly, not just because he's bloated with clothes, but also because he's carrying a ghetto blaster. He puts this down near Chicken Robert and then stands apart from him, at the front of the stage.

In the audience, Rebecca Miller leans forward from the row behind Tracey and Robert. She says, 'Why does Paul have a bin over his head?'

'Why are you asking me?' Tracey says. She hasn't seen Rebecca in years – but this isn't how she'd be now. It's the teenage version of her.

'I thought …' Rebecca waggles her finger between bin-headed Paul at the front and Tracey at the back.

'I didn't even know him then.' Tracey looks around. The room's full. Was it like that before? Everyone from camp's here – but apart from herself and Robert next to her, they all appear as they did fourteen years ago.

Teenage Kevin turns round from the row in front of her, and says to Rebecca, 'Nobody's supposed to know it's Paul. That was the only way Robert could get him to join in.'

'It's going to be obvious,' Rebecca says, 'when he opens his mouth.'

'He doesn't have any lines,' Robert says. 'That was one of his conditions.'

Up on the stage, Chicken Robert throws his head back, but instead of crowing, he stands silent, open beak waiting to catch manna from heaven. He looks down and points at the audience. 'Tonight,' he says, 'we present to you the folk music of chickens!' He holds his palm up to the side of his mouth, and adds, in a stage whisper, 'Medieval chickens. Mystical chickens.'

He points the spoon at the carton of eggs. He says, 'I shall play the salmonellaphone, while our mysterious friend here' – at this point, Paul steps forward – 'embodies the collective chicken soul. They possess him.'

'Unh!' Paul says.

'What are you trying to tell us, mysterious friend?'

'Yes, Paul!' Kevin shouts. 'We all know it's you.'

The bin flops from side to side. 'Ohh Au!'

'As I play the beautiful music of the salmonellaphone, which is of course inaudible to humans, our friend, enraptured by its heavenly melodies, will demonstrate the folk dancing of chickens. He will move as chickens move.'

Paul places his hands on his hips and makes a feeble effort to flap his elbows.

Rebecca says to the grown-up Robert in the audience, 'Shouldn't Paul be wearing the chicken suit?'

'That was the original idea. He wouldn't do it.'

'Yeah,' Kevin says, 'but you were secretly made up. You were desperate to put it on.'

Chicken Robert steps back behind the table. 'Quiet!' he says to the audience. He taps several eggs in succession. 'Each egg is laid to a different density,' he explains, 'so each produces a different ultrasonic note.' He taps one on the left of the carton; then moves the spoon over to the right. The only sound is the spoon cracking the top of the two shells. 'See!' he says, repeating the motions. 'Completely different.' He turns to Paul. 'Are you ready, mysterious friend? Are you ready to receive your instructions from the world beyond? To be … a chicken medium!'

Paul shrugs.

'We begin with a ritual.'

Mark stands up, near the front, wearing a Hawaiian shirt from his earlier appearance as one of the Abererch Beach Boys. 'Robert,' he says, 'I'm not sure I like where this is going.'

'Who made him the concert police?' Rebecca asks.

'He was my group leader,' grown-up Robert says.

'When we did "The Joneses" in church,' Kevin says, 'I said I couldn't remember this. I lied. This is the most exciting thing that ever happened at camp.'

At the front, Chicken Robert's voice makes its way out of the mask in reply to Mark. 'It's fine.'

'Is it fine?' Mark says.

'Yes.'

Mark sits down.

Robert reaches down into the plastic bag and takes out a piece of paper. He begins reading. 'When still, poised. Head movements involve strong neck movements too. Not just up and down: three-dimensional. Psychotic stare, but sideways.' He tilts his neck, so the dead eye of the chicken mask points out at the audience. Paul stands paralysed. 'When walking, legs held out at an angle, very slight waddle. Little wing movement, always accompanied by head. When running, stronger waddle, more wing movement.'

'Isn't this someone *watching* a chicken?' Rebecca asks.

'If Paul was doing the movements though,' Kevin says. 'Which he's supposed to be.'

'Didn't they rehearse?'

Tracey makes a sour smile. 'I don't want to see this,' she says. 'I didn't want to see it the first time.'

Paul's standing closer to the front of the stage than Robert, and the bin acts like a pair of blinkers, so Robert pokes him to get him moving and then continues, 'Primary motivation: insatiable, trivial greed. Think chicken: be stupid. Do not think egg. I cannot be a rooster, because the idea of "rooster" is different to the idea of "chicken", but I cannot be a hen either. I must be a male chicken.'

'What's he talking about?' Rebecca says. 'He's got a dozen eggs up there.'

'*He* didn't lay them though,' Kevin says.

Onstage, Robert continues, 'All chickens think the same thoughts. Food, food, follow the food!' Paul perks up at this, and jabs the air to his right.

'I think he's pointing at the dining hall,' Kevin says. He looks out the windows of the rec room. Tracey follows his gaze. No tents or chalets outside; no campsite. 'Where the dining hall *should* be,' he adds.

After a few seconds in prayer, Robert says, 'Thus concludes the ritual.' He steps back behind the salmonellaphone and picks up his spoon. 'Are you ready to dance, mysterious friend?'

Paul grunts.

The spoon moves through the air over the carton, touching eggs in a seemingly random sequence. 'Insects in the walls are writhing in ecstasy!' After thirty seconds playing on the silent salmonellaphone, Robert reminds Paul to 'Dance, mysterious friend! Dance like a chicken!' Paul capers from side to side and moans.

Robert keeps tapping eggs with the spoon in his left hand, and reaches down with his right to press play on the ghetto blaster.

Cacophony. Rebecca puts her hands over her ears.

'Jimi Hendrix,' Kevin says. 'Smashing his guitar and setting fire to it. "Wild Thing".'

'I know,' Tracey says. 'I've seen the film. But this is stupid. It doesn't even make sense.'

Waves of noise, lapping. Robert turns the volume up as loud as it'll go, and the crappy speakers on the ghetto blaster add even more distortion. He throws his spoon away and picks up the ketchup bottle. He takes the cap off the nozzle. He holds the bottle down by his crotch, above the carton of eggs. He pushes his hips forward, and at the farthest point of the thrust presses down hard with both hands on the sides of the bottle.

A whistle of escaping air. He thrusts again as the feedback on the tape starts to crackle and fizz; he grips the bottle tighter and squeezes harder. A congealed plug of ketchup shoots out from the tip of the nozzle and flies over the heads of the front row, who all duck. The bottle groans with relief.

Robert lets the air back in, and squeezes again. The bottle farts a thin stream of ketchup all over the carton of eggs, the table, the stage. From a distance, it looks like blood.

Mark stands up again, and extends his arms, palms forward, as if he's pushing against a wall between him and Robert. 'Enough! Stop!'

'Too late!' Robert throws the ketchup bottle off to his right. It boings off Paul's bin and falls on the stage. 'God wants a sacrifice,' Robert shouts, placing his hands on the craft table, one on either side of the carton of eggs. 'My instrument. My children.'

'His children?' Kevin says. '*He* didn't lay the eggs. I thought that was the point.'

The feedback on the tape sputters, but it resumes with a continuous sound like a foghorn, a blaring distress call. Except it's underwater. 'You can't,' Robert shouts, 'make an omelette!' He reaches into the carton. 'Without breaking some eggs!' He throws two eggs down on the stage, and leaps back as they splatter. He wipes his hands on the matted orange fur of the chicken bodysuit, then reaches into the carton again. Two more explosions. The front row have all retreated to a safe distance. Mark's still standing in the middle of the room, hands pushed forward, protecting the audience behind him. Paul jumps down off the stage, but only so he can turn around and see what's happening.

Robert picks up the egg carton and throws it down. He kicks the little table on the stage, and it skitters away and falls off the edge. He drops to his knees and forms his hands into fists, then starts bringing them down on the remaining eggs in the carton. Again and again.

Tinny applause on the tape from the audience at a pop festival in the sixties; none in the room here. The sound on the tape cuts off abruptly as it runs onto the leader at the end; the play button pings off. Robert kneels on the stage, surrounded by smears of ketchup, scattered bits of eggshell, drizzled slime.

Medieval slime. Mystical slime.

He rips his mask away. He stares out towards the back of the room. Unfocused eyes; face shining with sweat.

'I'm surprised they ever let you back on again,' Kevin says to Robert in the audience, who's slumped forward, looking at the floor. 'Church, here. Anywhere.'

'They didn't,' Tracey says.

'How do you mean?' Kevin asks.

'They let *me* back on.' She turns to Robert next to her. 'For the church concert, I had to promise my dad I'd keep an eye on you. So it wouldn't get out of control. But I never understood. What's the point of all this?'

Robert rubs his palms against his thighs. 'It's public, but it's still a secret. I'm the only one who can make sense of it all. More than that. Go up to the edge of what's allowed. Look over; lean forward. It's *safe* to do it. Because someone's always going to catch me.'

'Mark? But he didn't stop it. You carried on.'

'Not Mark.' Robert straightens up; looks at her. 'You.'

Tracey can't speak for a second. 'I wasn't even up there with you. So why are we here, now?'

'Because this is where I became a Christian. But it doesn't matter; it's already too late. Nothing can stop what's coming. Not even God can change the past.'

Jenny turns around, three rows ahead. She's wearing a bowler hat and a fake plastic moustache from the *Two Ronnies* sketch she did with Tracey earlier in the camp concert. 'You're wrong,' she says, holding a finger to her lip to stop the moustache falling off.

Everyone else in the audience turns round too.

'I can't deal with this,' Tracey says. 'I haven't slept for two days.'

'You're asleep now,' Robert says.

'When Christ died,' Jenny says to him, 'He went down to hell, to preach to the SPIRITS IN PRISON. And lead them out.'

Tracey looks at Paul, who's still below the stage, doubled over, surrounded by confused, abandoned chairs. Hands on knees, shoulders shaking. Bin wobbling.

'What's wrong with him?' Rebecca says.

'I think he's laughing,' Tracey says.

'What do you believe?' Jenny asks her. 'Say it again.'

'I'm not alone. I was never alone.' She looks at Robert. 'And nor were you.'

Someone's banging on the rec-room windows from outside. A naked child. It opens its mouth, ripples its throat, but Tracey can't hear anything.

'Is it singing?' she asks. Now the child's pressing its lips against the glass. Its flattened mouth looks like an undersea creature. 'Are we supposed to let it in?'

'No,' Robert says. 'We're not supposed to let it in. But it's too late.'

'It's not too late.' Mark primps the collar on his Hawaiian shirt. 'God *can* change the past. Forgiveness changes the past.'

'Bill's dead.'

'But you're not,' Tracey says. 'So what are you going to do?'

Robert moves to the windows; smears his palms down the surface of the glass. Over the girl's face, as if he's trying to smother her open mouth.

'I can't cast her out,' he says. 'But I don't have to live in her world. I can cast myself out of her.'

Robert, I'm so happy you came to camp with us this week. I know God has great plans for you. I'll see you at church tomorrow. Your oldest friend, Tracey

ACKNOWLEDGEMENTS

I would like to acknowledge the influence of two novels by Charles Williams: *Descent into Hell* (1937) and *All Hallows' Eve* (1945).

I am grateful to the University of Kent, which awarded me a scholarship for a doctorate in creative writing to work on this book. I am also grateful for the editorial feedback of my supervisor there, David Flusfeder – and the support of the external examiner for my thesis, Adam Roberts. Thanks also to my fellow students, especially Steve Noyes, Tom Ogier and Martha Schulman.

The Angels of L19 is a work of fiction, with an invented setting and characters, and an entirely speculative theology. However, it draws on my memories of church life in the 1980s, and several friends from Liverpool (and Glasgow) helped me to remember important details: (in alphabetical order) John Barker, Fiona Barrick, Jeanette Bowlay-Williams (née Allen), Richard Bell, Andy Cowen, Gaynor Doyle (née Morrell), Chris Ford, Kate Jenkins, Liz Kelman, and Neil Morrell. Jonathan Adams kept an old box full of letters and papers for twenty-five years, and sent it back to me just when it was needed.

Special thanks to Heather Briscoe and Darren Williams.

From Australia, where my career as a writer began, Kate and Nick Eckstein offered encouragement, and Mary Cunnane advised me on the contract.

With regards to the wider world in 1984, I have stuck to the historical chronology, with a few exceptions: chapter 2 alludes to 'William, It Was Really Nothing' by The Smiths, which wasn't released until August of that year; similarly, for chapter 11, I moved the release date of *Footloose* forward by two weeks. In chapter 7, the miners' strike also starts several weeks early. In summarizing and quoting films, I have omitted scenes and elided dialogue for reasons of concision; similarly, I have elided a Bible quotation in chapter 18 (but without, I hope, altering its intended sense).

I am grateful to my publishers Neil Griffiths and Damian Lanigan, who not only believed in the book, but helped to make it better. I'm proud to be one of the first releases for their imprint, Weatherglass Books. I would also like to thank James Tookey for his help in bringing the book to press, and my copy editor, Sarah Terry.

Thank you to our Founder Readers
for supporting Weatherglass Books in our first year of publishing

Kirk Annett

Andrea Barlien

Linda Barton

Therese Bernbach

Willa Bews

Kevin Bleyer

Geof Branch

Celia Brayfield

Sarah Brearley

John Brewin

Peter Burgess

Karen Burns

William Butler

Joseph Camilleri

Russell Chant

James Clammer

David Clarke

Jeff Collins

Joe Cooney

Matthew Craig

Alan Crilly

Ian Critchley

Stafford Critchlow

George Cronin

Kevin Davey

Gaynor Doyle

Kevin Duffy

Anthony Duncan

Timna Fibert

Sam Fisher

Marita Fraser

Emma French

Paul Fulcher

Graham Fulcher

Joseph Gallivan

Neil George

Sarah Goldson

Victoria Goodall

Susan Gorgioski

Bryan Gormley

Charlotte Green

Louise Greenberg

Paul Griffiths

Anne Griffiths

Ortelio Grillo

Ian Hagues

Daniel Hahn

Paul Hannan

Alison Hardy

Jack Hargreaves

Sonia Harris

Katy Hastie

David Hebblethwaite

Karen Heelan

Rónán Hession

Caroline Hett

Dirk-Jan Hoogerdijk

Stephen Hopper

Liz Houchin

Hugh Hudson

Bex Hughes

Robert Hughes

Joe Hutson

Dylan Hyson

Roy Immanuel

Jarkko Inkinen

Bijan Jalili

Daniel Janes

Alistair Jenkins

Dan Jenkins

Stuart Kirschbaum
Marina Klimovich
Justin Kurian
Alida Kuzemczak-Sayer
Simon Lewis
Duncan Lewis
Chiara Liberio
Alex Lockwood
Catherine Lowden
Anil Malhotra
Sarah Manvel
Kelsey Marcus
Oscar Mardell
Andrea Mason
Charlie Mawer
Jack McSweeney
Eloise Millar
Geoffry Missinne
Thomas Moloney
Ian Mond
Ann Morgan
Zosha Nash
Armen Nersessian
Amanda Nicholls
Vilma Nikolaidou
Steve Noyes
John O'Donoghue
Declan O'Driscoll
Anna Paige
Krista Parris
Debra Patek
Keirstan Pawson
Hannah Piekarz
Robert Pisani
Ben Plouviez
Lee Rodwell
Jonathan Ruppin

Josephine Sacks
Mimi Sahu
Dan Simon
Alan Simpson
Arabella Spencer
Han Smith
Jolene Smith
Valarie Smith
Peggy Starbuck
Elizabeth Stubbs
Daryl Sullivan
Sue Thomas
Tessa Thornley
Matthew Tilt
Pat Tookey
Simon Trewin
Nina Trivedi
Paul Tyrell
Mark Valentine
Jeroen van Dooren
Pauline Van Mourik
  Broekman
Steve Walsh
Xiaowei Wang
Emma Warnock
Venetia Welby
Sam Whaley
Wendy Whidden
Phil & Anne Whitehurst
Crispin Whittell
Christine Whittemore
James Wilson
Lucinda Winter
Lisa Wohl
Marcus Wright
Stefan Zebrowski-Rubin

First published in 2021
by Weatherglass Books

001

Text design and typesetting by James Tookey
(with thanks to CB Editions)
Cover design by Luke Bird
Printed in the U.K. by TJ Books, Padstow

A CIP record for this book is published by the British Library

ISBN: 978-1-8380181-3-9

www.weatherglassbooks.com

Weatherglass
Books